LOVE IS LIKE PARK AVENUE

Alvin Levin, early 1950s.
Courtesy of the Estate of Alvin Levin.

Alvin Levin

LOVE IS LIKE PARK AVENUE

Edited, with an Introduction, by James Reidel

Preface by John Ashbery

A NEW DIRECTIONS BOOK

I wish to thank Margaret Ratner and Barbara Morse, Alvin Levin's nieces, for their assistance in the preparation of this book. I would also like to express my gratitude to Christopher Lewis of the American University Library, my wife M. Lori Reidel, and an old confrere whose knowledge of fine and budget reds must appear in lieu of his name. —J.R.

Letter by William Maxwell (p.141) © 1941 by William Maxwell
Letter by Nicholas Moore (p.142) used courtesy of the Estate of Nicholas Moore

Cover design Ann Weinstock
Book design Sylvia Frezzolini Severance
Manufactured in the United States of America
New Directions Books are printed on acid-free paper.
First published as a New Directions Paperbook Original (NDP1146) in 2009.
Published simultaneously in Canada by Penguin Books Canada Limited

Library of Congress Cataloging-in-Publication Data

Levin, Alvin Frederick.
  Love is like Park Avenue / Alvin Levin ; edited, with an introduction
by James Reidel ; preface by John Ashbery.
    p. cm.
  ISBN 978-0-8112-1799-6 (pbk. : alk. paper)
   1. City and town life—New York (State)—New York—Fiction. 2. New
York (N.Y.)—Social life and customs—Fiction. I. Reidel, James. II. Title.
PS3523.E79915L68 2009
813'.52—dc22
                                                                    2009027741

New Directions Books are published for James Laughlin
by New Directions Publishing Corporation
80 Eighth Avenue, New York 10011

Contents

PREFACE

BY JOHN ASHBERY

J FIRST READ ALVIN LEVIN'S *Love Is Like Park Avenue* when I was about fifteen, shortly after it was published in the *New Directions 1942* annual. At the time I was beginning to explore contemporary experimental writing, thanks in part to the excellent collection at the Rochester Public Library, an art-deco gem still extant on the edge of the city's faded downtown. In fact I was looking not just for modernist writing but sexy writing as well, having already looked into Henry Miller and ignored critical warnings against combing *Ulysses* for the "naughty bits." Levin's narrative provided plenty of those, in graphic accounts of steamy sexual encounters that used such hitherto unprintable words as hardon, cocksucker, frenching and come (where were the censors?) in breathless run-on sentences that suggested its author too had read Molly Bloom's soliloquy. The biographical note on Levin mentioned that the text represented about one third of a novel. I waited impatiently for New Directions to publish the complete work.

Alas, that never happened. Occasionally I would remember *Love Is Like Park Avenue*, and sometime in the 1990s I asked an editor at New Directions if he knew what had become of it. He replied that after searching their files he had come up with Amelia Earhart's chinstrap, but no sign of Alvin Levin. James Laughlin was still alive then, but according to my informant had only vague recollections of the author. I resigned myself to the trail having grown cold. (At that time I hadn't seen Levin's lovely short story "Only Dreams Are True" in the 1939 annual. It could very well be a fragment of *Love Is Like Park Avenue*, though it stands beautifully on its own.)

A couple of years ago I thought of Levin again, and this time Barbara Epler, editor in chief at New Directions, was able to offer help. The extensive correspondence between Laughlin and Levin (mostly on Levin's side) was found to exist in Laughlin's archives at Harvard's Houghton Library. At the same time a friend in Cincinnati put me in touch with James Reidel, a poet and specialist in forgotten and semi-obscure American avant-garde writers, and the author of a terrific biography of the unjustly neglected poet Weldon Kees. Reidel has now done an amazing job of tracking down more fragments of Levin's oeuvre in little magazines and anthologies of the period, including some published by the Little Man Press in Cincinnati. For me the search seemed to come full circle when Reidel produced a Levin story printed in a British anthology coedited by Nicholas Moore, a brilliant poet of the 1930s and '40s whose work has fascinated me ever since I discovered it about the same time I first read Levin, again in the pages of a New Directions annual. How strange that these two forgotten icons of my youth had been in touch with each other, across the Atlantic in wartime, and that one had actually helped the other get published.

Moore has been recently re-evaluated in England, and now, thanks to Reidel's digging, readers can finally get an idea of Levin's writing. His stream-of-consciousness narrators, often women, reflect the yearning of lower-middle-class New York Jews of the 1930s for upward mobility of the kind shown in contemporary films and cigarette ads. They dream of "Vassar girl" sweaters and men's suits from Rogers Peet (the somewhat cheaper alternative to Brooks Brothers), of yacht clubs and supper clubs where sleek young couples dance to Glenn Miller, though they themselves have to make do with restaurant "dinners" of hot dogs and sauerkraut, and sweaty make-out sessions in parked cars. All this is conveyed in wonderfully caustic run-on sentences inflected by the cadences of radio commercials and movie "coming attractions." The voices at their most benign anticipate Woody Allen; at their nastiest Budd Schulberg's Sammy Glick of *What Makes Sammy Run?* Scabrous scenes of family feuding in the Bronx and crowded Coney Island beaches come at you with the leering verve of Reginald Marsh's drawings and Paul Cadmus' quasi-pornographic paintings. It's a confused, squalid, but vehemently bubbling melting pot, where, in the author's regretful words, "Only Dreams Are True."

INTRODUCTION

BY JAMES REIDEL

Have been reading the 1942 annual—many thanks—
the stuff by Alvin Levin has brilliant patches—...
—Tennessee Williams to James Laughlin[1]

*T*HE PROVENANCE OF THE following pages comes very close to my own "Custom-House" experience. The trail had led to a cardboard box in an unlikely place trapped in time—the charming home of the late William Kunstler on Gay Street in the Village. After getting to the bottom of that box, however, Alvin Levin's masterpiece, which gives this book its title, was not found. In its place are the surviving fragments and companion pieces, which appeared in anthologies and little magazines of new writing that are lost in their own way, shelved and largely unread in library stacks.

Levin belongs to that wave of young and often good writers who came into their own in the 1930s and '40s—as the Depression segued into a world war. Many were regionalists to the point of writing only about one town, one neighborhood or borough (Daniel Fuchs's Brooklyn)—or even just one block (Robert Lowry's Hutton Street). Some were experimental, even surrealistic (the early Weldon Kees), others radical-proletarian (Albert Halper), and others personal and *peculiar* (Carson McCullers and Jane Bowles). These aspirants were children in the 1920s and they identified with Hemingway and Faulkner, as others wanted to be aviators, oil tycoons, and screen actors. And there was Sherwood Anderson, whose *Winesburg, Ohio* encouraged this generation to fill in the American map with their sense of place. Almost every high school and college had some kind of

---

1   Tennessee Williams, *Selected Letters of Tennessee Williams* (New York: New Directions, 2000), p. 554.

journal in which to publish the work of these aspirants. Add to this the little magazines that flourished and the Federal Writers' Project and an adventurous reader could choose from a small army of voices before the Selective Service picked its army (which, of course, took away readers and many of the writers, too). From the ranks of all this talent Alvin Levin began to stand out despite being a bit reclusive, and despite having to use a cane.

ALVIN FREDERICK LEVIN was born in Paterson, New Jersey, on May 16, 1914, to Nathan Levin, the son of working class Russian immigrants, and Rose Botwick. At the time the elder Levin made a living driving a horse cart and delivering bottles of soda made by relatives. He went on to be a taxi driver.

In 1917, Alvin's sister Shirley was born. The siblings may or may not have been among the two thousand babies whom William Carlos Williams brought into the world, but like the poet-physician, Levin would come to write about what Dr. Williams simply called, and prized as subject matter, "the local." For Levin, however, this would not be Paterson but rather New York City, and, in particular, that borough on the north shore of the Harlem River, the Bronx.

There Nathan Levin bought a garage and opened a used car business with the inventory oftentimes being the family's already tenderly loved and well-used Packard. The Levins were renters and first lived on Ward Avenue and later on Grand Concourse. When construction of the Third Avenue El line reached the Bronx, access to Nathan's garage was blocked. This setback was soon followed by the Stock Market Crash of 1929. Looking more like a college professor behind his round, heavy-framed glasses than the shrewd salesman he never was, Levin settled into driving a cab for one of his better-off relatives to support his family and to pay for his son's frequent medical bills.

As a small child the younger Levin contracted polio, possibly during the widespread 1916 epidemic that struck New York City and the rest of the Eastern Seaboard. The resulting physical handicap—he would have to walk with some means of assistance for the rest of his life—and his frailness changed a rather key dynamic in his progressive but nevertheless traditional Jewish family. His sister Shirley outshined and overachieved in a way that eclipsed the "elder son." She filled a vacuum that he could not fill—even when he became the unwelcome center of attention during one of his many post-polio illnesses (for Shirley would be sent away to stay with relatives). She would later assume some guilt for being the healthy and "normal" child. Her brother, in contrast, took that leading role in the Levin household, which he was certainly aware of; this made girls the most interesting form of life for him to write about.

Levin was a brilliant boy despite his physical limitations. His lameness, however, certainly intensified his intellectual develop-ment, especially when it came to those solitary pursuits of vora-cious reading, keeping a diary, and writing little stories. He attended the beautifully gothic Morris High School and, like many of the Jewish middle class, he entered City College rather than Columbia and other Ivy League schools, which were then less open to the children of immigrants if not tacitly anti-Semitic in their admission policies.

By 1936 Levin had earned an undergraduate degree in sociol-ogy. During the next four years he studied at Brooklyn Law School when its law degrees were still conferred by St. Lawrence University, a small, Unitarian school in upstate New York. It was during this time he started to write stories that he thought worthy of publishing. He took this vocation seriously enough—although it was plainly a diversion from becoming an academic and lawyer—to write something novel-length, if not in the pure sense, a cycle of short stories. The title was chosen early and he kept to it if not its content or continuity—*Love Is Like Park Avenue.*

His "serious" writing began at a time when younger adults plan for their lifetime careers, marriage, and the like. Levin undoubtedly had trouble, largely because he was polymath—he was too gifted, too interested in everything to make a choice. From his few surviving letters one learns that he was already a scholar and social critic, writing and publishing papers on sociology and law in the thick journals. His politics turn up in notes and sketches: diatribes with himself, a few intimates, and even fewer friends.

> *I didn't like the Russian exhibit at all. It was all propaganda. Everything in the building was so happy. Every picture they showed you was of big people all smiling at whatever they were doing. You take the other foreign exhibits, France, say, there you see peasants working hard and looking like they were poor hardworking people. They try to show you the same kind of life in Russia except that everybody is laughing.*

Levin may have been, as he puts it, a "contented" Communist, rather than the good kind as many were in the Great Depression. And like many, he became disaffected with the Soviet Union, especially after the show trials and the Molotov-Ribbentrop Pact of 1939. But politics hardly provided the kind of sadness and disappointment as love did, and there was more for his life of the mind in the popular culture, especially swing music. There he took serious joy and even took up playing the clarinet. Together with his fiction writing, Levin's interests would almost seem to be a form of balance, the same as his need for three points of support—his weak legs and the cane he carried for most of his life.

Levin eventually put more emphasis on his fiction, perhaps with William Saroyan in mind as a model of success rather than as a literary influence. It is natural to look for the *Saroyanesque* in Levin's slice-of-life métier, in which he portrays his take on the Jewish American experience set in an insular and yet permeable Bronx (and Manhattan, which serves as an appendage, or afterthought, to Levin's center of the world). Saroyan is the writer whom Levin sometimes invokes. What he seems to borrow is the other man's spontaneity and confidence. In contrast to the California writer of Armenian ancestry, Levin is darker, more bittersweet, sadder. He is almost the foil to *The New Yorker's* H*Y*M*A*N K*A*P*L*A*N stories. He has a remote, touch-me-not quality despite how richly he peoples his stories and seems quite comfortable among them, like family. He prefers to narrate from inside them, from an interior and private vantage point.

Thought itself is what is unique to Levin. He has a good ear for it, especially the thoughts of women. He is very good at making such thoughts dialogue that either stays inside or surfaces for just a few moments as spoken. And a good deal of what his characters think about is the other sex. The avenues opened by Henry Miller, another product of City College, come to mind here and it is a name that Levin mentions in his letters. However, Miller is a writer whom Levin contradicts rather than imitates. There is none of Miller's rugged first-personhood here. Levin finds more honesty in how the first person is a little damaged, wounded, on the mend as he so often was himself. Further in the background, but overarching, too, is Dos Passos, save that Levin's New York is "de-Babylonized." Levin seems to be writing more of the Bronx, Jewish "Dubliners" in sentences to match those in *Ulysses,* and a personal dialectic that has this street music intelligibility that so many younger writers eschewed—or unconsciously *corrected* for the Irishman. In what he still called his "Work in Progress," Levin also fixed on what would be a very brief moment both in his life, from which he drew his stories, and the American scene. Both were the eleventh hour—the end of his youth and the end of a short period of peace.

Between 1936 and 1939, Levin was good enough to get into little magazines such as *Tempo, Literary America, American Scene, Parchment*—the kind typically edited by students like himself, rather than slick publications such as *Esquire* and *The New Yorker*. It was at this point that his work attracted the attention of James Laughlin IV, the publisher and editor of New Directions, who asked him in the early spring of 1939 to submit a short story for that year's annual anthology of new writing. After Laughlin accepted Levin's "Only Dreams Are True," one of the speculative fictions that Levin based on his sister Shirley, the editor asked Levin for something longer, that he knew existed, for Levin had published a fragment from his novel *Love Is Like Park Avenue* in *Literary America* almost three years earlier. Rather than quickly turn over the expected opus, for such a work-in-progress had to have grown since 1936, Levin demurred.

> *I haven't got a book around, but I wager I could put one together by just cleaning out the drawers. This is no evidence of talent; only an irritating desire to put a million thoughts to paper. I am twenty-four next month. The only achievements I'm proud about this far are the B.S. in social science degree and the LL.B. degree, both won in the same year—1938, and a hundred dollars prize money from the American Society of Composers, Authors and Producers for a killer of an essay, bedecked with footnotes and all, on "The Legal Nature of Literary Property."* . . .
>
> *Besides writing stories, "finishing" the work on social mythology, book reviewing for The Modern Quarterly, writing a legal text-book for a Southern correspondence school (at so-much a thousand words), suffering, staying up all night, I don't do very much. In other words, I don't do very much.*

I shall be glad to send you what material I have here.
Will you let me know the expected date of publication of
New Directions 1939. I hope Only Dreams Come True
comes out ok.

It took Laughlin another letter to coax Levin to send more work. The understatement and modesty on Levin's part continued—but he was not immune to the flattery he was receiving. Nor did he keep it a secret that he wasn't just sticking his work in drawers or that New Directions was not the first to discover him. He even let on that he had picked up a girlfriend in Kansas on the strength of his writing—and that he was really well informed about contemporary American fiction.

Lately the mailman brings copies of little magazines
around with my name on the covers. The latest one is
Parchment with "A COOL DRINK IS REFRESHING"
story in it; I like the story but it gives me the creeps—
about a little brother and his sister frying in their own
rancid fat up in the Bronx one summer and both of them
aware of it. . . .

I havent read White Mule but I recall some reviews.
Passaic, the river, children, young couple, German back-
ground, child psychology, pregnancy, real stuff. It
sounded good and I liked Williams face and shirt and
tie. I want to read it and see what you mean. I am send-
ing you a copy of something I wrote a long time ago
with an idea for a novel. Tanya Foss of Robert McBride
wanted to have the completed book but she only sends
me post cards and that seems awfully bare in the way of
encouragement. I need somebody to put me on the top
of my mess. Do you think there is anything in the piece?
Is that what you mean? It's a lot of breast beating and
that's the way I feel, starry-eyed.

The way Levin responded to Laughlin suggests that he considered all of his stories to be part of the work-in-progress that had, since 1936, borne the title *Love Is Like Park Avenue*. Structurally fragmented, plastic, even modular, it could be strung together or broken apart to have something that a little magazine might publish under whatever title might suffice until the fragment was reabsorbed or left a one-off. Laughlin's interest and his offer to publish a longer work was the encouragement that Levin had long needed. In July he sent a 20,000-word manuscript and then offered to write more under Laughlin's editorial guidance.

> *What do you think of it for a book? I would like to tell you how much more of this same thing is jumping around in me and, better, how eager I am to put it all down on paper. But I am worried about what you will say for the material thus far.*
>
> *What you had to say about a plot is okay with me. I feel great trying to fit into the groove you created. Which style do you prefer: the one about the girl ditched by the guy from Davega's or the Julie prom thing? They are both the same to me, the only difference being that the public would want to make reading easier. [...] I like the Julie method better because I think it permits the author to stay out of the picture. A comma or a period and a capital is an author's invention.*
>
> *Will you try to communicate with me as soon as possible? I know I can give you above 100,000 words by September.*

Enthusiastic about the novel-length book, Levin nevertheless felt "less and less a novelist." His sociolegal mind had been moving right along with his fictive imagination. Never minding that

Laughlin published avant-garde literature, Levin proposed that
New Directions print his monograph on social order and the law.
"We could skip the law review stage, I think. I mean, would you
be interested? Its solid stuff and dynamite enough to get talked
about. Footnotes and all."

After *New Directions 1939* came out in the fall of that year,
Levin looked for other venues that would be hospitable to his stories, usually places beyond what would seem to be his home territory and natural audience. He placed a story in Lillian Smith's
North Georgia Review and with a new avant-garde press in
Cincinnati, Ohio, The Little Man. Levin probably learned about
The Little Man in the advertisements that appeared in the back
pages of the New Directions anthologies and he probably saw its
quirky little pamphlets in the Gotham Book Mart. The Little Man
books were designed and hand-printed by its publisher Robert
Lowry and often illustrated by his partner, James Flora. How
Levin and Lowry connected is unknown, but Lowry began to
publish Levin's stories in 1940, in separate issues of the Little Man
series and in what turned out to be the first published collection
of Levin's fiction, *Little Alvin's Storybook*. This comic strip appel-
lation and graphic art would not have been chosen by Levin but
rather by Lowry and Flora. The Little Man, if it had a mission,
was exposing the world of the American neighborhood and a people whose literature really was the funny papers.

Working with Lowry, first as an author and then as the dis-
tributor of Little Man books in New York City, is partly what
encouraged Levin to start his pamphlet business. The difference
would be that his publications would be utilitarian rather than
unprofitable and ephemeral limited editions. Undoubtedly Levin
had in mind the success of the Little Blue Books published by
Emanuel Haldeman-Julius. In mid-1940 Levin founded the
Pamphlet Distributing Company to serve the library reference

trade by publishing bibliographies, book lists, and the like. Working for himself, Levin soon took on an entrepreneurial intensity that borrowed liberally from the careful economy of passion that he had given his fiction.

Levin submitted a long passage from *Love Is Like Park Avenue* to New Directions in the fall of 1941 but had missed the press date. Laughlin now had what he wanted—including what may be the most notable literary example of a *dry fuck*—a once-common vulgarism to describe that near-consummation often performed in the front or backseat of a car before the Sexual Revolution. And like Levin's other stories, what might look to us as a kind of New York World's Fair time capsule, this transition-al, pre-postmodern writing offered a naturalistic and sublimated self-reportage that included anthropology and social commen-tary. Or, to use Robert Lowry's words in his ad for *Little Alvin's Storybook*, the "kinds of ginks, goofs, and nice people in New York City."

The writing is reflexive, automatic. Levin probably typed his stories without revision and without looking back, a method more like verbalized photography. According to one of the Little Man biographical notes, Levin had actually taken up photogra-phy during the time he wrote the New Directions fragment of *Love Is Like Park Avenue.*

The pamphlet company was one reason why Levin had been late with his manuscript and why, unlike, say, Bellow or Salinger, he was more like an outsider artist. He would even change hats on Laughlin. Rather than turn in his novel, Levin proposed busi-ness ventures such as publishing full-color ads for Pepsi or Coca-Cola to subsidize a new fiction magazine. "Could be done?" he speculated. "Revolutionize publishing? They tell me Simon & Schuster tried it some years ago and it didn't work. But I don't remember. Anyway, I like the idea and so I don't want to think it a bad idea." The other new business that Levin wanted to bring up had already become a reality and he knew it would not be well received by the editor who would put up his own money first to publish his writers.

> *Is there anything wrong with it? I publish a great deal of pamphlet material, stuff people bring in with a flame in their eye and the printing costs in their pockets. Call it vanity publishing, we do. We don't promise anything, we don't overcharge, we do everything we can to sell pamphlets. We run an ad in the Sunday Times Book Section. We charge $3.60 a page per 1000 copies, 6x9, 10pt type, 60lb Book paper. Reasonable. The job is clean, utilitarian.*

Levin was not using the "we" to suggest he was writing from a suite of offices in a skyscraper instead of a post office box in Times Square. In 1941 he opened up a law office with his brother-in-law, Abraham Cohen, Shirley's husband—but their partnership really became the William-Frederick Press, derived from the proprietors' middle names. This new company eventually absorbed the Pamphlet Distributing Company and published clothbound books as well as the ephemeral chapbooks and bibliographical listings. The press was modestly successful, enough to boast a staff, an advertising manager, an executive editor, and an office manager—all of them Levin. For many years the press specialized in finance, printing stock market analytics for Wall Street traders and such classics as Edgar Lawrence Smith's *Common Stocks and Business Cycles,* whose reputation Levin once defended against *Forbes* when the magazine suggested that Smith's 1924 book had inspired the speculation causing the Great Depression. As for literature, William-Frederick would publish it if someone wanted to pay. (Levin did not avail himself of his own services,) There is one conspicuous name among those who hired the press—James Purdy, whose first collection of stories, *63 Dream Palace,* was published by subsidy in 1956.

In the fall of 1942, James Laughlin published sixty pages of *Love Is Like Park Avenue* in that year's New Directions anthology. To his surprise, Levin received a note from William Maxwell of *The New Yorker* in November asking him to submit some of his stories. And in March of the following year, the English poet Nicholas Moore asked Levin to send a story to London for a representative anthology of American fiction. Levin enjoyed the attention, but he also preferred to putter about his apartment and personal life.

Dear Laughlin:

I'm working in work shoes and heavy stockings and dirty pants and drinking lots of coffee and getting up at 5 in the morning and getting hard all over and shave only twice a week. I could quit and be fancy again in an office but I like this because I guess I never did it before. Maybe I'll really write after this. Thanks for the check for the New Directions section. I can't find any reviews so far, except a garbled listing in the Times Books Received list and note that the Book Clinic of Graphic Arts selected the book for its appearance. Also a letter from New Yorker stating that Clifton Fadiman liked my piece and thought that I might find New Yorker a congenial place to publish my fiction. Were there any reviews yet? I'd like to look some up. Did you know that love is a fever you can't subdue? Your heart will catch the flame? Anyway, its very interesting.

Alvin Levin

Levin exchanged a few more letters during the war years with Laughlin. These disclose how much of his passion for arcane details had been redirected into building up his pamphlet business and writing an occasional piece, such as an essay on the "nature of legal property" for ASCAP at a time before there was such a phrase as "intellectual property." The young author who had shown so much promise turned away from it. The reason could be one thing or many. Perhaps he had found love, as he intimates in the letter above, and no longer needed to write about it. Perhaps the accident he suffered in March, 1943, when a car jumped the curb and knocked him to the ground, left him with little energy to spare on his fiction. Perhaps his subject matter had dried up. The model for some of that was now married and her husband was his business partner. Stories like his might require disclosures, and everyone involved needed to be comfortable with that.

Perhaps Levin, as he became more and more the serious man, saw his Little Alvin years as childhood and saw his stories as a form of play, something a serious young lawyer-scholar and a publisher should not do. Perhaps he thought the lost souls who came to him to publish their own little books were embarrassing themselves. So why should he? For us, Levin closed the window that he had opened on his private world and his imagination. Soon he found ways to enjoy himself with another kind of theater, lending his cane to one of his sister's daughters to perform a tap dance routine. For another precocious niece, as a gift, he used his press to publish her stories.

Laughlin presumably returned the used and unused sections of *Love Is Like Park Avenue*. And, as though filling a back order for his pamphlet service, Levin culled a love story—his favorite subject—which was practically radio theater from his family life. He mailed it across the Atlantic with the convoys to the anthologist in England who, like the publisher of New Directions, wanted to be among the first to discover a writer good enough to appear with the young Saul Bellow, Lawrence Durrell—and Henry Miller whose candidness Levin rivaled, although he pulled back on the master's excesses and gave it all a Bronx pathos.

After this, Levin seems to have stopped submitting his work or sending his personal narrative-like letters. In libraries, one can find mostly his business correspondence with librarians. The manuscript for the novel disappeared and no one looked for it or asked him to write again during his lifetime; it might have made another Henry Roth-like comeback. Whatever James Laughlin read was not among the papers that filled the lone cardboard box, that family members used to clean out his rooms following his death on September 20, 1981.

A Note on the Text

I HAVE LOCATED AS MUCH of Levin's published and unpublished fiction as possible. (Other fugitive stories may turn up as more library holdings are digitalized and obscure little magazines come to light.) This selection is arranged chronologically to mirror the way Levin probably assembled *Love Is like Park Avenue*, that is, as a record, a documentary. The stand-alone stories serve to give a *semblance* of the missing parts of Levin's grand design, a method that seems to work well here if not for dinosaurs in the Museum of Natural History. That is, I believe Levin took passages from the longer work and had them titled when the need arose to see his name in print. (I have supplied the titles for all the unpublished sketches except "Law School.")

Selections from Levin's correspondence interpolate the stories. The goal here is to provide a narrative in Levin's words about his life and intentions. This makes for another documentary, a small window on the writer, the narrator.

For the most part, I have preserved Levin's "style." One can only imagine how the copyeditors of his day, who were famously severe, must have seen Levin as the ultimate challenge. Something, however, stayed their red pencils and we, the publisher and I, have only lifted ours a little. For the most part, I have left intact Levin's "stetted voice," his syntax, his idiomatic spellings, his "house" Yiddish- and Bronxisms, the lack of punctuation, words maddeningly run in and apart. He has forced "a while" together more than Gertrude Stein did *alright*. No documentation exists thus far where Levin forbade changes and his scholarly writings and reviews prove he could follow a style book. The manuscripts I have seen indicate that he did go back and sparingly cross things out and make insertions. What he is doing is not automatic writing. I take it to be a kind of naturalism, where the unnatural presence of the author, anything of his "invention" and discipline, to paraphrase his words to James Laughlin, wither away—like capitalism being debated by his friends and relatives. Levin is a people's author in the true sense, for he has tried to imitate how they might think or write out their narratives. He streamlines (there was a mania for this in the Depression) when the voice is on a roll, ditching commas and periods. Levin can also slow the tempo of his streams of consciousness, like the swing bands he loved, and even wordily "wait in line" (as people also did in the Depression). This naturalism did not exclude Levin. He, I think, factors in the means of production. Where a hyphen should go for a compound adjective, the ergonomics of a spacebar trumped the dash key of the typewriter that was either second hand or worn out.

Thus, only judicious corrections and revisions have been made where the reading experience is truly impeded. Also, some notes have been provided at the end of the book where certain unfamiliar names, places, "mistakes," and the like are explained.

—J.R.

LOVE IS LIKE PARK AVENUE

Love Is Like Park Avenue
(1936)

*W*HEN I SIT HERE alone and so full of weary sadness and I think about myself with plaintive yearnings my heart is heavy and all I can do is sit on the hard chair and look out of the window up at the sky. And I can sit here forever and feel so miserably at ease, thinking, making up things and making everything go on so wonderfully for myself, and all along I know it's only make-believe. But I don't care. I like to do it so much.

And when I'm not making things up I think about real things and then I almost kill myself with the saddest joy when I think how nice this was and how nice that was and how homely and familiar and peaceful that was and how the day was cloudy and later it began to rain while we were inside in the darkened room where the girl I made up said you're such a dope but I don't care.

I just want to sit here by the window with my cold hand against my face and just let me alone a little while so I can think awhile. And if no one will bother me I'll have such a lovely time. There's so much I want to think about and lay out nicely so I can refer to it again and again and again. Because that's the way it is with me. I can have such a good time and it would be so unfair and stupid to deprive me of it all for really no reason at all.

And so I remember all things thinking this way, the class where a fellow could actually rest and enjoy himself amid the semblance of a serious seminar in the social sciences. So slow and quiet and comfortable a class, doing nothing sitting and listening and looking around and everything went on so nicely and quietly with nobody bothering anybody like everybody came purposely to sit on hard chairs in the dusty room and be by themselves for an hour to sit still like they made you do in public school for punishment when you were bad only this time you weren't bad. Fragments about Briffault and the origin of the family and the Polynesians had such beautiful bodies and it was always raining and you could look outside as long as you wanted to and watch the rain roll down the big grimed windows and the wind shake the drops off the strong slender clinging vines around the edges of the sill and the cars making tire marks over the wet streets stopping two blocks down for the red lights while beautiful sad-faced drivers blew smoke against their windshields, and the little fast torrents of rain water forming and charging hell-bent down the insides of the trolley tracks going across town.

Oh, it was so nice to sit there where it was so quiet and you didn't have to say a word and everyone was so quiet like well mannered children in church on Sunday only the student in the teacher's big chair up in the front reading droning away his term report to the class and the professor sitting in the back with you happy and quiet too and smiling quietly and sadly and listening to the report of the great book he read fifteen years ago when he was studying at Columbia.

And after awhile it grew dark and you couldn't see the rain any longer, even when the lights came out on the campus. Only the street glistened under the College lamps and somebody got up in the classroom and looked around the room and everybody looked up too and he went to the switch in the room and put the light on, and you knew then pretty soon the bell would ring and you would go out into the rain in the dark and ride home.

Some days you had to go to the museum for the class and you didn't like that at first. But you did afterwards. It was so much like the class in school—there in the museum. You did the work yourself in the big dusty rooms filled so carefully with so much truck. And you copied the models and copied the labels and made believe the Indian girl in the case was your squaw and that the tepee was yours, and she had beautiful breasts and it was cold outside the tepee and you made a big fire while she helped you, bending over, and then you and she went inside and she took her soft black hair down and you both lay down to keep warm in front of the fire while the wild Dakota wind howled outside.

Everything was so quiet and orderly. You could sit on the high stool for hours and nobody would go near you. You could sit by the Eskimo exhibit and the kids with their mothers or fathers would stop by the other cases and the kids would never get their questions answered correctly, or most times the kids would never ask the questions but the fathers and mothers would tell them the wrong answers anyway. And the girls and fellows would come to look at the exhibits and they would go out very soon. And old men would come to look around. And sometimes the curators would take smiling visitors around. And everybody would look at you as if you were some special high class student or somebody making plans for a new addition to the museum, perhaps.

It was all so nice. Especially late on Friday afternoon when the place became empty and the attendant said they were closing up in five minutes and he started pulling down the old green shades over the high dusty windows and you walked down the quiet deserted halls into the roadway up to the long street and you could see the Park and the cars racing through on their way downtown for dinner, and the traffic on Central Park West racing the other way, up into the Bronx, uptown for supper.

You sit here now on the hard chair and think about these things and you don't know whether you are happy or sad. And you wonder if you'll ever think some day about now, and if then everything happening now will be nice to think about.

There's so much, so very much, to think about. It can drive you crazy with frustrated desire, all this, all the things that happen and you know about and feel about, even when they don't happen to you like people would say things happen. It's too much, really; too much to know about and feel about. You have to do too much to know and to feel all that. And when you think you do know and feel, it's even worse. You don't know then what to do about it. It's so much, you say. If only you could have it now instead of have it later when you think about it in the past.

Walk on Fifth Avenue at 7:30 in the evening. Ride through the Park about 9:30 in the morning. Drive through the Grand Central Station about six o'clock, past the old Murray Hill Hotel and around the turn past the Hotel Commodore. Or pick up a girl on Southern Boulevard or on 120th Street, or ride across the Manhattan Bridge, on the topmost level from a foreign city called Brooklyn, after the *Jewish Forward* sign lights up in blazing yellow, or see Tudor City and Sutton Place and race up Exterior Street in back of the Medical Center, and stop, like a crazy man, to hail the barges on the river after midnight.

It's like standing on the rear of the ferry, crossing the Hudson, with the strong wind slamming your breath down your throat and choking your life down into your belly.

Round and round the room the girl goes, stopping here and here and here, to say this and that and laugh nicely and lean back and sway this way and that way and blow smoke round and then go over there for awhile. And the music goes up and down throwing your heart this way and that way and throwing your arms out in slow motion, rocking your body and pushing you through a sleepy heavy mire of drugged consciousness. Drifting sands and caravans and music tense and sharp and full of tiger rhythm. While the clock ticks on and moves its hands and the girl goes on and on and the others sit and sit and talk and laugh and worry about themselves to themselves, August Heckscher, now eighty years old in an old thin body and under that white head of his, sits and thinks about his Foundation and

his birthday cakes, and the pretty silly little manicurist holds the
hand of the Bronx matron and hums the happy tune, da de de
de tum la de da, she learned in the good old days when from
Harlem she went to the Heckscher Foundation Camp for two
weeks one summer long ago.

Round and round it all goes, beating its rich sullen tom-tom
against your chest. So cold it was outside and so warm it was
inside, with the radiators steaming quietly away; and in the huge
dark hall shadows and dying dust and the small yellow lamps
and the bright sun bursting through the colored glass in sharp
beams, lighting up the corners for awhile and disclosing the path
of the dying dust, and then dying out leaving the same corners
dark and dusty. The professor looked in and then came in and he
shifted his dead cigar around, munched at it, held it in his freck-
led old hand, chewed it; and he searched for a pencil in every
pocket making faces like an angry Santa Claus until he found one
to make rough messy lines on the graph. It took him so long to
make a few lines from the notes it took him so long to make out
from the back of the envelope he took from his pocket. He
looked happy when he finished and he set the graph aside and he
looked around and he too heard the music the instructor was
grinding out of the victrola for the students who sat and listened
for the bell. He heard Haydn playing the brave and mighty music
to the mountains and he sat down heavily in a corner near me
where he smelled so strongly of the dead cigar and peppermints;
and there he sat and listened and wheezed and dreamed away
and all of a sudden the music stopped but the professor, staring
ahead of him, his eyes dead fixed on nothing ahead of him, never
knew it and the instructor changed the record to let Haydn go on
playing to the mountains, and the professor dreamed on with his
cigar tight in the corner of his old mouth, sitting in the dark corner where it was so warm, near the quietly sizzling radiator under
the big stained window that looked out on the cold hard cracked

ground of the campus.

On and on and on, and Christmas comes and ten thousand plaintive hopes and plans take form while the cheeks are cold and the lips are bright and dry and the eyes grow clear and bright and anxious, and the cold air wets the nose and the girls all look alike only their eyes showing how they feel, and all their powders smelling alike, and all of them so beautiful and so marvelously nice to think about from far away. And Christmas means the red and green and blue neon lights with the cold sidewalks and the frosted windows and the red tinsel all over the small wrapped-up bundles and the candy and the peanut brittle and peppermint chocolates and cigarettes and tea and cocktails and Shirley Temple movies and gloves and shows and the telephone and the restaurant downtown and the library and the Christmas tree in the strange lobby and the swinging doors and the trolley car and the pictures around the top and the friends and New Year's cards and some Christmas cards and going out and boy friends and girl friends and the light in the window upstairs and the smoke coming out of the apartment chimney and making up the uncertain sky that has no sun or moon or stars and parties and nickels and quarters and hot chocolate and cars running by as fast as the wind over the trolley tracks and down the avenue sometimes steaming from the radiators and always smoking out of the back and hopes and plans and wishful waitings and maybe maybe maybe's, this time it will be better. It's Christmas and, oh, the tremendous overwhelming love for me and the sweet nostalgic longing, yearning for more and more of the titanic spectacle to have and feel and know before me. Within me, the wondrous splendor of all the ordinary life before me, within me, that weaves and weaves about me.

The night is cold, the trees are bare, and the naked spinster limbs bend against a sky, clouded, clear and bright beneath a clouded moon. A hundred miles away, south and far from the snowy bleakness of the Berkshire Hills, the red brick apartment stands itself, five stories high, against the sky, clouded, clear and bright beneath a clouded moon. And from a window, from behind the very latest cheapest cross-knit curtains on the window peers the face of the girl who sits with her head cupped in her hands, who sits and sits and wipes the window clear of her breath against the cold pane of glass and follows the path of the people as far as she can, and lifts her head and silently, wildly, screams her anguish against the sky, clouded, clear and bright beneath a clouded moon, the sky that goes on and on and on.

And high above the lights of Manhattan, in the Rainbow Room, on the sixty-sixth floor of the RCA Building, the rich and gorgeous splendor of a Joan Crawford supper club makes itself real to the merry merry merry and so beautifully well-dressed boys and girls, from Harvard, Princeton, Yale, Cornell, Syracuse, Vassar, Smith, Adelphi, Woodmere Academy, that the swift gilted elevators carry up sixty-five floors from the amazing subtle richness of a Rockefeller Center, up to hear immaculate aesthetic Ray Noble arrange his orchestra through "Moon Over Miami." And rich and happy, jolly wise guys home from school and happy happy happy sweet smelling daughters, all laughing laughing at nothing, at something, when it hurts, when it doesn't, till it hurts; nibbling costly pretty food, spoiling wondrous, gorgeous, expensive concoctions of sickening painful fluids.

And all this the girl in the window yearns for and plans for, and on Christmas yearns for and plans for more than ever before. And on this Christmas she sits and listens to the radio, to Ray Noble from the sixty-sixth floor high above the lights of Manhattan as he leads his diabetic orchestra through "Moon Over Miami," and she can't sit any more, it's too much, but if she stands up she'll have to do something, and what is there to do? But she can't sit here, she just can't, that's all, can't can't can't, do you hear, can't. The night the darkness the cold the lights the music, oh me me the boy a nice one, oh so nice a boy and like her, show her he does every time too, oh show her he likes her. But you can't sit sit sit always sit and listen to the radio and look out of the window and that's all. Damn the radio and I'll break the window. Christmas, God-damn Christmas, God-damn it to hell. And the girl in the window stood up in the dark room and she didn't know what to do then but she crossed the room and flung herself across the bed and cried and cried and her body jerked while the radio was telling how Ray Noble sixty-six floors above Fifth Avenue was finishing "Moon Over Miami" and how you'd better make your New Year's reservations at the Rainbow Room as soon as possible.

So it is. And so it is. But how it hurts and hurts and never ends, and how it fascinates. It's because life is fundamentally so miserable an experience. And everything you hope and pray for never sees the breath of the day you hope and pray for. And from such beginnings and ends of dreams remains no heart that sings, but a mind and consciousness that learns once more and grows to hope and pray anew. And therein lies the fascination—to hope and pray anew.

My Son
(1939)

I LIKE MY WIFE BECAUSE she takes such good care of my son. When she bathes him she bends over the large tub in the bathroom and her body makes the sweetest turns. When it is hot she takes showers with a bathing cap over her long thick hair, and she puts my son in the tub at her feet, and he claps his hands under the cool spray that dashes off her glistening body. It is wonderful to watch her dry herself and my son at the same time. Then she powders her body and his at the same time and a wondrous smell hangs over the bathroom, and my son helps his mother rub his soft belly that is growing harder every day. When my son laughs out loud, my wife grins happily and talks back to him as though he were a man already.

She steps into something that isn't bloomers and still isn't running pants. My wife tosses her long hair back of her ears and begins to tidy up the house. I sit in my chair and watch my son swaddle on the floor in front of me on his throne of heaped towels. The curling smoke of my long white cigarette takes my son's fancy, and he rolls off his throne to grasp at the smoke. I can only sit and watch him. My wife passes by the door of the room and rushes in suddenly when she sees my son on all his fours looking for the smoke. She pats his behind in scolding, and settles him once more on his throne before me. My wife throws me a silent glance that is full of weary disgust at the way I take care of my son. I grab her to me and set her on my lap, and my son waves his hands when I touch her lovely shoulders and she lays her damp head against my neck.

I feel like a million dollars and I watch with fascination the slow regular rise and fall of my wife's breasts. She tells me it is time to feed my son, and then we have to stand up. My wife hunts in the dresser and dresses my son in a white panty that hugs his belly with a ribbed elastic band. A little roll of flesh hangs over the top. He is very good to look at too.

We take him into the kitchen for his supper. He is very hungry and I sit back to watch my son put an end to his farina and zwieback. My wife sits before my son in his brown highchair, resting her elbows on his small table and feeding him calculated spoonfuls while he proclaims to us on the ways of his life. There is a trick my wife knows to catch my son between paragraphs and let him have a spoonful. My wife miscalculates occasionally, and my son gets only three-quarters of the spoonful and a blob of farina lands on his manly chest. My wife uses the zwieback to scoop the mush off my son, and he laughs in a ridiculous mood. I toss over my handkerchief, but my wife sticks her red tongue out at me and uses the big napkin with the word "Bobby" stitched in red across the corner.

My son takes his time with the glass of milk and the rest of the zwieback, devoting long intervals to his discussion of Neo-Kantian idealism. My wife puts everything into her job now, bending over to my son, and her shoulders are like handsome apples, and her strong chest bone shows just below the long line of her graceful neck. My wife explains to me the nature of child guidance from nursery to college, and my son doesn't interrupt her but keeps up a conversation of his own.

My son is like a clock, regular and constant. When the glass of milk is really empty he becomes drowsy, like a tired old man, and he begins to pout and stops talking so much. My wife picks him out of the highchair and hugs my son to her with her head tilted back—then suddenly leans her head forward behind my son's left ear, as he urges his fat arms around her neck. My wife's hair falls over her face and my son carelessly musses it with the last fancy of his day. I could do a better job of it than my son does.

A Cool Drink Is Refreshing
(1939)

MIMI WALKED DOWN THE main corridor, smelling the heated dankness of the place, feeling the conserved poorness of the whole school in the strained pretentiousness of the wide rectangle flagged on either side by small classrooms and dingy offices, a few class display cases and several small hard benches under the traditional class plaques.

A tall, haughty, grinning man passed out of one of the offices, distinguished under his shock of soft white hair combed straight back, his rimless glasses protected from a fall by a black cord around the starched whiteness of his collar. Everyone near him shriveled into insignificance as he strode down the hall with a huge relic of a meerschaum held tightly between thin red lips. The heat meant nothing to this splendid specimen of English perfection, and Mimi, in the stickiness of her wrinkled blue linen dress, despised the professor for his smug complacency as he greeted a colleague with a boyish wave of his arm, or stopped to exchange a few choice quips with a sweating student who managed to hold the receiving end with a series of foolish grins.

At the end of the hall Mimi stood around under the clock trying to make out whether the red gash, in the center of a rather silly and pretentious wall mural of learned men of ancient times, was an electric bulb or just an extra blob of paint. It lay over an impressive double door cut through the mural and Mimi figured whatever it was it must certainly have some symbolic significance. And who cares, she told herself.

She was tired and warm, she wanted to sit down somewhere.

A shrill bell rang out for a full ten seconds and the hall suddenly filled with yelling mobs of students in suspenders and fancy polo shirts with undershirts showing through. Mimi picked out a nice boy wearing a suit and white saddle shoes and asked where room 316 was. He directed her and she walked to the elevator, but when the professors began collecting around its small grating she decided to walk the two flights.

The soles of her feet burned in her sandals. It smelled pretty bad on the staircase. The banisters were sticky under her hand, they felt dirty under her hand as she grasped to keep her balance in the midst of so many eager students bent on getting down to their classes on time. For Mimi was unwittingly using a "down" staircase to get up to the third floor.

Upstairs she found the room finally, and waited for Henry to appear. She stood leaning against the wall, her feet crossed at the ankles, watching the fellows pass in front of her. Most of them noticed the girl and looked back. She met their glances with the semblance of a small mysterious smile, relishing their curiosity over her presence in this man's world, aware as they were of her breasts pushing tightly against the thin dress, of her bare legs. Then Henry came along, toward his classroom.

"Hello, Henry," she said quietly, with a happy laugh as he passed into the room unaware of her.

"Gee, Mimi, hello. What are you doing here?"

"Are you surprised to see me, Henry? You look so scared."

"I'm glad to see you, kid, but what's the matter?" Henry stood there, scared and then comforted by what he saw in his sister's face.

"Oh, I came down to see the president, that's all," she kidded, twisting her face nonchalantly. "No really, I've got news for you, good news I suppose. Come here," they were blocking traffic through the classroom door. "You got a job, for the summer, I mean. Papa got it for you this morning. He called up in the candy store and mama spoke to him." She looked at him in the dungeon gloom of the hall.

"Yeah, what kind of a job?" Henry asked, the flash of riding up the elevator of the building, telling everything to some secretary, finally talking to the boss for the job—the sickening agony of it all—passed through him.

Mimi paused. Then: "On a milk route, you'll be helping the milkman with the deliveries," she said quietly, watching her brother from under serious eyelids. She added quickly, "You only work a few hours each day, at night, you know, in the early morning."

Henry could feel her opinion of the job. He could only feign cynical disgust, but also cynical resignation. He loved her for her attempt to shield him, for her understanding, because she was so like him.

"Well, that's O.K.," he said looking back at her.

"It's not so bad, Mimi," he told her, "I guess I have the whole day off."

"Yes," Mimi said, her turn now to be critical. "But Henry, you'll have to get up so early, three o'clock in the morning, every day."

"Oh, that's O.K. It'll be fun getting up so early, I never did it before." Now the important question: "Did papa say how much I get?"

Again Mimi was on the defensive, "Papa said they paid the other fellow seven dollars a week. He said you should ask the man for more," she said.

"But isn't it settled already? I mean the job is certain isn't it?"

"Yes, I guess so, but you got to see the man, this afternoon. That's why I'm here now. The man wants to see you this afternoon. We knew you wouldn't be home until late so I came down to school to tell you," she explained, writhing in the sudden realization that no amount of compromising could wipe out the awful defeat of Henry's job for the summer.

And Henry, who knew this for a long time, sickened because he saw Mimi knew too. A dollar a day and Mimi had to come down to school in all this heat so he wouldn't be too late for the job. Go on, make some joke up about the job, something to show you don't care, something to show her it's only for the time being, say something funny. But it was no use, it was too hot, you feel lousy enough as it is.

They stood there watching each other. The late bell rang and the doors were being closed and latecomers kept racing past them making for their classes. Two instructors came along, their little red books under their arms, talking. They stopped outside one of the open doors, talking, one of them playing at the door stop with his moccasined foot while the class waited. Then he went inside closing the door behind him and the other teacher went to his room. Then they were alone in the long curving corridor.

"Don't you have your class in here?" Mimi said finally.

"The hell with it," Henry grouched. He acted sore, like things were too hard to bear. "I wouldn't go to class today. I wouldn't miss anything anyway." He wanted to do something for her now, something to show her everything was all right, to show her how things would be pretty soon for all of them. He wanted to casually take her someplace now where it was cool and buy her a drink, as though it meant nothing and wasn't planned beforehand.

Gosh, seven dollars would come in handy every week, you could buy things, go some place—that's if papa didn't take the money for the rent or insurance.

He had some money with him, but he wouldn't take her into the smelly cafeteria downstairs for an amateur soda they called the "radical flop" and have her drink it standing up before the high kitchen tables with a mob of slobs and greasy lunch bags and *New York Times* all around them under the dirty yellow bulbs. You couldn't be casual and important there in all that familiar dirt. He stood there with her, letting precious minutes go by unchecked. He wanted to sit down there right on the steel steps for a minute and rest his back against the wall in all that dark silence.

"Come on, let's get out of here, Mimi," he said moving off.

Mimi laughed, following him. "Some school, you can go to your classes whenever you want to, just like the movies." They went downstairs together. The halls were empty. Henry was glad she thought it daring to cut a class just like that. A slight breeze came through the high dirty windows of the staircase from out of the west, from the Hudson, stirring up a little dust. Mimi stopped on the landing, catching the little wind, her eyes closed gently.

"It's a nice view from here," she said watching the panorama from the window.

"That's the Riverside Church over there," Henry pointed to the tall grey tower way over the top of the stadium, "Rockefeller built it. You ought to see it at night, its got a red signal burning on the top."

"A church with a red light," Mimi ridiculed. "I never heard of such goings on, pretty soon you'll be telling me the madams live in the vestry rooms."

"Well, to be perfectly frank about it, Mimi, they do live there, that is every day but Sunday. That's the day for services, you know," said Henry seriously, falling into Mimi's mood joyously.

"Some town," Mimi remarked, watching from the window.

The small campus lay boiling in the afternoon heat. Some students crossed the streets slowly. The pop man sat on the stone railing under the shade of the WPA shack, his white box of chocolate pops, kept hard like bricks by artificial ice, between his legs. Over in the stadium some fellows were taking the blazing sun as they lay stripped to their underpants on folded newspapers on the stone tiers, making every inch of the place look like the Roman Senate after the patriots got through with Catalinex and his followers.

"It's hot, all right," said Henry, "do you want a drink, Mimi?"

"A drink? Yes, anything that's cold," Mimi wanted a drink.

Henry remembered a German soda parlor up near Broadway; he once passed it and liked its substantial devotion to the business of serving ice cream sodas without the cut rate innovations of the candy palaces. It was a long walk from school and Mimi wanted to stop in any one of the candy stores on the way but Henry was adamant. He brusquely told her he would not enter those dirty little places that were as bad as the school cafeteria; she could go in herself, not him though.

They finally reached the place, lying comfortably under its awning, off the wide sidewalk. Inside, amid the quiet, orderly heat of the darkened place, Henry debated whether to sit at a table in the back, but when Mimi climbed a stool at the fountain he followed next to her. Mimi scrubbed her face with a handkerchief. "That was some walk, Mr. Henry," she told him primly.

"But worth it, kid," he told her scowling. "I can't stand those other places. Do you want a malted?"

Mimi said no. She liked this kind of a place better too. Henry was a swell guy, she was sure. He ought to get the breaks, though. She watched his hot face, he looked bad, all grey and pale. Gee, she daydreamed, if I ever marry a rich guy the first thing I'll do is get Henry fixed up with some swell job. She sat with her elbows on the counter, staring away at the mirror along the wall, all plastered up with menu suggestions, dreaming away, fixing everything up for the family.

The soda jerker stood in front of her. Henry asked her again what she wanted. She came back to reality. "I'll have a coco cola." But Henry would have none of it. "Like hell," he whis-

pered to her fiercely, "you'll have an ice cream soda or something, not a lousy little coke. Now don't get me sore, Mimi"—
when she shook her head—"you take a coke and you'll drink it
here yourself."

"But I don't want a soda, Henry," she protested laughingly.
"I just want a drink."

The soda guy never heard such nonsense. He waited impatiently. Henry ordered two sodas, chocolate, with a dominating
mastery that made him proud of his manliness. They watched the
jerker perform. The sodas were sweet; Mimi said so and Henry
half wanted to order the guy to add more soda to it. Mimi said
it was all right. They finished in silence. Mimi asked for another
glass of water; she drank it watching Henry over the rim of the
glass. He wanted a drink too but he wouldn't give her the satisfaction of asking for more water. Mimi watched him pay the jerker thirty cents. He took her elbow and they went outside into the
glaring sun. Henry was still thirsty.

A trolley jerked by. Some mothers were shopping over sidewalk vegetable displays. The street was quiet. The kids were still
in school. They stood under the awning.

"Was mama all right when you left the house?" Henry wanted to know.

"Yes, but she's afraid the work will be too hard for you. She
don't like the idea of you working at night." Mimi retreated
under the awning, leaning against the plate window.

"It's all right. I'll take it easy."

"You know, Henry, you don't look so good. You really ought
to have a rest."

"Don't worry. I haven't got the job yet anyway." Again the
mean horror of interviewing for the job caught him.

Then: "Well, I guess I better go if I have to see that man. You
got the address?"

She searched in her pocket. "Here it is. He's the manager.

Tell him papa spoke to the man in the office this morning."

"I know, I know," Henry said, taking the card and sticking it in his pocket.

Mimi reared herself. "Well, I guess I better be going home, Henry," she said, peering at him from under a bent head. "You'll be home for supper pretty soon, won't you?"

"Yeah, thanks for coming, Mimi." Why did she have to act like a woman all the time, making it so hard, acting like it was a funeral and you had to keep your chin up? Go on home!

"It's all for the family, my dear brother," she pointed out with her finger.

He raised his chin in mock derision. The crosstown car rumbled down the hill. "There's your car, have you money?"

"Yes, I got it here. Now I wouldn't have to wait in this heat for another one. Come home early, Henry, and lots of luck—" She wanted to ask him if he had any money for his carfare but she figured on his hot, angry face. "Goodbye, Henry," she called over her shoulder, cheerfully, as she ran for the trolley stopped on the corner.

He smiled back. Maybe she didn't want a soda, maybe she really only wanted a coke instead. He was sorry he acted so rough. He loved her as he watched her climb the trolley steps, so small, so familiar, really a little girl, the back of her knee showing as she lifted her foot high to make the step. So poignantly a part of everything he knew and did and felt.

April 22nd, 1939

Dear James Laughlin,

Thanks for your swell letter. It would be something really big for me to appear in NEW DIRECTIONS 1939. Big enough to make me get a new typewriter. Or a new ribbon, at least. ONLY DREAMS ARE TRUE is bright and sad. It's the way I feel most of the time. . . .

Sincerely,
Alvin Levin

ONLY DREAMS ARE TRUE
(1939)

*T*HIS IS A TRUE STORY about life. It is simple because life is simple for all its troubles. I speak of a girl who wanted peace, peace of mind. She was pretty and sweet, with lovely legs and good taste. She gave her all and was satisfied with little in return.

This girl was riding in the subway of a great metropolis one afternoon. She slipped and fell. The guard picked her up. Her brother was a young lawyer, so she said to the guard, I want a doctor. The guard called the hospital and she suffered the stares of the other subway riders as they glanced at her seated on the wooden bench near the tracks. The ambulance came and the interne examined the girl. He said, where does it hurt? It didn't hurt anyplace, it was just a scratch, but she said, oh my foot, it hurts terribly, and she raised her brown eyes to his. The interne was awfully nice looking. She said maybe we ought to go to the hospital, but he said, lady I only see a little scratch and a bruise and I don't think you ought to go to the hospital, but if you insist … By this time the girl was getting cold feet and she said, maybe you're right, but I don't want to go home alone like this. So the handsome interne said, I will be free in another hour, so if you want to wait for me someplace I will call for you and take you home, that is unless you live somewhere in Brooklyn.

By this time the girl was getting cold feet and she said, maybe you're right about the hospital. But she didn't think it would be comfortable waiting in a subway for an hour, and anyway it wasn't at all proper, so she said, thanks, I'll manage myself. She kept her self-respect.

The handsome interne made out a report, and when she was riding home in the subway alone she thought that if he wanted to get in touch with her he could because he had her name and address in his report. So she arrived at home and she figured out that in another half hour he would be free and if he ever called her he would call in a half an hour because now he had a good excuse to find out how she felt after her accident.

So she hoped and hoped that in a half an hour he would call her. And even if he didn't call her then, she would see him in court when her brother had the case. And then she would wear the new skirt and sweater she was thinking about all week that matched her new winter coat so nicely, and she would get a hat to match the sweater she saw in the window; or maybe she would wear last year's outfit which was more sophisticated. What she was going to wear was going to depend on how she was going to act toward him.

Now, if she was going to act friendly, as if she wasn't angry that he hadn't called, and maybe even ask him how he had been, then she'd want to look sophisticated and then she'd wear her last year's outfit. But if she was going to pretend that she never gave him another thought she would want to walk into court in a carefree manner as though she was just going or coming from a football game, and then she'd wear the skirt outfit.

So she sat near the telephone in the foyer and thought about what could be. Because you can never tell with fellows, just what they like to see on girls. So she thought she better play safe and wear the dressy outfit from last year. It never fails. They always like to see a girl dressed up. They may say they don't like you to use lipstick, so you don't use lipstick, and they remark that it is good that you don't use lipstick, but when you do put lipstick on they always say how much prettier you look. So she settled the matter: she'd get the skirt and sweater anyway and she would wear it when she went visiting and she could feel comfortable in a chair and when she stood up in the living room. And if it was warm in the house she would take her suit coat off, she should really get a tweed suit, and pull the sweater sleeves up over her elbows, like the Vassar girls did. With a simple string of small white beads around her neck. But she'd wear last year's outfit when she went to court. Only maybe she'd get a new hat and she'd wear very sheer stockings. She'd buy two thread with a sunburnt color, but with more orange in it.

The minutes passed for the girl and the importance of the accident faded as far as the family was to be told, because a scratch is after all only a scratch and telling about it means going over to yourself all the incidents of the scratch which cannot ever be told to the family. You can't think with so many people around. Because there are too many things to think about. You have to corner your thoughts in a narrow space somewhere in your mind like when you go to your room and lay on your bed and put your arms over your eyes and pick out each thing to think about separately. You arrange them orderly in rows and you try to get rid of the bad things first, and when you have only the good things left the bad things come back and the good things are no longer there or even good anymore.

What if Johan had a friend who had a bookstore. Then he'd tell his friend about you and that you were looking for a position, and you'd go down to the Village to see him, but you wouldn't know what to wear again. Its always safest, though, to wear black. It makes you look older and it makes you feel stronger. He'll be an old man, about sixty, in dusty clothes, and he'll be very pleased with you. You'll tell him you were a literature major at college and you'll hope that he won't begin to discuss the classics with you.

Then, after you are there a few weeks, you'll take off your high heels and you'll buy those brown gum-soled shoes for three dollars you saw yesterday on 14th Street. Then you'll buy a cashmere sweater, but it won't be a cashmere sweater really because you'll only make about thirteen fifty a week, because he's poor. And maybe after awhile you'll cut your hair short all around, and he'll grow to depend on you more and more in the bookstore, and you'll grow more efficient and charming everyday, and you'll have a quietness about you.

Nice men will come into the place. A man will come in one day in a reversible coat and a mustache, and he'll be impressed with you after you talk to him awhile. And he will invite you out to lunch after talking to you until about eleven forty five all about literature and books. He will be about forty, and you will go to lunch with him in a nice place and there will not have to be any effort on your part because you know he already thinks that you are charming and he is forty anyway, and he is going away in a few days on a long trip.

Someday a young writer will come in and he has an apartment right around the block from the bookstore and after coming in a few times he invites you to a party he was invited to. You go and you have a few straight drinks so you will not be afraid and everybody thinks that you are wonderful. And he is very proud but also very jealous, so you don't bother with the other people anymore and you and he leave the party and he takes you home to his apartment and you look out of his window and point out where the bookstore is. He says that he loves you and you think of all that he has done and who he is and you think that he is wonderful.

So you muzzle a little bit, and it is very nice. And then you say, it isn't very late, I'll go home alone. Because by this time you're pretty much an independent woman, and if he were just an ordinary fellow you wouldn't think of going to his apartment in the first place, but with him anything seems all right. But he wants to take you home in a taxi but you don't let him, and then a great understanding springs up between both of you and you are both really in love with each other.

I speak of this pretty girl who wanted peace, peace of mind. When I walked in on her she was seated at the telephone in the foyer, and I said, why are you sitting here in the dark? And she looked up at me with a silly laugh and said, I don't know, I was just thinking how a girl must feel if she hasn't got as much as her friends have because none of the guys make passes at her in the subway, and even though she says to her friends, isn't that terrible? she is envious, not of what happened, but because it didn't happen to her and maybe she hasn't got what it takes.

June 13, 1939

Dear Laughlin,

Its great getting a letter from you. Im a sucker for the postman anyway. I don't get much mail, except offers to have the summer rugs cleaned before laying. I once was very lonely and answered a personal note in the Saturday Review of Literature, *and now even though I don't feel so bad about being lonely I cant get out of the correspondence. Shes 36, divorced, lives in Chimney Rock, North Carolina and makes rugs and baskets for tourists on their way south. She has a beautiful body, red hair and a stubborn head, thinks Thomas Wolfe and Erskine Caldwell should be ashamed of themselves and William Faulkner should be lynched. She had me get her Bercovici's Tour around New York City because the metropolis "fascinates" her and when I told her the WPA guide was much better (I didn't think so) than Bercovici's sappy travelogue she told me I must be a radical because I could say the WPA did anything good. She said Roosevelt wastes our money building houses for the poor whites because they can ruin a house quicker than a nigger can. She says her husband drank too much and lied too much and one day he drank too much and lied too much so she took the key, put the dog in the back of the car and drove away. Then there is a wonderful girl out in Lake Quivira, Kansas, who read a short piece of mine in the University Review a few months ago and had to write and tell me what a masterpiece it was. She is very sad and brilliant and it makes her suffer a lot. I didnt want her to tell details*

about herself because I liked her so much and I felt
that you only want to know things about people you
dislike and the more you dislike them the more you
want to know about them, sort of spite (and if you
hate people in a mass you want to be a sociologist
about it and that makes you want to be a writer), and
if you like them you want to live in a suspension about
them and be able to dream how they are; but this
Harriett started asking questions and before I could
stop her she told me she was 29, plays piano and is a
member of the Kansas bar, though she practices nei-
ther, has a father who is a college professor and a
mother who was a D.A.R. (but it didn't take on
Harriett) and a handsome brother. She is a lightweight
except when she drinks beer. She offers to build me a
tree house on the estate and bring apples, ale and
cheese, and I tell you she is quite wonderful, like Ella
Fitzgerald riding on down. That is about as far as my
correspondence goes. . . .

> *Thanks,*
> *Alvin Levin.*

August 29, 1939

Dear Laughlin,

A lot of trouble here. I'm writing a great deal but I don't think its all what you want. I have laid off interior monologue and it seems that the next thing is travelogue and editorial comment; Like: "Well, let's see what they're doing in Europe these days." I mean, reading of Leonard Q. Ross's latest book, THE STRANGEST PLACES, reviewed this past Sunday, I suddenly recognized that Mr. Ross was stealing my thunder and undoubtedly carrying it off much better. There is the brittle cleverness of New Yorker stuff in his material and I can't attempt measuring up to that. Also, each piece of his is centrally located, like today we will discuss the Cafe Royal on Second Avenue and tomorrow we will take a trip to New Orleans and its all connected under the theme: THIS IS AMERICA, HAVE A LAUGH. I don't want to offer a free advertisement to places of local color; I want to fit feelings and emotions and despair and faith into background, but I can't decide, so far as construction goes, whether to fit background to feeling or feeling to background. Why can't I make Hemingway simple? Why can't I break down the studied construction of Hemingway or Caldwell so that we might really understand how men feel in the struggle against losing control of their world? In the choice between suggesting and proclaiming I choose the latter, but I feel that this choice implies a million characters and a million activities and I don't know how to put the characters and activities together for the reader's benefit. Main characters and central plots are out. At least I think so right now. But otherwise, as you say, "It gets a bit thick after a while."

As it stands I have a general concept of some twelve sections each devoted to a phase of New York life, under headings Society, Science And Health, Fashions In Dress, Sports, Manners, Europe, Love And Sex, Revolution, Religion, World's Fair, Five Boroughs. Hell, it sounds like a super WPA Guide Book. But my point is that guide books contain no feelings and interpretations and heavy mixtures of Waldo Franks and Saroyans.

Go on, Laughlin, go on and rush me into something definite. Tell me when we go to press, if we're heading that way anyway, or should I stick to my legal tomes?

Alvin Levin.

November 26, 1939

Dear Laughlin,

I saw New Directions 1939 in books received in the Sunday Times this morning. That's nice. I saw Henry Miller there too. That's not so good because when they get to looking at New Directions to see Miller they figure they might as well read his whole work under separate cover and thus New Directions is neglected. It would be better if the Miller book came six months after New Directions, to give New Directions a break. Anyway, I read Miller and he is good, just as Saroyan is good, but I am better. Not that I write better yet, but I'm better because without writing I'm funnier than Miller and smarter than Saroyan because Miller isn't so funny and Saroyan isn't so smart in writing anyway. Love Is Like Park Avenue is piling up in pages but it still hasn't plot and I doubt if it ever will have plot in the sense that novels have plots. Its like a newsreel and the daily papers and talking about things, like a journey to the city and back. . . .

Its cold here and the full moon is shining over the clothes line. It was a bountiful Thanksgiving and I am full of red wine, sweet and Jewish. I am doing record reviews for a very arty magazine and I get passes to the Savoy Ballroom. I am a champ at Chinese checkers. I will buy a clarinet. I feel that I can blow out in the four-fourest time.

Alvin Levin

AND I TOOK A WIFE
(1939)

SHE'S SUCH A NICE little girl. Appealing like. I love her very much. In the wintertime, when she has a cold, her nose is wet, like a sassy puppy dog's. I like her all year around, though, day and night. Her shoulders are like ripe apples. Her tummy is round and hard and soft, too. When I think of her I think of jasmine because I don't really know much about jasmine, but it must be very wonderful. Sometimes, when she walks down the street, she struts. But she is not like a girl who would strut and refuse to admit it. Nothing like, say, Madeleine Carroll in the movies. She's more like Gypsy Rose Lee. There is a steady ripple under her dress high up on her hips right to the sides of her round button when she walks.

I ask her, I say, why do you go out with me? I go out with you for my mother's sake, she tells me, and then she laughs out loud, drawing off to take a roundhouse sock at me, and I duck in all seriousness. Sometimes she is sad, real sad, like as though she wanted to die. It's only when she feels bad about things, and then I feel lousy, too, because I would like to believe that with me she feels great all the time. I wish a hurricane would blow *us* all up, she tells me. Hurricanes are no fun, I say. That's all right, they smash things, she tells me. She says, I wish that I were dead. She says it feeling her breast and looking like it hurt her there. It's not right for her to be like this, I think to myself. I want her to go with clean sunshine and clear, fresh water of mountain streams like writers write about when they call things pleasant and oddly exciting. She has soft, black, curly hair that sweeps off a neat rounded forehead.

You have nothing much to feel bad about, I try to tell her. Yeah, she says, nothing but me and life to worry about. You have nice clothes, you smell so nice, I say. And I want to go on. So what, she says with that solemn look girls have only when they are looking into their mirrors, what's it all for, anyways. It's all right to wear gingham if you have enough colors. Do you see what I mean? I say that I do. You go to school, and that isn't too difficult to swallow, I urge her. And what if I do, she says, her eyes mad and big; I don't learn anything. I waste so much time there, she says. I only remember nonsense, like the Palisades are ignias intrusions of the triacic era of the Mesozoic Age. So what? Does it do the Jews any good to know that the Catskills are a dis-ected plateau on a pene plane? She pauses and stares out of the window, gazing recklessly at rain falling in a million drops from an empty sky. If you understood me you would know what I mean, she says slowly. I feel like hell then because she feels like she does and she thinks I don't understand how she feels. If I try to tell her that I know she only gets sore. She says, finally, ah, go out and lay yourself in the alley down there; I'll come down later in my raincoat and step on you. And I don't want her to say such things because that means she wants me to go away and leave her alone for awhile, and I want to stay with her all the time.

I love her like I love a thick, soft snow before it melts and grows stale and dirty with garbage in the gutter. Sometimes when she is happy and her face is full and open, laughing and happy, I feel so wonderful that I can't keep that heavy lump out of my throat. Then we have great times together. We go to Chinatown, on Mott Street, and we order Wor Tep Hor, which is nothing but bacon and shrimp. She drinks a lot of tea with what we are eat-ing, and then she has to keep going all the time. She gets up from her bamboo chair and walks slowly to the ladies' room, and I sit around waiting for her to come back. Most of the time she forgets her pocket book and I sit playing with it, feeling the heavy leather and smoking cigarettes, and I am very sad sitting there until she comes back slowly through the door. The room is very ugly, and it makes me think of her when she is sad, but it shouldn't because we come here only when she is happy again, and when she keeps on talking about anything. She tells me that two hundred out of the five thousand nine hundred babies born every day in the U.S.A *are* illegitimate, and she tells me a long story about an actor out in Hollywood who refused to hold an actress in his arms in a scene in a picture because everybody in Hollywood knew the actress, who was a very famous glamour star, had syphilis. She tells me a lot of phoney stories, her mouth full of rice and her eyes dancing all over me. I listen and listen, and I finally cut her short, telling her, madam, I could give you my decision in psychological terms, but in plain language you are a screwball. She likes that and she laughs, and we are both very happy.

She holds her fingers of her right hand against her cheek in a thoughtful pose and doesn't talk for a few minutes. Then she withdraws her fingers and leaves three little white marks on her cheek. The flush spreads over them. It's like ripe wine. I am a modern disciple of Orpheus, she bursts out; I am a member of Radio's Happiest Family, too. I have nothing to answer her with. I was born in the May month, the springtime, that's me, she tells me, and I seek my guidance from celestial augeries; in fact, I am just one colossal microbe. I say to myself, what's so wonderful about her? and it comes to me like a flash: it's the way her hair falls down the back of her head, the way it fluffs about her ears, the way her shoulders move under her clothes, the way she changes from an illusion to a commonplace and carries over the illusion to the commonplace.

She talks a lot, like she had to get it out of her system. Like it was gnawing at her moiling insides, like some people have to shout and run all over the place to get some final peace. You are a phoney, she tells me; your mother should have dropped you on your head when you were a baby; the Devil is sitting in your eyes; go tie a flatiron around your neck and take a running jump into the Hudson River for a change; my home is my castle—I'll throw you down the sewer; I'll go see the mayor and have him raise your taxes; you're so crooked that when you die they'll have to screw you into the ground. She goes on and on. Then she cools down and confesses, her head buried in her arms; it's a wonder, a miracle of God's goodness, that my tongue isn't stricken dumb with the words that fall out of it. Twelve months from today I will be dead just one year, she tells me.

We go home later, and it is not important at all what she wears underneath that is so fascinating. It's the snug intimacy of what she wears underneath, or even on the outside for that matter—because a crumpled little handkerchief or a bent bobbie pin or a deflated pair of stockings lying tossed over the chair is just as lovely—that counts. How she rolls over on her side with a long night sigh, sleepily brushing a curl of hair off her face with the back of her hand and languidly drawing up her knees, twisting the blue faded pajamas under her, and her coat falls open and I watch her gold chain, the one from my watch before she bought me my wrist watch, slide from the nexus of her breasts and slip over her breast and dangle with the weight of my college key from around her neck. How she slips out of her pajama pants in the early morning cold, dropping the warm pants from around her hips and stepping lightly out of them with the graceful step of a naked leg and a calculating glance into the full-length mirror on the bedroom door—deep-rooted satisfaction quietly registering for the warm bed-fragrance of curving multicellular delights. She clucks her tongue in appreciation and turns to me on the heel of her foot. Every girl is Isadora Duncan in the quiet of her room, she tells me. And she dances, prances, weaves and flirts, and in her naked wanton splendor seduces ten thousand reckless men. Is it any wonder that I had to marry her? I lay there praying for a happy day today with her.

August 9, 1940

Dear Mr. Laughlin:

. . . It was pleasant receiving a check for my little piece in NEW DIRECTIONS, 1939. Are you still accepting material for the 1940 issue? I have some stuff around, from the novel. You may recall: LOVE IS LIKE PARK AVENUE. I haven't been able to get around to a definite plot for the thing. I believe that it has a wholeness as it is and I am constantly adding to it. I think that plots are an easy way out, anyway. I think you can lose a great deal by sticking to a plot. I like the sociological novel, but sociological over novel. I know that it gets a bit tedious, all this Saroyan stuff, but I think that he plus direction is the only true writing. I don't like understatement, unless Hemingway does it. I want to put the cards flat on the table. Would you care to see the ms again? . . .

I am with Robert Lowry of LITTLE MAN these days, as associate editor. You may have seen LITTLE ALVINS STORYBOOK, of the second issue. We have a beautiful thing coming out in September: STATE OF THE NATION, a pamphlet over 100 pages. I want to hear from you.

Sincerely yours,
Alvin F. Levin

LITTLE ALVIN'S STORYBOOK
(1940)

Fall Guy

By the time they were ready to close the library for the night only a few stragglers finishing up the chapter and Sam, Al, and Muriel were left at the tables. Muriel spied a tall thin fellow way back in the corner behind a bunch of books piled in front of him, looking like he was about to pass out cold.

"Look, isn't that Sidney whatshisname?" she roused the others. They looked at the corner. Recognition.

"Yeah," said Al, "Sidney Morse. I haven't seen him all term. I wonder what he's been doing with himself."

"Looks like he's practicing for the cemetery," remarked Sam, the fountain pen jigging from the side of his mouth as he diagnosed Sidney's exterior. They all waved to the tall guy. He had been watching them and now he got up laboriously and stumbled over to their table nearly tripping over himself on his way across the room.

"Hello," he said neatly from behind a weak smile. "How you all?" He stood there one hand on his hip, a cross between a Spanish refugee and Fourteenth Street day life.

They all looked up at him and Mabel said, "What's the matter? You look sick." Sidney flopped into a chair. He looked like he was going to cry, this fall guy. Once he met a woman old enough to be his mother; she let him fool around and he swore he was in love. She lived in Chicago and when she went home Sidney followed her half way across the country. She got scared having the kid around and told him to go home or her husband

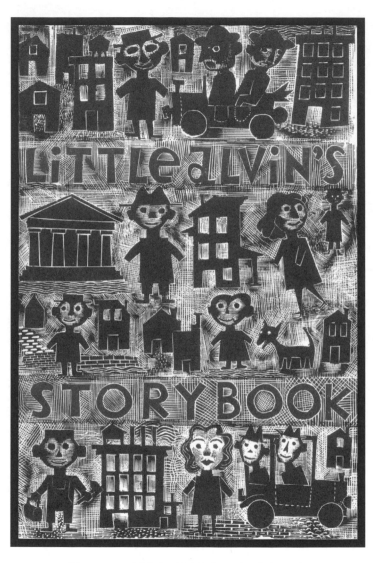

The cover of *Little Alvin's Storybook* (1940).
Woodcut-illustration by James Flora.

would get after him. He was broke so she took him to the Western Union and paid for the telegram to his mother to come and get him.

Then he went to College and they threw him out in his junior year. But he couldn't tell his mother about it, so he sat in the branch library near his home every day for a whole term, leaving the house every morning with his bag of lunch and notebook, making straight for the subway and then doubling back to the library. At first he was going to write a book and he even started several rough outlines and references for a work on the nature of social disorganization that would pop their eyes out down at the College. He was very busy for a while but the library didn't have all the books he needed, and for one reason or another he gave up the idea for the time being. Then he planned a course of study for himself in contemporary American letters, and he was the first to read *The New Yorker* and *Vanity Fair* and the rest of the magazines as they arrived in the library; he started *Ulysses* with his mind set on doing it carefully; he circulated a petition for a subscription to *New Masses* and *New Theatre* and the *Labor Monthly*, and he complained bitterly to the librarian because James T. Farrell's *A World I Never Made* was not purchased for the library. At 11:30 each morning he would wash his two cheese sandwiches down with a coca-cola in the candy store next door, sitting at a small cluttered table near the telephone booth; when it became warmer he sat outside on the library steps sucking up the coke and watching the mothers bring little kids home for some lunch. In a little time he made up his mind about a half a dozen mothers he would be willing to go home with and lay around with on their warm beds and living room couches. He would grow warm and shortbreathed just sitting there watching any one of them pass with their kids—just so long, of course, as they were not too far gone. Then when the street became quiet again he'll go inside again, maybe to try to get the prettier librarian to read a good book for a change. To the three o'clock crowd of high school kids he was quite an imposing figure when it came to the spelling of a difficult word or a complicated homework question in history, what with his deep books before him and his ready, willing and able manner; some of the girls were real beauties too.

Finally the dean let Sidney come back to College, and he never had to let on to his mother though he had a hectic time catching the mail before she laid her hands on it. He was still behind that term. So he sat at the table now, worn and dreary, his Adam's apple bobbing up and down, his eyes glazed as his fingers toyed nervously with a pen, as he related the newest account of the troubles in his life.

He gazed around cautiously and leaned over the table to talk low as he conceded to his friends that he was carrying two full programs, 16 credits at the day session and 9 credits at the evening session, without either session knowing he was attending the other. The scary thing about it was the hell to pay if either session found out. Both would when the records were checked up when Sidney tried to register again next term. It was driving him crazy, the work and the worry and the anxiety what they would do when they found out. Here it was the end of the term and he had so many examinations coming up he couldn't count them off for himself without referring to his schedule. All he could do was sit hid out with the books in front of him and try to figure out what they'd do to him this time when they sent him a letter to report to the office. He finished his story and remained sitting there in dumb silence, ready to drop dead with the anxiety, weariness and frustration of his life.

They could only sit and digest the enormity of Sidney's daring. "But why did you do it?" Sam queried. "Even if you pass everything and they do give you the credits, why did you want to try such a thing and kill yourself with work?"

"I'm doing it to justify my mother's faith in me," the kid told them solemnly, bent down with the full import of his mission.

They looked at him, not knowing whether to laugh or try to comprehend. The lights dimmed in the big room and the librarians looked warningly at them.

"I guess we've got to go," Muriel said looking around. She watched Sidney. He looked back at his table stacked with the unopened books.

"The days go so fast and I don't get a bit of work done. I can't study; it's too hot and I have too much to do. It was all right during the term, they were all lecture courses except a few and all I had to do was sit there, but now it's all piled up." He looked at them pitifully, Then he let go in soft jerky sobs, gaping at them, suddenly released from the wretched swollen tension of his life. "I'm so tired," he gasped, "I know they wouldn't give me the credits—they'll throw me out for good this time. Oh, I'm sick of life. So sick, it's all the same, everything is so hard and mean. I want to die, I want to die." He buried his head in his arms over the table that had felt only the weight of learned works on the social sciences and psychology, a thin weak guy alone with his troubles.

This was more than the boys figured for. Only Mabel could take a hand now. "Sidney, you got to stop that," she mothered him, moving into the seat next to him. She touched him on the arm, urging him up. "Come on now, you're acting like a baby."

"Yeah," said Sam rising, "let's get out of here." He looked around the place, self conscious of the scene his group was making and not altogether sure whether to be glad or not that the library was practically empty.

"Yeah, come on, Sid," said Al. "What you need is some sleep."

"My books," Sidney whined, still shot to pieces.

"Go on get his books," Muriel told the boys. "We'll meet you downstairs." And she led Sid to the door. Downstairs, they

stood on the dark sidewalk; a Negro couple on skates and holding hands rolled down the Terrace around the curve down into
deep Harlem. The College across the street was dark except for
an occasional light shining through the staircase windows. The
watch on Sid's bony wrist beat out loudly; the only other sound
was a couple of pairs of shoes making their way down the
Terrace to the Eighth Avenue station. A car stopped at the corner
to the click of the red light and then started off again before the
green came on again.

"That fellow could get a ticket," Sid said making conversation. He turned a shy, sad face to Muriel. She was ready for
action not conversation; she looked him over in the most searching analysis Sid had received in a long time. "Look," she told
him, "I know what's the matter with you, you need an interest in
life. I mean it, Sid. You can forget about your troubles, and I
know you have lots of them, if only you could forget them doing
something else. Listen, you're radically inclined, you're sympathetic to our work, aren't you." Sidney nodded certainly. "Why
don't you join the Party? You know about the movement and I
think you know it's the only way out for everything that's wrong
in society. If you join up you'll be working for a better world, Sid.
You'll be working together with your friends and you'll realize
that the things you've been worrying about aren't really important." Sidney Morse listened importantly.

The boys came out then, full of questions and full of advice
on how to clear Sid with the administration and prepared to
lend their friend any of their term reports that he could use.
They all moved toward the trolley. Muriel listened to them in
weary participation. A bunch of kids, she concluded. She had a
much better plan for Sid. Sidney dragged along, listening and
arguing the various points of attack and defense with foresight
and understanding. With someone to know his troubles and to
worry with him, he already felt better.

At Hunts Point they broke up; Sid promised happily to get a lot of sleep before his exams the next day and not to worry because he knew like they knew that everything would turn out O.K. Mabel took the opportunity now, after sitting on pins all the way home in the crosstown trolley as it made its determined way connecting the Bronx and Manhattan, to strategically invite the tall guy to their next circle meeting, and Sidney promised to come. He danced around them shaking their hands and expressing all kinds of thanks. They watched him turn the corner.

"Gee, that guy is always in some kind of a jam," said Al.

"I don't know how he's going to get out of this one. I never heard anything like it before, twenty-five credits in one term. Gee, what a guy," marveled Sam.

"He ought to join the Party," put in Muriel. They were walking her home, down the Boulevard, passing the still lighted store fronts with their red, blue and yellow neon signs flowing on and off. Under the Loew's marquee couples, young and nearly young, and stray singles, were trickling out of the lobby, some entering the cut rate candy palace next door as part of a social obligation to complete the evening according to form, while anxious-eyed female fans, all alone, figured it a waste of time to get a soda alone, the kitchen sink is good enough if it's only thirsty that you are.

"The Party doesn't want his kind. He's just the kind of a student to become a Trotskyite," said Al as they passed the red front of the five-and-ten, its doors closed tight for the night.

That started them off and they were holding a regular faction meeting by the time they got to Muriel's stoop. She finally said goodnight; that left the meeting up in the air. The boys watched her sturdy legs climb the steps into the renovated modernistic lobby of the apartment house.

Al wanted to have a beer, but Sam didn't want to; he was taking Edith out tomorrow night and a nickel was a nickel. So they said goodnight, "See you in school Monday for the Gov exam, Al."

God Made Harlem for Kids

My cousin George lives in New Jersey. He graduated this year from Rutgers and he's entering law school in the fall. In the meantime he helps his father in the silk dying factory during the week. Over the weekends we go around together here in the city. He usually brings his car in and we have a pretty good time.

Last Friday his mother and father wanted to use the car so he came in by ferry. I met him at 125th in my old load, one of them 1930 Packards, seven passenger and eight miles on a gallon.

After supper we're sitting around and George says, "What'll we do tonight?"

Well, it's hot so we finally decide to ride around awhile. George wants to drive. "You can't drive a New York car with a Jersey license," I tell him.

"It's all right," he says, getting behind the wheel. "Nobody will know the difference." O.K. I figure, wait till he starts law school, he'll have enough time then to breathe with one eye on the Character Committee.

We're riding up around City Island, the traffic is terrible and the load is throwing plenty of heat. I want to take my coat off but you can't pick anything up if you look like a pair of bums. "How about riding down to Harlem?" George says, disgusted with the country.

It's hot enough up here, Harlem must be swimming in sweat. "What's the matter?" I ask him. "You sorry you're healthy?"

"We'll try anything once," he says turning the house around. "We'll pull the curtains down in the back, nobody'll know the difference."

"Nobody but us," I tell him, spoiling the fun already.

We're back in the city again, passing through the East Bronx. About a dozen hefty dames with gold teeth give us the eye. We ride by just like we didn't see them.

"Somebody's mother, her," says George as we pass one.

"Yeah," I tell him, "maybe she only wants a lift somewheres. You know, quick transportation."

He laughs, he knows better. In Harlem it's plenty hot, but they seem to take it in their stride down there. We're across the bridge now and George heads for Eighth Avenue. It's a real jungle here under the elevated, dark and dingy, piles of dilapidated houses falling all over each other.

We spot her standing on the corner ahead of us, across the street from the bank. She was very small but beautifully put together. A black satiny dress hung to her ankles. She wore rouge, her black skin showing up a soft purple. Right away George slows down. He began to turn around through the elevated poles as we pass her, about half a block up.

"She's beautiful," he tells me, as if I can't see.

We rode back past where she was standing, slowly walking around under the street lamp. She just smiles quietly, tilting her head at us as we pass her in second. George is blocking traffic behind him so he pulls ahead when they start blowing their horns. Two blocks up he turns back through the poles again and we come back.

She's not alone this time. A bunch of fellows are standing around her on the corner, talking, laughing, slow like. They didn't see us, or if they did they thought we had left. One of them had his hands on her hips, facing her and looking down at her. He says something and we see she laughs and puts her arms around his neck and draws his face towards hers.

George curses. We're riding close to the corner now. They see us. George throws her into neutral and we roll along a few feet past the corner; we're in the middle of the intersection now.

"Don't traffic lights mean anything to you?" I ask him.

He does me a favor and moves up out of a ticket. I look back. The fellows have moved around the corner, sitting on the stoop on 128th Street. They don't bother with us. She looks at us, smiling softly. I notice three sets of pawn balls set next to each other on the street, one over the front of each of three gated stores.

She crosses the street toward us, walking slowly like the girls you see modeling those fur coats up in the window on Fourteenth Street. I never saw such a dainty little thing.

She cocks her head, standing on one foot, the other arched behind her, lifting that crazy dress.

"Well?"

"Come on in the car."

"Come on, it's a swell night for a ride."

"I know it is," she laughs.

"Don't you want to come?"

"Sure, but I caint."

She stood there rocking slowly. "Do you want to come upstairs? There's a nice girl for you too," she tells me. She's having a swell time anyway, something is making her feel good.

We don't want to go upstairs. We got that much sense.

"I like you, daddy," she tells George, rolling on the balls of her feet.

That's all he needs to hear. Some fellows are suckers for a straight right; George is different. So he sits there coaxing her to take a ride.

She figures we're not getting out of the car; she gives us a merry look and walks back to the corner slowly mincing her steps, swishing that party dress around her legs. The fellows come back then. I guess she tells them about it. They look our way expecting us to get moving. We do, but they don't know George. He kept driving around the block, trying to make the lights and then slowing up when he gets close to her corner.

They looked at us with blank faces. She just watched, that same mocking grin all over her. But she didn't budge. Four times around my cousin went.

"What is this?" I ask him.

"What the hell," he tells me. O.K. I figure you're driving the car tonight.

Fifth time around, he parks the car where they don't see us and we watch. The fellows go back to the stoop after awhile, only she and this other boy left. They carry on there against the window of the pawnshop. Then she laughs and pushes him away and looks up and down the street. Once a man passes and she walks to the corner and looks at him with a smile as he passes. She comes back and that boy is waiting for her in the shadows of the store.

She gives him a playful push toward the stoop and he goes.

She walks around and we blow the horn at her and she sees us, just laughs and looks the other way, walking around. She knows we're watching her. She ignores us, just smiling soft like.

I say, "Let's go, George."

He's for trying once more. He rides up to the curb next to her. That black boy rushes up to the corner, straight at the car, one of them pocket knives with a long blade open in his right hand, yelling, "Goddamn them bitches—keep coming around here just poking their noses around here!"

George shifts into second, forgetting all about first, and we make off. I figure a flat would be perfect right now.

He kept talking about her all night. We pick up two kids in a tavern on 86th Street later and he keeps telling them all about her. The girls got sore listening to him.

Her Friend's Brother

Ida walked with Sam and Dora over to her friend Charlotte's house, and as she drifted through the soft thick snow that fell through the evening dark the plan danced in her head that maybe Charlotte's brother would be home when she walked in through the door and removed her hat and shook back her hair snow-dewed where her beret did not cover. Anyway, sometimes, when she would see him again and he would sit by her.

At Charlotte's house he wasn't there, and they all sat around in the living room and consciously talked themselves out in little time because on the war in Spain and the German steal of Sudetanland and Hague in Jersey City they were of one mind. It was impossible to really talk because Sam was with them and a fellow is not for real conversation with the girls. It became shamefully silent, a time to watch each other smoke the cigarettes Sam had with him, until Charlotte stood up and asked if they wanted to hear some music. Everybody said yes, that it was just the kind of a night for Beethoven. Charlotte carefully selected the concerto pieces and everybody recalled that the collection in Charlotte's house was very good but the symphonies were not there and everybody knew that a really good collection starts with the symphonies first and then the concerto pieces. But Charlotte's brother was still not home.

But when the dreary time came to leave and they were standing in the hallway with their coats on, he came in, laughing and bursting with the brittle glow of the night outside. And when he saw Ida he asked her not to go yet and would she come into his room he wanted to see her and talk to her. It was wonderful to see how they obeyed him because they removed their coats and went back into the livingroom, and Ida followed him into his room carrying her coat with her because she said she was leaving in another minute, she told him.

He had his room fixed up like a studio with a daybed heaped with big pillows, and one of them had a jagged cigarette burn staring up at her as he switched the small lamp into a cozy glow. He was very wonderful and his sketches on the walls could be sold to anybody who really understood painting. He wrote one-act plays and he was very clever and he did well in college and maybe he would even get a Phi Beta key when he graduated. He had a swell room because it was off from the rest of the house and it had its own bathroom besides.

He sat her down on the daybed and he sat next to her and told her she was grown up and more mature and that their relationship was fine. He told her they really understood each other and fitted together like twins. She liked what he said and took a cigarette from the box he held out to her, though her throat was dry and burning from the cigarettes she had smoked all evening. She was thinking how he must have heard from Charlotte about how Herbert was always calling her up for dates and how he thought she was rushed, and she looked at him like she thought he thought about her. On her calm face was a girl who goes out three times a week and formal nearly twice a month; she was a girl to whom dates are nothing to worry about.

He was swell and he was holding her hand and sitting closer to her on the daybed. He told her that she should not give herself to anyone. She should keep herself for him because after all he liked her best and she was for him and he was sure that she liked him a little bit anyway.

It was her turn now and she told him that she did like him but that he treated her without consideration for her feelings. She told him she felt hurt but not hurt enough to worry about it, and that if he felt her attitude was only casual it was his fault because she could only feel for him the way he made their relations turn out. It became involved, but they seemed to understand all about it. Finally it was seriously agreed that they would both be more than glad to see each other very often. But, she warned him, she would have to get more respect from him in the future than she got from him during the past year.

He agreed with her again and he moved closer, not really, because he couldn't move any closer by this time, but it felt closer because he rubbed his shoulders against hers and he moved his feet on the floor. She turned her head to watch his face as he told her that their friendship would turn out swell, she should wait and see. His face was smoothly shaven, only a little red around the neck. He looked very clean, his starched white shirt fitting snugly around his neck and bound carefully with a knitted tie.

He told her their friendship would turn out swell but it would have to be physical. That was absolutely necessary because it was nonsense to think that any real friendship between two people of the opposite sexes could be without the physical part of it. He told her that it would not be a real friendship if they were both unwilling to kiss. She answered him on another track, telling him she wanted to be his friend but that he had to prove that he was really in earnest about their friendship. It was her signal to leave and she stood up, telling him it was late and they were waiting for her out in the other room. He said yes it was getting late and he reached up at her to kiss her. She twisted out of his grasp and very properly refused to comply.

She told him it wasn't right for him to take advantage of her feelings for him. Even if she liked him, she wasn't a fool any longer, she pointed out. She was older now and had a better understanding of things. It was a neat exercise in double talk, and he fell for it because he leaned back on the daybed and laughed with great force and he told her he was a fool because she wasn't acting at all like a grown up; he was a fool to think she was mature now.

She saw that she had him now and she finished it off by saying that she had to be getting on home. He got up and made a pass at her anyway and she let him hold her close around her shoulders but she twisted her face away when he tried to kiss her. He finally landed in her hair behind her ears, with his hands stroking her arms for a good ten seconds or so.

They were calling from the living room by now and she had to go and he let her go. And she walked home with Sam and Dora crunching the soft thick snow under her shoes. She kept thinking how if she saw him again, because she knew he would call her up maybe even tomorrow night, that she would let him kiss her like he used to do. Under the clear bright sky of winter night she thought how it was kissing. Planlessly she put her hand to her hair and face and she caught her breath hotly with a delightful pain somewhere in the emptiness under her brassiere. The daybed and how he would make her take off her blouse already mussed under his hands and how they would both have to help remove the brassiere, and with longing Ida thought of her friend Charlotte's house when Charlotte was not home and her brother would be there in his room.

Freddy

Freddy awoke feeling loose around the belly. His mouth was parched. He crawled out of bed after awhile, but standing on the balls of his feet made him light in the head. He remembered it was four steps to the window, and he decided this very morning to do it in three, just for the hell of it. It was worth it to die near the opener spaces. He jumped three times and nearly made it, except that he had to lean way over to touch the window shade. It jerked under his grasp and went racing up the window, flapping around the top.

He stood in front of the bay window ready to puke down the sixteen flights into Fifty-Fourth Street. Mother hollered from the next room, "What the hell's the matter in there? Can't you get up without bringing the house down?"

Freddy ignored her. He was busy creeping out of his pajamas; then he stood in front of the open window doing breathing exercises. He felt much better after a few puffs; he danced around, sending out a few left jabs and taking back a sweet one, right on the kisser; then he blew up his chest and started pounding the air out in a rat-a-tat beating with both fists. This exhausted him and he had to sit on the floor recouping enough energy to suddenly let go a blood-curdling Indian call produced by clapping a palm against his mouth as he issued a long oval shriek.

"Shut up, you pig, and let somebody sleep," Millicent hollered from her room.

Freddy gave a clear robust Bronx cheer. "Mother!" Milly yelled, "he's still drunk. Do something, I want to sleep."

"Freddy, you're not drunk, are you?"

"No, mother, I'm not drunk. I'm just healthy, that's all. I think Millicent is drunk, though. I can smell her breath in here." He began to shout, "Everybody come in my room and smell my sister's breath, come one, come all."

Milly began to scream, "Make him stop, make him stop somebody, or I'll jump out of the window!" Father's voice drifted in over the din: "If you both don't stop I'll come in there and knock your teeth out, so help me I will."

"Freddy, please shut up," Mother called tiredly, "I'm going to have a nervous headache today so please try and be quiet."

"Mother, what you need is a drink," counseled Freddy from the depths of his chair. He reached out for the pack of cigarettes and took one. Now watch me die, he figured as he inhaled deeply, die on an empty stomach like a crum without a pot to piss in. He examined the fine printing on the tip of the cigarette. "Yes Mother, what you need is a nice long cool drink."

"Freddy, don't you dare touch a thing until after breakfast at least," Father called out. "Go downstairs and see about breakfast anyway. My God, he wakes up with the sun and drags everybody up with him. What time is it anyway?"

"Who the hell knows, who the hell cares," Freddy chanted, making his way downstairs.

"Ha, wait till he remembers that he has an examination today," Milly screamed, "then he wouldn't be so glad he got up so early."

Freddy stopped dead in his tracks. Sure enough! He felt sick again. All the exercise didn't do a bit of good, and just when he was feeling good too. That little bitch, reminding him even before breakfast. "You little stinker," he called from the stairs, "I bet you put a little note under your pillow last night so you wouldn't forget to remind me."

Milly appeared with a towel over her shoulders. She looked at Freddy with interest. "You're still naked," she pointed out.

"Gee, I don't feel so good," Freddy leaned against the brass banister.

"You're an awful sissy, Freddy. You can't even take an examination without being sick about it."

"Listen, I don't give a good goddamn about the lousy exam. They could hold it in the French Casino and it wouldn't make any difference to me. I just don't like going down there and sitting around with a bunch of phony flopheads and waiting for the papers to be passed out and looking at the clock and counting off the questions still left to be answered and figuring on what word to use. My God, for three hours straight, too. When I get all through, I don't know how in the hell I ever did it."

"Freddy, what do you want to be a lousy lawyer for anyway?"

"I don't know, you got to be something I suppose, don't you?"

"Yes, I guess so," Milly hugged herself. "Gee, I'm glad I'm a girl."

"Huh, that reminds me of the flossies in my class. They're glad they are girls too so they can be lawyers and knock the judges dizzy—if they ever get into a court." He threw Milly an approving stare, "So help me, Milly, you're getting prettier every day."

Milly looked pleased. "Huh, you must be feeling good again."

"Oh, I feel all right. I feel fine. I'll be right back," he turned and made off down the rest of the stairs.

"If you have anything to drink before breakfast I'll tell on you," she shouted after him.

"Freddy, don't you dare," Mother called out.

"See about breakfast, son, see about breakfast," Father put in.

Freddy caught Williams laying out plates in the dining room. He doubled back through the kitchen and found what he wanted, under the closet shelf. Feeling uncertainly at ease, he encountered Williams in the dining room on his way back. They engaged in some smart repartee, most of Williams' smartest comebacks being accomplished in expressive silence.

Freddy quieted his stomach with a roll from the table and made upstairs for the bathroom.

In the next half hour the upper floor was a mess, the bathrooms particularly, and by 9 o'clock Freddy, fully dressed and feeling perfectly swell, stood receiving in the dining room, beating a dishpan over the din of a swing record and yelling that as far as he was concerned breakfast was good goddamn ready.

Father came in and asked for a bicarbonate. "These late telephone calls," he explained. Mother watched him drink it down and said she'd have one too. She was a nervous little woman with grey hair, short behind her ears, and full strong little breasts and the neatest figure. She wore a bandana this morning. Standing next to Milly they looked a lot like sisters.

"Mother, you're prettier than my sister this morning,"

Freddy was working on a baby lamb chop.

"Your mother was a beauty when I met her," said Father gargling orange juice around his mouth dissolved in seltzer.

"I feel like hell," Mother commented, "just like lousy hell."

"Didn't the bicarbonate help?" asked Milly spearing some toast and looking all over the sideboard for the coffee.

"Bicarbonate! That stuff is a joke, believe me. I think your father is crazy. I should have what my Freddy had this morning."

"Me? Me? What did I have? Ask me, what did I have? Do you by chance refer to my orange juice? Williams, pour Mother some orange juice!" Freddy pointed to his empty glass.

Mother brooded.

Father suddenly shouted, "No. No." He was at the sideboard, heaping his plate. "You got to have a full stomach first. It's the best way to start the day right—have a good breakfast first, plenty of good food for the empty stomach. You hear, Milly!"—he looked at her plate—"Is that breakfast? What the hell's the matter with you? Are you sick? She comes down after a long night and takes toast and coffee! Eat something, you hear, my child, eat something. Here, take some nice soft livers or these sweetbreads, take both they're wonderful. Here, do you want some bacon? Williams, make some bacon for Millicent."

"I don't want anything else besides toast and coffee, I tell you," Milly kept repeating, drawing her plate away. Williams hovered around, pointing out the food quietly.

"It's your fault," Father pointed his finger at Mother stirring restlessly in front of her full plate, poking at a bun with her knife. "It was your idea sending her to a school, to a nunnery, I mean, with lettuce and spinach three times a day."

"Well, I came home, didn't I?" Milly countered.

"Milly, take some kippers," Mother compromised.

"They stink," Milly said. "Keep the cover over them, Father."

"That's Williams' fault," said Freddy, his mouth full,

"Williams and his stinking kippers. And that's why Edward left
the British Islands. He couldn't stand them either, he's like Milly
that way. It's the British pride that made up the story about Wally
Simpson. They wouldn't admit it was kippers that made him give
up the crown. Am I not right, Williams?" Freddy was expanding
now. "So they pulled in an American and shifted the blame on her.
And we stand for it. I tell you if we had a stronger man in the
White House this insult would not go by unnoticed. First they
take our money and forget to repay us, then they castigate our
women, castigate, I say. We're fall guys, that's what we Americans
are, I say throw the kippers and Williams out. No," he reconsid-
ered, "let's keep Williams and only throw the kippers out."

Williams smiled, working efficiently all over the room.

By the time they got through, the place was a mess. Father
on a full stomach debated the future of the day with Mother who
sat at ease with a three fingers before her. Milly was going shopping, there were so many things she had to take back to the stores
from yesterday. Mother didn't want the car but Father didn't
want it either, so everybody urged Mother to go for a long ride
in the country for her sick headache, and Father suggested that
William drive carefully, but Mother didn't want to ride alone, she
said it gave her the creeps, so they all suggested that she call
someone up. Mother said the hell with whom she could call up,
and Freddy agreed and said for two cents he'd stay home and go
with her. Then everybody talked about Freddy's exam, except
Father who only commented that what must be must be, and
what must be done can be done so that Freddy had nothing to
worry about with this examination. They sat around until
Williams stood almost on top of them, his cautious manner suggesting that they get out and let him clean up the room. So they
all got up giving him dirty disgusted looks.

Father left with Millicent; Mother left for her appointment
with the beauty parlor on Broadway, and Freddy drifted quietly

into the kitchen. Williams was out shopping and the girl came in and started cleaning the upstairs rooms. Mother returned about eleven and joined Fred at the kitchen table. She was looking swell, she was thirsty though. They both talked for a while until, amid Mother's best wishes, Freddy left for school full of the very best intentions.

Riddles, riddles, it was all riddles, this law crap. How in hell did they ever sit down and think up so Goddamned many puzzles? What a bunch of flat heeled stinks these lawyers were! If tonight was the last exam for the year it certainly was something to celebrate about. Do you celebrate before or after, though? Frederick stood on the street and figured it out. Both, you celebrate before because it's going to be the last exam and after because it was the last exam. See, he concluded logically just like a lawyer, if people would only realize it they could be celebrating all the time! He figured if that's the way it is he'd better not take his car with him. A car is like a wife that way; if you're celebrating you've got to be free to do it the right way, you can't leave a wife on the corner and you can't leave a car there either. That's why they call a car a she. Of course some wives were different; take Mother, for example. You'd never want to leave her anywhere, by Golly. That's what Freddy decided, all of a sudden; got to get a wife like Mother at my side, by my side, to my side

He looked up to the twenty-ninth floor, his floor, to wave bye-bye to Mother in the kitchen. The leaning back nearly knocked him off his balance. "See," he pointed to Joseph, the doorman under the green canopy, "that's my window, without the Venetian blinds. Yes, I know it's difficult to see that window"—when Joseph glanced up, reaching only to the third floor—"but come out here into the street away, it's worth seeing, it's the only window without those blinds, it's what makes this house unique, Joseph." Joseph would come out only a little way. "You're not interested, Joseph. I'm sorry for you. You haven't a soul." The doorman smiled just like Williams smiled. "Are you related to Williams, Joseph? You look like him a lot."

Freddy trailed Joseph back to the door. "O.K. Joseph, don't look. Soon, when Mother finds out about it, she'll take the window shades off and have the blinds put back and you'll have never seen the unique in life, and you'll always have this to remember, that it was right under your nose all the time."

Freddy decided he'd better take a last look himself because Mother would surely be in his room during the day. He reentered the house and rode upstairs. The elevator made him feel light in the stomach. Inside, Mother was on the telephone. He made upstairs for a last look; still there, drawn neatly over half the window. "Beautiful," he breathed.

Then he sneaked down, into the kitchen. Some of Mother's stuff in the closet, not that piss water out in the dining room. He sneaked out unseen while Mother was still on the phone.

Downstairs, once more, he walked stiffly past Joseph. "It's still there, my friend, you can see it yet for another hour or so I believe, so make your hay while the sun shines."

Rosie Got Married

I give you the story of Rosie. It is short because the truth can be told briefly and to the point. This story captures the deep essence of Rosie the woman and projects her truthfully as the eternal femme fatale. Her story is her own; I tell it as she thinks it:

Rosie got married. She knew how to cook because for the last five years at home all she did was cook and wash dishes and clean up the house. She had a partner in her mother, that is in her campaign for marriage. But her mother was a limited partner to this enterprise because a girl in a big metropolis is really an entrepreneur in the real Adam Smith tradition. Can you tell your mother everything? I mean everything. Rosie was actually the

agent for the partnership. The mother came in only for the critical attitude, only to pass final judgment and set the tempo.

When Sam came along and it began to look serious, really
serious, Rosie's mother stepped in to put the finishing touches to
the negotiations. Rosie's mother said to Sam, only after she knew
that Sam was going to marry Rosie, my Rosie she never dipped
her hands in cold water. It'll be lucky for you, Sam, if she boils
you an egg in the morning. This was after Sam had been investi-
gated with an economic acumen as efficient as Dun and
Bradstreet. A salary and an expense account in a big business that
was the only corporation in 1933 to give out a dividend. That's
what Sam said one night. It was a forty million dollar concern,
and it sunk in. Forty dollars a week in a forty million dollar concern. Forty million dollars! Rosie, grab it before somebody else
does. You'll have a good home.

Mother could even joke about Rosie's ladyness: I suppose
you can make the coffee yourself. Or maybe I'll have to be in
your house every morning to fix up your breakfast? In this
remark was contained two essential propositions: namely, one,
Sam was getting a bargain; two, it would be best, nay it was
decided, that the couple live near the mother. My Rosie is such a
lady she wouldn't know a potato from a lemon. Rosie, you know
the difference? And Rosie flustered in a glow of bustling pleasure.
And Sam lived in dreams of a rosy lady in bed all night with him
and mornings in his own home.

So Rosie and Sam got married. And the truth is that Rosie
loved to cook. But she wanted Sam to think she was a lady. A
person is what people think she is, and people think she is what
her husband holds her out to be. Did she want Sam to think she
was used to washing floors on her knees and washing clothes and
darning his socks? Better she shouldn't darn his socks. Let him
walk around with holes in his stockings. You are what you make
yourself.

Rosie was such a fine lady. And oh so good in bed! But should she tell Sam she was in bed before? Just like she should tell him she knew how to cook? And it was easier to fool him about this than about the cooking. All Rosie had to do was to remember the first time and each time with him for the first couple of months should be like her good memory told her the first time was. But she carried it too far, because Sam said after awhile, Rosie, I know this is hard on you but there is a limit to how long it should hurt. So when Rosie realized that she had made her first mistake she tried to remember a little more and figured it was time now that it shouldn't hurt anymore. So it worked out perfectly and Sam figured he married a real lady and it was wonderful.

And it was time already that Rosie should have learned to cook too. So Sam could say one night, Rosie, you pick things up so easily, and he smiled happily and patted her as he chewed on his toothpick after supper and scratched himself, a happy lord in his own home. And Rosie could say then, ah Sam, as the years go on you'll learn what a wonderful woman you married. And Sam was in the mood then to agree, and that was how love came to this couple.

To herself Rosie talked philosophically, it is a virtue to keep your mouth shut because a wrong word can make so much trouble. She couldn't help thinking dimly how much smarter are women than men. Men are such dopes, but Rosie figured it out that it wasn't that women were really smarter. It was just that they were forced into telling more lies than men and when you tell a lie you had to live up to it. And that's why a woman's life is more complicated and that's why men were dopes and why women were much smarter.

MY BABY NEEDED A MOTHER
(1940)

I WAS SITTING IN THE sun on the porch of my house in a great metropolis. The sun was very strong in the afternoon and I could not keep my eyes open on account of it. I looked very peaceful, believe me. I was feeling good too.

A girl came up the street. She was carrying a baby in her arms. She stopped at my house and then came up on the porch. She looked awfully hot and uncomfortable. But she looked pretty good.

You're its father, she told me and she held the little baby out to me.

It was a cute baby and I took it in my arms from her. He danced on my lap.

I'll be around sometimes if you want, she told me and she turned around slowly. She does everything slow. She walked down the porch steps.

The kid was saying something, She turned around on the steps and said to me, If he says war-war that means he wants a drink of water.

I have ice water and cubes in my house, I told the girl. Real ice, I says.

Well, I don't think ice water is good for him on a hot day like this because he is so young yet, she told me. He's only a baby, she says.

She went away, but you see she forgot to tell me the little baby's name. So I had to spend most of the afternoon calling him every guy's name I could think of and waiting for him to make a sign that that was his name. It was no use, though, because he thought I was just talking to make conversation.

He played with my face and when he suddenly let out a yell, war-war, I took the little baby inside to my kitchen where my refrigerator stands, and I took out the ice cubes. I found out that the baby likes ice cubes very much. It's good if you drink ice water slowly on a hot day.

In the nighttime I had to go out. I let the baby sleep in the bedrooms where I live. I put pillows on both sides of him because I didn't want the little baby to fall out of my bed. I gave the key with a quarter to the janitor's wife named Sarah, because such a little baby couldn't run downstairs if the house caught fire. My cousin is visiting me for awhile, I told Sarah. He is a sound sleeper, I says.

The girl was hanging around the corner when I got down there from my house. It's a big corner and they have a traffic light there. It's a crowded street, especially at night.

A little baby like that shouldn't stay home all alone at night, she told me. Even in the daytime, she says.

She looked a little cooler now but she was still tired. She was good to look at though. She has slow ways.

He's not so little, I told her. He looks smart, I says.

Did he have his supper? the girl said. Did he eat? she says.

We both ate, I told her. That was more than she did. He ate well, I says.

She had nothing to say to me. She stood there with a slow look on her face. Her face reminds you of something when she looks like that.

Well, don't hang around this corner, I told her. The cop is particular around this neighborhood, I says.

She just closed her eyes at me, quietly. I stepped into the candy store for cigarettes. When I came out the girl was gone. I had some chocolate for her. It's five cents a piece, but if you buy three at a time it costs you ten cents.

The next morning I woke up about eleven o'clock. The little baby was all tangled up next to me on my bed. He was crying to beat the band. Shut up, I told him. Keep quiet, I says.

He was in a mess too. It was a good thing I got up when I did. Shut your mouth, I told the baby. He looked at me scared. I did the best that I could with him but it wasn't good enough, I guess. Then I shaved and in the mirror I saw how the little baby sitting there in the bathtub looked like me. He was like a lifesaver in the tub. After he got used to the water he liked it a lot. After he learned not to lean back too far. In my refrigerator I found an orange for him but I forgot all about the pits until it was too late. He had some coffee with me and I let the little baby chew on the end of a loaf of bread.

He was sitting with me outside of my house in the sun. I rigged up a rope around his belly and tied the end to my chair so he wouldn't bother me when I closed my eyes in the sun and thought. I knew she would come back to my house in a little while and when she came up on the porch slow like she always walks I looked surprised.

You again? I said to her. You back again, I says.

The girl touched the little baby's head and made little curls out of his hair with her fingers. She was a beauty, you could tell by the shape of her behind. I reached over for my coat. Here is some candy for you, I told her. Chocolate is good for you, I says.

She took the candy from my hand. She peeled a bar like a banana and broke a piece off and took a little bite. She broke off another little piece with the nuts in it and put it in the little baby's mouth. He liked it and grabbed for some more. She squatted down near the little baby, her skirt was down on the ground. She broke another little piece off and fed the baby. She looked up at me slowly with her eyebrows up and held out the rest of the bar for me. It's alright, I told her. You eat it, I says.

You gave me two more bars, she said. Take some, you like

chocolate, she says. She knew I liked chocolate. Her shoulders are like round apples and she never laughs.

Then the little baby hollered war-war and that meant he wanted a drink of water. I got up to take him inside to my kitchen and she untied the rope around him. I opened the door for them and she looked at me when she carried the baby inside to my kitchen, and I followed them inside to show her where I keep my glasses and how the cubes come out of the tray in the refrigerator.

I Bet You Think Life Is a
Merry-Go-Round
(1940)

A FEW DRINKS DOWN MY girlish throat and I am very popular. That's the way I feel right now. I don't feel sad any longer and everything takes on the glow of the Good Life. It's not the ideal existence of an intellect, like an intellectual. See, I'm not an intellectual any more sitting here with a shine in my moiling sides. Not like that intellect of a professor at college. Her story was that she lived her life by Shakespeare. I was that kind of a fan too but I was always suspicious of William's verities, and anyway Norma Shearer as Juliet finished my affinity with the Bard of the Avon.

This professor, by the way what is the feminine of professor? Don't bother really, this professor had another yen. It was a slot machine picture frame on the wall opposite her bed. The masters captivated her aesthetic senses and she would lie abed many hours staring fixedly at some magus opus until her fancy would be taken by some other reproduction and then zip would go the slot machine and out would come the old picture and zam would go in the new picture and then bang, bang she would lay there for hours going on days staring fixedly at her new love. She would lay like this, with her arms peeking out of her virgin night-ie and tucked under her head against the pillow with a beautific smile on her map. That's one way to take up space in bed and I always say every woman to her choice. Isn't there a brilliant sentence about paying your money and taking your choice?

Of course, you understand that with her you can't associate the word boudoir. Not even bedroom. Something like sleeping chamber, I would say. I used to sit in her class and think of sex and you know she would stick in my mind like a neuter noun. I couldn't place her for the love of money. I used to have her hollering to a bunch of little kids, you are all the slips of my pessary, just fortuitous slips, but, friend, it was no use.

Well, as I was saying, a couple of drinks doesn't give me an intellectual frame of mind. It's not the company, mind you. You over there can feel as intellectual as you damn want to, and personally I don't like that Phi Beta look on your profile. It's too damn patronizing. If you would care to retire to the seminar room I would gladly exchange a few historical facts with you. But frankly not now, lug. Because frankly right now I feel like the *Daily News* toward the close of a party. Yes, it would be nice if you called the waiter over. He could bring a bottle and then we could be our own bosses. Bosses, now there is a vicious word. Entrepreneur is so much nicer, more distinguished, and classy. I always like the French, don't you? I mean, they have such nice terms for things. Like *cherchez la femme* and *vive la guerre*. I mean, don't you think they have their feet on the ground?

Now I don't want you to get the wrong impression, because really I do like the better things in life. The man I marry, for example, he must smell of woody fragrances, he must be a subtle combination of lavender and lilac and Russian leather. When I lay against his rough tweed shoulder, I want his cleancut grassy smell to knock me out. I want him to stink of tumbleweed.

Of course, appearances aren't everything, I realize. Love is deeper than that. But still and all, a woman has to be careful. "Love is a credulous thing." Didn't Ovid say that? "Love deceives the best of womankind." Homer made that truism up. You see I was an English major. I culled the best of antiquity, I did. And if they ever give a teacher's exam in English I shall make out very well. That's what I tell my parents and they got me believing it too.

In the meantime I try to make the best use of my background in esoteric antiquarianism. For practical purposes, you know. Thus where but in Tennyson can a puny woman find an ally? Don't you recall where he says, "I am ashamed through all my nature to have loved so slight a thing?" Frankly now, don't you honestly believe that women are better than men? I mean really. No, I'm getting sad. It's only that no one really appreciates us, except Robert Briffault. He wrote a book about us. Two volumes and he called it after me, *The Mothers*. I'm a potential mother.

If I should write a book it would be about myself, as one woman to another. It would be the story of my young life. It would be a short parody because I have lived and died within the short space of . . . but no, I must not divulge my age because that is part of our code of honor. Anyway it was a short time indeed to live. What I am doing now is not really living because I'm really just coasting along on the last bitter dregs of Bertrand Russell's second law of thermodynamics.

Now I don't really know why you over there should be pouting. You are very handsome, my young man. You do look like a lump of ectoplasm, but you are a really nice piece of ectoplasm. I myself now am indeed a lovely *baggage*. Certitude is not the test of certainty. Somebody said that but it is true nevertheless, yet I am fully convinced of the absolutes of my own form. But please don't try to pay me any compliment, friend. The truth is annoying after awhile.

You take my friend now. One of my dearest friends. She is an awfully nice girl. But she has a child's body. Yet her legs are full and womanly. Once she went out formal and I said to her, Hortense you have lovely gams so why don't you splurge this once and buy a pair of single thread stockings. Well, Hortense did so purchase and a peek at her legs that night made you want to reconsider her body. It was very impressive. And whatever the public might say about her, I know for a positive fact that she will make one swell wife for some lucky young man.

Her escort for the evening was a dental student at NYU. Now I wouldn't say he was proverbially wet behind the ears, but frankly he wasn't all dried up there either. Anyway he had his pop's car and when he drove my dearest friend home he finally let out the burning question whether he could kiss her goodnight and Hortense said sure, all my friends kiss me goodnight. Well, I guess he's a dentist by now. No, it's a four year course, isn't it? I guess they're letting him clean teeth by now. Anyway my dearest friend never saw him again. I told Hortense it was because he was looking for a girl who could open an office for him, but she said no because it was a new Buick his father had, but I said nevertheless.

When I get married . . . Isn't that sweet, though? I want the chance to write to the *Times* about my marriage. They'll print it, wouldn't they? I'll have them put it on the society page, opposite the book review so then I can read both pages with out turning a page. They'll say the bride-to-be graduated from college in New York City and attended Mr. Jacob Shapiro's classes in Steno and Typing at the WPA school in Harlem. They'll add in the same paragraph that the bride-to-be was an applicant for a relief position prior to the announcement of her marriage, and following the ceremony the couple will retire to their residence close to the relief bureau in order to be close at hand for their joint relief checks.

Ah, marriage. But love is where you find it, I always say. It's a song, isn't it? Just signal the orchestra to run that one off for me, will you, chum? Oh, it's a slot machine victrola? Well, don't bother. No, don't bother, really. It's just as well, really. Mildred Bailey only makes me sad. Four-four time grips me. It's not good for me.

You know, sometimes I think to myself sitting here, what am I wasting my time with you here? But of course I didn't mean that crack. You know a joke when you hear one, don't you? You're intelligent, aren't you. Look, I'll soothe you with another one.

The jockey started to whip the horse who turned around his head and yelled in anger why are you whipping me, there's nobody behind us. Isn't that clean and good? Or the time I didn't mind losing at the races, but when the horse came up to me, in the grandstand and asked me which way the other horses went it was too much. Don't you feel better now, handsome?

Now what was I saying before reality hit me between the eyes. Oh yes, marriage. One of my dearest friends got married a few months ago. It was a big family wedding on a hot July afternoon. I looked beautiful. The bride looked nice too. But she wore a black dress. Now that's quite irregular, isn't it? I mean black, after all. He has red hair and a Civil Service job.

You know, security and all. I can't imagine myself with a red-haired man. I mean does that mean he is red all over?

She claims to be sickly. Personally, it's a good line if you can pass it off. I mean, if she wasn't married she could pass off as a member in good standing of the women's javelin team in the Olympics. But now she can lie in bed and pout. I mean, the things women use the beds for. And believe me, pal, it's not getting her anywheres because Joe, that's his name, Joe is wandering about of late. It used to be music with concerts all over the city, and now it's the Trotskyites. Joe, you see, is sympathetic and he wants to know all about it before he joins up. He even went out and paid something like three dollars for a book on the Moscow trials and he knows now that the trials were a fake. He'll tell you about it if you ask him, even if you don't ask him. But look, if he joins up that will make the party membership 116, wouldn't it?

And there's a very intelligent girl who is always around their house lately. It's a room and a half with Joe's records and pamphlets in every corner and this very intelligent girl in the center of the room looking very intelligent. She's a part of the family already. She's Leon Trotsky's emissary from Coyoacan, that's in Mexico, you know, and she carries around a membership blank with a pen ready for Joey to sign up.

Last time I was there Belva, that's the wife, she was sick
again and I said to her, where's Joe and she said he went to a
meeting tonight with Miriam. That's this dame with the pen. So
I said to my friend, I said, look here Belva, I know that that
Miriam is a fat slob and all, but still and all she and your Joey
got the same frame of mind these days. And my friend agreed
with me and even more because this here Miriam she told me, in
spite of her heaviness of body and the bovine aspect of her puss,
I mean her face, has had affairs with every big shot in the party
from national directors down to faction chairmen. She wins them
with her mind.

I don't like the looks of it, personally. Let me give you an
example: He calls up he wouldn't be home tonight because he
wants to hear them discuss Stalin's deviation from the third chapter of Marx and it's too bad Belva is ill again so he is going with
Miriam and he is going to send up some detective magazines and
chocolates, the kind she likes. See what I mean? He reads Lenin
and she is told to read detective stories. And Miriam is there
chewing her cud. I wouldn't give a damn, that's life I would say,
but you see Belva is my friend. And how can I say to her, Belva
get up and don't play sick anymore? Maybe she really has got
heart failure and then it would be on my conscience if something
happened. Life is hard enough without taking on more troubles
for myself. See what I mean, bud?

Oh well, I think I'll have some more of this. Oooop, there
goes a spot on my skirt. Oh that's all right, don't bother, really.
A spot or two is all right. It shows that you are living. Tell me,
pal, you like poetry? I mean poetry, not pap. Gee, what if Mr.
Auden and Richard Aldington walked in here right now? I tell
you no matter how beautiful you are to look at I would stand up
and leave you to walk at their side and perhaps sip a Scotch or
two with them. You know how it is, can you resist God?

"Not with a club the heart is broken, nor with a stone: a whip so small you could not see it." Dangerous, is that? Or this: "I've come a long way to prove, no land, no water, and no love." How about, "Will you die for a female mammal, two breasts and a curled slit?"

If you'll light this cigarette for me I'll tell you how once when I was walking through the English Department the head of the department stopped me, putting her ringed hand on my soft arm, saying we like your poetry so much, child, that if you hang around this dump for a year or so we'll give you a chair. A camp stool? I asked in disbelief. No, she said unto me, a real chair in the department. And sure enough they had the men working away in the cellar knocking nails and building me a chair. But I couldn't sit still, I tell you.

I bet you want to hear about the dormitories at school. Frankly they didn't appeal to me. But the dormitories at Harvard, ah but those were okay. I bet you think I'm interested in men. Well, I'll tell you, I am in a way. A girl friend I have, she isn't. I had a nice fellow for her. Richard was his name. It still is, though. She said, I'm not interested in men. Good, I said to her, then you'll be interested in Richard. How did it turn out? Frankly I don't know.

No, I feel quite all right, honestly. I was just thinking. When I surrender I shall surrender voraciously. But I can't help thinking of the look on his puss, I mean his face, when if there was a moralist who thought that he had married a virgin and finally went to bed with her and she suddenly sat up in her nightie and laughed out loud at him, ha, ha, I fooled you, I fooled you, and he lay there the victim of a perfected fraud. I would like to see all the men get a good kick in the pants like that, wouldn't you? Gosh, I keep forgetting who you are. I always think you're a friend of mine. Of course you are, but I mean a girl friend.

But for myself, by the way, I want to lead a full life. I want to have ten children in ten years. And I want to have enough money to have them right. I want a full house with a maid for each kid. I want to lay in lavender and silk in a big white bed and give the world children. I want to have to check up each night to see that they are all at home. I want to walk arm in arm with my husband at night from bedroom to bedroom, peering at the nameplate on each door to see which kid belongs inside and then looking inside to see if the tousled head is against the soft pillow. I want my husband to say our son is a fine boy and I should answer which one do you mean, dear? And then I should retire with him to the master bedroom.

I would like to get a position or a job. Something to do in the meantime, you know? My friend, I can call you that, can't I? My friend, it is most difficult to find a job. I have a gentleman friend who is supposed to have done a marvelous piece of work editing a college paper out west somewhere. Frankly I don't know what that means, but anyway, he graduated and got mixed up with a bunch of wealthy liberals, the ones who worry about the youth problem and European refugees. They can't sleep nights just worrying about these problems. Anyway, now he is the office boy for about a dozen long-named organizations and he runs around as busy as a cockroach. And he gets more out of it than just twenty dollars a week because most of these ladies, I understand from reliable sources, are very sexy. Right now, as I was saying, he is the one who gets jobs here for the German refugees.

Only this morning I woke up with a German accent and I felt just like I was tripping on down the gangplank of the boat from the fatherland by way of Norway. I put up my lovely brown hair in braids and I was all ready to go down to see this friend when I suddenly realized that we weren't on speaking terms any more. We don't stand eye to eye on certain issues of fundamental importance. No, my friend, I can't tell you at this stage of our friendship. Perhaps the future will provide the opportunity for more intimate confidences on my part.

Yes, oh yes, I have studied the employment situation very carefully. Most carefully. I know, for example, that a *Herald Tribune* under the soft girlish arm is much more appropriate than the *Times*, and a cross around the graceful girlish neck is a great help, especially in the employment agencies. One night I dreamed that I was successful and was sent to work with a light heart and a willing hand. But I soon found that the conditions of my employment were not at all to my likings and inclinations. My mistress was not progressive, not in the least. And I prided myself on my modern outlook. She would have the beds made up in the most peculiarly outmoded manner. She would come in on me and yell, this way Marie, this way you dope. But you see, I was trained in the newer, functional method. And peeling potatoes, it was the same story all over again. My friend, I awoke in a sweat.

Sure, I go to all the department stores. I am so sweet to the personnel directors and they are so sweet to me. They are personality girls in beautiful clothes behind desks with two flowers on each wilting away. It's their smiles that get me. Did you know they give a special course at Smith in how to smile no? You give full with the whole face and your heart and last night's supper. Sometimes you catch them off guard and they stare at you blankly for a moment thinking about if he will call tonight, and then she wakes up suddenly and throws you that 1,000 watt gleam, I tell you it knocks you right off your feet it's so powerful.

Whose manner is cynical? Me cynical? Why, I have the time of my young life looking for a job. When I finish with the personnel gang I go shopping in the store. I try on the better coats and I say to the girl, have you anything more expensive, and we have a fashion show and I look beautiful, I do. You ought to see me. They think it's Gloria Vanderbilt down for an outfit. Then I say, I'll take your name miss, I want my mother to come down and decide for me. And the girl tells me where to find her tomorrow with my mother.

No, I don't want to dance. My present condition doesn't warrant the light fantastic. I may trip. I tell you I just want to sit here and think out loud. I want to be young again and play with my rosy toes. I want to be in 4A-1 again and have Miss Kinney for a teacher. I tell you we are all little children with filthy minds. My brother has a filthy mind. He says go chew a piece of paper. He uses filthy words like chew. I am only two years old and I have a friend who plays with me all the time. When my brother uses filthy words we do not play with him anymore.

Say, did you ever notice how when it rains in the Village it is very beautiful there? The streets are old and quiet and the city is clean and fresh. And the men walk by, so strong and intelligent and so full of manliness. Many of them who are quite young wear Van Dyke beards which I would like to stroke. It is advisable to pick up one of them and even bring an extra one home for a dear friend. You know one night I was riding in the subway with my friend who next to my dearest friend is my dearest friend. I was saying to her how unhappy I was and a gentleman overheard us. He tried to strike up a conversation seeing our frame of mind but we girls did not pay him the slightest attention. In fact, our close attention was directed in another direction where a most handsome man was seated. He was almost made for my friend in every detail, in every respect. You see, she is tall, a big girl, and that makes it difficult to get her together with the few gentlemen in our circle because they are usually small of stature. Frankly, they are usually few in number, besides. But see how chummy I am becoming with you. You should be proud, *msieu*. Are you, though? I would certainly be proud if I were you. I would not let me go.

Let me tell you about this friend of mine. In my lighter moments I call her Mollie off the Pickle Boat. She has atrocious tastes, especially in clothes. And unless I go with her on her shopping tours she is bound to turn up in the most ridiculous clothes that do not become her in the slightest degree. Academically, she is beautiful, but you know what that is worth. I always say that it is what you bring to your can and to your *rondeurs* that really counts, if you follow me.

Of course I like her. Honestly. Well, to tell you the truth, she does irritate me at times. I don't think that she has any class, if you know what I mean. It is not a matter of being a lady, it's a matter of not being a lady with class. Now take me. I have class all right. I have class besides the foot men love to kiss. Me and Marlene Dietrich. But haven't you noticed? No, I mean the class. Oh, the foot? Well, I'll let you see it sometime. Remind me of it in one of my off moments. But come now, have another shine with me.

May 22, 1941

Dear Dr. Levin:

Of course I remember LOVE IS LIKE PARK AVENUE. We all thought it was interesting; but rather too "experimental" (for lack of a better word) for the general public.

If you should ever write anything more conventional we'd like very much to hear about it.

> *Sincerely,*
> *Maria Leiper*

June 4, 1942

Dear Laughlin,

*Thanks for the note on ND42. I'm glad you're taking
something from PARK AVENUE for this issue of ND.
Simon & Schuster is after me again. They want something, something "new and fresh". You take something
from PARK AVENUE, anything you like best. I like it.
You like it too. For me.*

*I've built up quite a market in pamphlets. The
libraries throughout the country are buying a lot of
stuff. Then I'm putting out something called NYU
INDEX TO EARLY AMERICAN PERIODICAL LIT-
ERATURE, 1728–1870, a series of bibliographies. I
have 5 books out so far, the latest is RALPH WALDO
EMERSON. WALT WHITMAN was no. 4, and
EDGAR ALLAN POE was no. 3. No. 6 is FRENCH
FICTION, with introductions by Prof Howard
Mumford Jones. They sell for $1.50 each, with a pretty
good profit. Are there that many scholars in the country? So now I'm going into something slick: how about
fiction, original works (not reprints), in pamphlet for-
mat, but large size, like ESQUIRE or FORTUNE, with
ads in the back, full page color jobs, like Pepsi Cola, or
Coco Cola if we want to be high class. One grand a
page, lets say. And sell the novel for 25 cents a copy.
Could be done? Revolutionize publishing? They tell me
Simon & Schuster tried it some years ago and it didn't
work. But I don't remember. Anyway, I like the idea*

and so I don't want to think it a bad idea. Is there any-
thing wrong with it? I publish a great deal of pamphlet
material, stuff people bring in with a flame in their eye
and the print cost in their pockets. Call it vanity pub-
lishing, we do. We don't promise anything, we don't
overcharge, we do everything we can to sell pamphlets.
We run an ad in the Sunday Times Book Section. We
charge $3.60 a page per 1000 copies, 6x9, 10pt type,
60lb paper. Reasonable. The job is clean, utilitarian.
Your poetry pamphlets are class. LITTLE MAN's
Robert Lowry tells me he's going to do one for you,
and Lew Ney says he to[o]. Lew can do a strong rough
job, heavy. He hikes over a page. I'm doing okay, I get
my gasoline. I made one mistake. I bought out the
JOURNAL OF SOCIAL PHILOSOPHY reprints and
can't get rid of them. Those professors are out of this
world and I fall for them. Let me know when ND42 is
ready and I'll give it plenty of space in THE PAM-
PHLETEER MONTHLY. I'm anxious to see what part
of PARK AVENUE you chose.

ALVIN LEVIN

LOVE IS LIKE PARK AVENUE
FRAGMENTS EXCERPTED FROM
A LONGER WORK
(1942)

*J*F I TELL YOU ABOUT THEM, as much as I know off hand, isn't that enough for you to know about them? Don't you really know them then? Do you have to be a hen to know a rotten egg when you see one? If I tell you it is a pleasure to stand still on the street, say down on Madison Avenue, when a woman goes by you so you can count three after she passes you, holding your breath all the time until three is up, and then inhaling deeply, do I have to go into a long dissertation on perfumes and womanly charm and libidos and the background of this particular scented female? Can't you agree with me then and there that it was a pleasure? Do you see what I mean? If you don't we're both wasting our time so far as both of us are concerned with each other. And let me go elsewhere with what I know.

———————————

We live for holidays and the fourth of July comes with a list of deaths that compare well with the list of last year, with California leading, Pennsylvania second and New York was fourth, losing out by some 22 persons. The kids hoped for fire crackers and had to be satisfied with sparklers. National Independence Day it was and it was for a revolution subversive and bloody and very radical with some people making a lot of money and others taking an awful chance with their necks and it was very cold at Valley Forge and it still is, no doubt. The Boom, Boom, Waldorf-Astoria shoots out Old Glories resplendent in starch and ironing and every civil service employee decks out his flag for his security and those damn radicals and news from Europe must be very gloomy, who will be our next President? Little kids may be radio stars someday they sing like Kate Smith Thank God For America by Irving Berlin who says swing is on the downgrade and he is glad because in a year or two we will be back to normal again and they will be ashamed to swing any of his songs. This is the day for the high class Jews to get on the radio and spit very authoritatively at all isms like fascism and communism except americanism and secretly feel pretty good about circumcision and the *Rothschilds* by George Arliss. Oh, the poor kid who wanted to shoot something off so it could make a noise like he was the creator of fire and splash and he could do things everyday to think about afterwards when he was putting his shoes on. A holiday and you get dressed in the morning like it was a holiday in summer with white shoes polished with all-white in the kitchen with a rag and you don't know whether to whiten the soles and heels too because your hand slips a little and some of it gets on the heel and it all dries on the window sill where the sun is hot through the screen and the shoes cake while you take a shower, ah life is good under the shower luke warm sprouting down on you and I dare you turn on the cold water all the way like they talk about a cold shower. We will go to the beach where the WPA made a beach for the public and everybody can swim in the water and eat lunches of delicatessen and pickles but they charge ten cents for soda when you can get it in the candy store for a nickel but they have to do it because their season is only two months. If we could find a place there where it isn't crowded and maybe we got a sun umbrella cheap and stick it in the sand down deep and it looks like in the movies so you could get out of the sun and go to sleep later in the warm sand in the shade. Its so nice if there was somebody you liked and we laid there together smelling clean and salty in the warm shade with our arms around each other with our eyes closed softly and kissing dry lips and feeling

each other in bathing suits, all alone on the clean sand, and then
we had a new car at night and we drive not home but in the country with the top down in white pants and a turban around her
still wet hair and we come to where there is fireworks real ones
not making noise but shooting up into the sky with a sharp puff
and spreading out in all colors of stars and slowly dying away as
they fall in the night. A girl who isn't a girl any more because she
is over twenty six and everybody else is married already by this
time hasn't a date because there isn't anybody she could think of
or could think of her as though she were alone in her own world
and there just isn't anybody, not when you go with a person for
three years and its serious, so serious it was nothing to go away
to Atlantic City for the weekend that time and even meet his parents another time even though it was by accident and you even
used to come home by yourself at night because it was so serious
that he could say he had to get up early the next morning they
were expecting a shipment of goods and he had to fix the window and it was all right just as though you were both figuring
out the insurance together, its so serious it didn't hurt you to hear
that someone you knew was getting married because you felt that
way too and you could even figure out that she wasn't marrying
so well because your Joe was making a better salary than hers
was making and he was a go-getter besides. And when it happened and he said he was getting married it wasn't like you
thought it could be because you didn't feel anything but just a little panic for awhile like you were on the subway platform and
you looked in your pocketbook and there wasn't even a nickel
there only three cents change from the paper. It worried you most
what you would have to tell them at home as though you didn't
know where to start telling them as though they couldn't believe
it even if you spoke for a whole day, you wanted them to hear
that it was off that's all, just like you took it, but they would
want reasons so that they could understand it and if you said it

was because he said he had to marry a girl with money, if he said it frankly to you so that you could feel if you wanted to that he would rather marry you if you had some money instead of the other one who had money so he could go into business for himself you can't get anywhere working for somebody else all your life they can go broke any day and then where are you, though it didn't seem possible that Davega's would go broke but he said there was no future there for him, if you told them that they would believe it because it sounded so logical but they would expect you to carry on more than you did as though it was also logical that a girl doesn't go with a fellow for three years and god knows what and even starts making a trousseau and then lets him walk out as though it was nothing at all. But you were so tired by that time there was nothing to do about it one way or the other and it didn't pay to carry on even for them. You wanted to come home and act just like you did before it happened and they didn't let you.

Even when you hear he is married and has a baby it doesn't mean anything and what if you grow older every year and nothing ever happens, what are you going to do about it? Things can give a turn over night and you are married and settled down and having your own babies and there you are. That's the way it is, God that's the way it is. You can't really blame him, I would do the same myself, or would I? A woman is a woman, and there is nothing to it as though its like in books where love is something special. A man wants one thing and he don't care where he gets it. I know. And with a woman its the same way. With him I didn't lose a thing but time and it was no different with him than it was with that buyer from Chicago. You just got to see that you take care and you can really have some fun out of it if you try and he is the least bit congenial and not an ordinary bum. There's nothing to it, there's nothing at all in life and the quicker you find it out the better it is for you.

So its the fourth of July, I'll take the kid to the pool with me
it'll do us both good to get in the sun for the day, if that sister of
mine will let her go, believe me if I had two kids like her I'd know
how to bring them up. I'd give them something to eat and I'd
bathe them once in awhile. They stink, in this day and age a kid
should stink! But I'm not supposed to say anything, I'm the old
maid of the family, the one who let a man walk out on her, I don't
know anything but the five dollars I give to the house every week.
What the hell, let them stink, but I'll take the kid with me this
morning and on the beach they will look at me and Charlotte and
figure I am her mother, a young attractive mother and it would
be nice if we both wore the same kind of bathing suits and I put
her hair up like mine instead of that mop of curls my sister makes
her wear in this heat. It's a good thing Shirley Temple doesn't
wear a wig, my smart sister would get a wig for Charlotte too. So
Charlotte went some place on the fourth of July and didn't have
to stay on the street in her wrinkled play suit and the little kid
fussed all morning getting ready, like a little old woman getting
ready telling her mother what she wanted for the lunch to take
with her, she wanted delicatessen and she got one lox sandwich
tougher and saltier for its night in the refrigerator, a soft banana
turning black at the end, a solid piece of coffee cake dumped
together in the brown bag and Charlotte glorying in the class and
opulence of this basket lunch the grease beginning to blot the
brown bag in luscious spots. It was beautiful to tell at a glance
what the bag contained just like watching a little kid vomit on the
street near the curb you could tell what he ate for the last seven
hours. Charlotte was in the street passing the word along that she
was going to the beach for the day, passing it off as though it was
nothing new, she and the salt water, she was born in it, mother
lay in the big lavender room overlooking the water when I was
born, the room she had done over when father brought her home
as his young bride in 1912, the same room from which grandfa-

ther Morris paced up and down up and down staring through the big windows at dat ole debbil sea that took seventeen ships from under him year in and year out because he could never tell the north from the south even on a clear day. Yes little Charlotte wore her bathing suit under her play suit and it itched terribly and she stank more and more as she grew hotter and hotter and beads of sweat stood out on her lip as she told everybody how she was going swimming today and they were going to take her lunch and have ice cream at the beach and she could swim a little bit if somebody held her up in the water and once she was in the pool and a man wanted to teach her how to swim and mama said it was all right because she knew the man, he worked in the appetizing store where they used to live and he held her under her stomach and he squeezed the big part of her leg and she got scared and started to cry and anyway she admitted she wasn't going into the water she was going to sit on the sand and rest like her mother did when she went to the beach it was just as good for you as going into the water where anyway all kinds of people went in and they had germs and you could get sick from them even if you just went into the same water especially if any water got into your mouth or even in your eyes she was going to stretch out on the sand on a cover and get sunburned. And Charlotte impressed the other kids because she was going to the beach for the day with her aunt who lived with her because it was even better to go swimming on such a hot day than even to go to California way across on the other side of the United States like Helen was on her way there with her father and mother and sister whose father was a teacher in the high school and they bought a new car to go away to California with to visit Helen's aunt in California and stay there all summer because it is so nice in the water and Charlotte said it was even better if you just rested on the sand like her mother always did, with her varicosed legs sprawled out leaving her wide open and her arms over her head showing two patches of curled hairs drying up in the slight breeze and retaining their odor forever and forever. Then Jean was ready, ready she was fit to be tied because of it all and besides her sister wanted her to take lunch for herself too because she said why should you buy something to eat, I got for you too in the house, I got enough in my house all the time to feed an army and you know it, nobody can ever say I didn't have enough food in my house, thank God my husband makes a living for me and my children and that's more than some people can say, and some people should even talk, but Jean had to plead, please, I don't want to carry a bag of lunch with me, I'll eat at the beach, it's enough I have to lug that bag of stuff of Charlotte's. My, my, such a classy person my sister turned out to be that it doesn't fit her to take lunch from the house. Maybe you don't like what's the lunch, I should have back for one month's time the money the good money that I spend for my table in a week, I know what people eat, I see everyday what they buy and you got the nerve to tell me my lunch is no good, you hear Sam what my sister tells me in my own face, my lunch I make for my own flesh and blood is not good enough for her, the princess, the king of England should have seen her first, the lady, and Sam looked Jean over from head to foot over his cigar and Jean was going to scream and she felt like a god damned fool in her linen dress and white sandals and yellow anklets with the yellow band around her head looking awfully sweet and hot and smelling nice and warm. And she rushed out of the house carrying her beach bag and Charlotte's lunch in each hand and walls painted light green and dirty with the baby's fingerprints and unmade beds and hideous furniture and egg-marked dishes and stale coffee followed her with her sister on her heels, I don't think I'll let Charlotte go with you, it's too crowded today anyway, a fake statement done with a serious turn of the mouth the eyes figuring a deep mathematical equation, I should let my Charlotte go where she isn't wanted!

Oh, don't be a fool, I said I wanted to take her didn't I? Leave us alone and the day will do her good. Her sister ran on ahead of her down the hall to the street, Charlotte, Charlotte come here quick, say good bye to the children, are you ready to go with Aunt Jean to the beach? I have your nice lunch all ready for you and go with Aunt Jean. Charlotte left the children, hollering so they could hear as they watched her, I'm all ready, mother, is Aunt Jean ready by now? She wanted to know where her lunch was and she took it out of Aunt Jean's hand and then put it back. She wanted to know where her towels were and everything, the little lady, so efficient, like her mother the spitting image. Don't go in the water, Charlotte, sit on the sand. Jean, don't let her go in the water, it's better she stay on the beach.

She's afraid of the water anyway, ain't you, Charlotte. On the beach she'll mind all the things when you go in the water, all right, so go already Christ in heaven, keep me sane, the neighbors on the sidewalk, where is your boy friend on a holiday you have to go out by yourself with your niece only? you're old, I don't think you'll ever get married, there's younger girls looking for husbands a fellow wants an old thing like you, I don't think you'll ever get married—on bridge chairs in the shade of the house of bricks, the super using the hose on the street the hose curving from the court of the house the spout in the rough hands of the silent blond haired Swede in his union suit and pants his fat wife in her hoover apron leaning against the house watching her man sweep the sidewalk clean with a curve of his arm the water charging out catching the dirt in the sidewalk cracks and throwing it into the gutter, its nice using the hose watching the water come out I'll do it when he gets a job next month on the milk wagon nights, he goes away at night at one o'clock so we will have to fix it so he can do it to me a different time, it can't be when he comes home about ten in the morning because the kids will be around it's no school until September again and he wouldn't want to at one o'clock before he goes away he likes to sleep after we do it if we did it now, right now, run inside right now and do it, George, do it to me hard and I'll hold you tight till you holler. Charlotte ran after her Aunt Jean and said wait for me why are you going so fast there is plenty of time, and Aunt Jean saying to herself shut up you little bitch, shut your lousy little mouth you damn stinking brat.

We're having supper in the left lounge, the girl called turning her head as she hurried on.

Two Negroes wishing each other a happy New Year on the street corner.

Sure, in another year the Dionne Quintuplets will be able to tap dance.

Skating in Radio City, reading letters from Trotsky in Coyoacan, Mexico. Picking up a woman on Pelham Parkway who's trying to get a divorce, and is afraid she's being followed, thinking about yourself with no respect whatsoever, visiting the Municipal Court, Bronx 2nd, where a nifty little nurse in uniform and all is telling the rosy judge that it's winter and her landlord doesn't send up any heat and the rosy judge looks her over and remarks it doesn't seem she needed any heat, the tall trees creaking as they swayed in the winter wind to and fro slowly leisurely like the masts of a heroic whaler out of New England ports, fine round hips delicately powdered and smoothly swathed in purple silk, swaying like an efficient tank, knowing that when you desire you are not kind, writing a letter, starting, dear honey suckle, believing that the only clean thing about being promiscuous and living promiscuously is the baths you take, trying to find the Broadway where a million lights flicker as a million hearts beat faster, trying to knock off a piece of romance, standing at the tip of Central Park West watching 59th Street send Columbus

around in circles, looking forward to the day when New York's
subways will be sunken things of beauty, with La Guardia's help,
two muted trombones calling and courting a lonely clarinet,
three o'clock in the morning the kid yelling 'Boppa, Boppa, I
wanna go pishin'!

Julie is a fine girl, a beautiful face full and laughing, and a body
like God meant it to be a body and no kidding around. A mouth
like a steamshovel's and a vocabulary she didn't get at the
Ethical Culture School. Now shift because Julie wouldn't take
any lip from you or anybody except the time he made her cry in
front of him and it was no act either because Julie couldn't cry
if she didn't feel like crying. No floating movie actress this Fresh
From The Cleaner's fresh from the cleaner's accent, the word
cleaner's breaking into two parts *cle* high and *ner's* coming
down like you're calling somebody named *cleaner's* living across
the street, it means more than a song, it means the night the dental student in the Professor's class in dental school who was introduced to Julie by the Professor because she didn't go out enough
and there was a prom the dental student was going to and he was
a likely enough young fellow he had possible political leanings
and a good family that is money and pretty good grades so he
was all right to take Julie to the Prom of the senior dental students to which the Professor got the tickets because a junior who
is still cleaning teeth doesn't even think of going to the senior
Prom a real nice boy with a car the family let him have for the
night and pretty cute in his dress coat too a real nice boy because
he thinks of kissing girls and how it is kissing them in a car or
anywhere but better in a car because it's all set for it there on the
front seat and dark and all alone oh the little piss baby still surprised about having to shave three times a week it's a joke fresh
from the cleaner's fresh from the cleaner's the whole thing was a

joke and Prof was a damn fool because the prom was a bust like they all are and Julie let slip a few cracks that weren't in the rules especially not for delicate-minded dental students in steel-framed glasses with sweet girls who hoped for a doctor and willing to settle for a dentist with a location for an office all figured out already and maybe a post graduate course in teeth straightening there's money in that and pretty soon this baby's friends thought she was vulgar and the fellows figured her through their glasses as easy for what you wanted and the girls didn't like her except one girl from Hunter who knew about Julie from there and was a little bit afraid of her not so much as she would be if it were in school now in the crowded stinking lunchroom on the second floor where you had to be a big shot just to eat your lunch of tomato and lettuce sandwich and milk in peace with the Trotskyites sitting on one side and the Communists on the other, and the really really above it all intellectuals in the middle all throwing daggers at each other and butter stains growing on the open pages of the loose leaf note books where the lecture notes in Mental Hygiene 252 are being copied and Julie had to be friends with her and she was already engaged to her dental student. Oh crap this night would never end this ballroom a large room in the hotel and he had so much trouble parking the car without enough sense to put it in a parking lot neat and dark with brilliant arc lights and crunchy stone under your feet and walk on the outside nearer the curb when you're with a lady you dope and let everybody see how beautiful I am in this thirty-five dollar dress too beautiful for you you drip pot with nothing to say because I scare you to death and make you hot in the pants at the same time here on Times Square with a million people passing by us and you have to make me tell you to park it on the lot and now you think I'm a gold-digger for no reason at all but just because a nice girl should keep her mouth shut and let you twist that clean neck of yours out of its socket looking up and

down the streets for a space to park in but you can't figure me
out can you? because your professor introduced you to me and
that should make me Joan of Arc if you knew why you sissy if
you only knew why you would lay down and die to think such
things could happen in this democracy of ours, you would forget
all the dentistry you ever learned you would forget how to clean
a measly little tooth if you ever knew Mr. hot in the pants and
Prof wasn't he there when all the professors came in and everybody clapped to see the professors in evening dress at their Prom
smiling to beat the fillings in their teeth and good jobs too and
didn't he come over to Julie and shake hands with the child and
look at Julie as if to ask her how it was with a fellow her own age
for once a little anxious too the old bugger as if the child might
be better than he was as if he thought that could be possible
would he flunk this mother's hope out and leave him knowing
only how to clean the front teeth? and she smiled back like he
was a good friend of the family's well wasn't he just that? ah the
bitch the old bitch maybe you want to dance with me maybe
that's why you fixed it up this date with sonny so you could
dance with me? Sure you dog sure I'll dance with you why not?
what shall we talk about after I ask sonny boy to excuse me for
this dance? Shall you ask about my family mother is complaining
about that tooth again shall she come over to your office Friday
late afternoon or shall I come in her place like every Friday late
afternoon you let the nurse off early like half a day and you took
to the girl big for her age from Larchmont who lives with her
aunt and uncle in New York after her graduation from
Larchmont High School so she can go to Hunter College you
took to her maybe because she looked so easy even then because
she was the first one in Larchmont her age to know where babies
really came from and how you had to fall off regularly or you
were in trouble maybe you went for these perfect teeth or these
lovely hips neater than those of your matronly wife with a den-

tal professor for a successful husband maybe you figured no
mother and father around it was a cinch and it was wasn't it
could you ever find such a one like me so quiet and discreet and
so young why you would think you were living in India you old
bugger, you and me, I'm there every Friday late afternoon and
every other time possible and when I can't help it anymore when
I'm sick just thinking about it I send you special delivery letters to
the office and the time you weren't in the city all week and I had
to write to you in Larchmont and I printed personal on the envelope I just had to write to you and then I was sorry because anything can happen to mail and you were scared too and angry oh
you dog you miserable dog you raped me the first time you did
you did and I loved it I love it I want to go to you Friday late in
the afternoon when you hold me like a man does like an old man
not a boy a fellow with your barrel body and strong hands and
the grey at your temples the way your clothes fit you heavy and
good the authority and you know so much and you know what
to do and no kidding around and no jokes and everything is settled like cement oh love me all the time so I can rest back against
you feeling easy and safe close my eyes and breathe deep and long
one two three four one two three four against the smell of your
starched shirt right over where you have that ugly cut from when
you fell and broke your ribs when you were young if I act so bold
it's because I love you so it's not really because I only want your
love whatever it is against me Fridays late in the afternoon.

No I know love is like a piece of bread with marmalade
spread dripping over the brown edges and most times bread
alone is enough and when you're finished you're full and no more
even to you I can't tell everything because you're so old and just
good for one thing like a rock in the middle of the bounding
ocean it was so stupid that night in the waiting room we were so
good with the lights out and the magazines stacked white on the
table with my bag and we said you were going to get a divorce

and break the whole thing open and we would get married you
talked like a kid like sonny boy would talk and later I was
ashamed for you you were like such an earnest college boy and
you sounded ridiculous like a funny old man and you were sorry
afterwards too like you forgot all your communism all of a sudden and it was love love love with hearts and roses Christ I
wouldn't couldn't marry you it would be so funny you old sap ah
you're a great thinker those wise eyes of yours thinking all the
time and it's time to settle this thing because you like me so much
and you mean well in an unwell world so you want me to break
it up on my side and get a fellow a nice fellow and marry and
then you can say to yourself that you made a wonderful woman
out of me and prove the Marxian theory of sex and marriage and
go back to your classes and an occasional nurse and more steady
with your wife and I fall for the general idea because the whole
thing is cockeyed I know like a blind alley and George is a swell
guy so different from you being young does that to him and if he
never kisses me it's because he is afraid to or because I scare him
coming from you but he doesn't know and never could know
because that's sin the way he sees it if he knew and you did it all
because I wanted you to do it knowing it was sin but not sin if
you are a communist even though you're not a communist in
Larchmont only a communist in the secrecy of the branch of pro-
fessionals who make enough to pay more than a dollar a month
to the party that's why I cried that night when he came and sat in
my living room and acted so sweet that night when nobody was
home and I wanted someone like you so much to be near me then
hell everything seemed so rotten that night my mother and father
visiting my sister in Larchmont and playing with the baby and
the young married couples dropping in for a drink and talk and
pushing around and I was so all alone in the living room and
mother saying her teeth were bothering her and she would go in
to see you during the week you were the dentist with the big fam-

ily up on High Street who taught in the dental school and must
be good and you belonged to the Jewish Center and came with
your wife to meetings on Friday nights sometimes after you and
I were finished on Fridays late in the afternoon and sometimes we
had dinner together afterwards in that Italian place eighty-five
cents and wine too and then you walked me to the entrance of
the subway on the corner and said goodbye holding my hand
lightly in your new hat and swell shoes watching me walk down
the ugly stairs taking a nickel from my bag for the turnstile oh
you god damned sonofabitch you and your Engels on the family
its not your fault though even though you raped me the first time
you don't like that word but you did and I'm not sorry, honest
I'm not only it makes it tough when all is said and done and I get
to feeling lonely and lost and when George sits there opposite me
looking miserable and I can't do anything about it I cry like I did
that night burying my face in my hands and sobbing till my
whole body shakes it's a joke honest a joke and I can't laugh
because it has no point and Mr. hot in the pants wants to get me
alone and try what he has been thinking all night and if the night
lasts long enough he'll finally grab at me finally especially if he
takes me somewhere for a drink when there is couples starting to
leave the ballroom in groups to go somewhere else planned
beforehand but he's not in the senior class and so we don't go
with them because he doesn't know any of the other fellows and
he tells me about the Junior Prom they are going to have in a few
weeks and it sounds like he is going to invite me to it if I don't
shock him too much or in his own mind he goes for me more
than just wanting to kiss me some because to your prom you take
more than just a casual girl especially if you are studying a profession oh anyplace a drink don't be so classy showing you never
drank before except a beer once in awhile with your sandwich in
the delicatessen store or some brandy a little bit in the house
when you had company relatives over on a Sunday from

Brooklyn really let me order my own drink I know what I want
and you don't I was pie-eyed before you entered dental school
because you couldn't enter medical school you never made Phi
Beta ah this is good for me and you don't really know how good
this is for you too my drinking so don't worry so much about the
thirty-five cents pieces I'm drinking up because for every one I'm
more receptive to your hot in the pants in the car later when you
drive me home get me there safe so I can go to sleep and find a
little peace in my own bed if I say you are a nasty brat and you
will make a good husband as far as they go do you know what I
really mean? ah the cool breeze in my face and through my beautiful hair as you drive me home it was a lovely prom such nice
people you go to school with they will be good dentists but not
as good as my old bugger ah that's a laugh he is so good in so
many more ways than filling teeth and home so soon? you drive
so well you should really be a doctor in a big black Packard with
your satchel on the seat beside you and the MD on your plates
and a trim mustache and your pants covering your behind tight
but right now you stop the car and don't know whether to shut
off the motor let it idle gas is cheap right now who thinks of gas
when here I am slunk down in the seat too far away from you
and so so desirable and not a word spoken until ah you brave
boy you shut off the motor what does that mean I can read it in
your eyes and the way you look up and down the street to see if
people are around but it is late and this is a good neighborhood
west side you know only tall houses and some brownstones with
nasty stories about them and everybody inside asleep now only
the classy street lamps and the apartment entrances lit up and the
traffic light changing red to green to red on the corner and some
cars passing and stopping there minding their own business and
you sitting there with a circus charging around inside your pants
see now you throw the cigarette away that means something and
now count up to three one two three all right do it again on three

this time you will do it one two three and you grab at me as
though I were running away from you and here I am closer to
you and you are like a jumping jack it was so easy and you plant
a kiss on my wide mouth and you mumble like a baby god knows
what you are saying I don't and don't care either and how I turn
my face to yours like in the movies ain't I beautiful see you
shouldn't be scared you can kiss any girl especially with your
technique sonny boy see only don't talk keep that mouth shut
maybe I can teach you something yet and a kiss isn't enough you
like my neck and those fingers are like busy little ants what do
they want anyway how they wander like excited little beasts
peckin peckin ah they want to come inside underneath my wrap
my aunt's wrap bought in Best's don't kid me bo that's my dress
you're touching, you don't want that you want under that where
it's soft like a sponge ball did you ever play hand ball fellow soft
grows hard and tight if you do it right but you wouldn't know he
knows though he knows Christ he knows what you don't know
and you creep and creep till it makes me sick you're creeping, no
I'm not sore I was just thinking about things and all like who
won the Wimbledon matches in 1923 and why don't you go
home but you're too far gone now aren't you if it don't come out
down there it'll come through your mouth and that's pretty
messy too isn't it so come then if you have to come so then come
like a good little boy but remember one word out of you and I'll
tell you what I think oh come on I can feel for you you slob your
leg over me in desperation and quiet frenzy in one final burst of
glory hold me tight in sweaty hands leave go with your hand you
can go away now as long as you're so high just the suggestion of
touching is enough for you right now and swim boy swim and
charge through space and fall deep deep deeper and rock this is
your party all your own I'm not in it I'm just the accommodation
did I ever tell you about him that could really do it what you're
trying so hard to do now puffing like a dying fluke fish in the bot-

tom of the boat off Rockaway shore? come on let's talk now just
you and I and you can tell me all about your collection of false
teeth every molar known to the profession in your neat little cab-
inet at home do let's talk or am I being foolish? this is the crisis
isn't it? I mean it's now or never or is it beyond that? I mean it's
now now isn't it? I look pretty real don't I I mean laying back like
this all submission and passion should I puff a little too? look I
will not lie to you I do feel something when you put your hand
there but not enough to really want to feel more you disgust me
really so please have it over with wouldn't you dear? do I ask too
many questions? I have a habit of talking to myself when I am
alone like now I ask myself questions for you oop look out you
moved into the critical position then that damn thing of yours is
out in limbo don't you keep your underpants buttoned you had
a feeling this was going to happen why didn't you pad yourself
you dirty pig now you're going to ruin your pants it's good it's a
dark suit prom suit it wouldn't show but you'll swim in it till you
get home you'll probably catch pneumonia too you little devil
only here wait a minute I got to think of myself too of my aunt I
mean her wrap here let me pull the wrap away from under you I
bet you think I'm doing this to get closer to you well go ahead
and think Christ there you are as neat and cosy as a bug in a rug
you're riding my left leg fellow in case you want your location
and you're jutting out like a barber pole on Saturday night this is
Saturday night isn't it? damn you if you come through I'll spit in
your face the one with the red marks around the neck where you
can't shave so well you bitch why can't you hold it between your
legs and out of the way it'll come through damn you it'll come
through on my dress up there on my leg or I'm cockeyed but I
can't tell you can I I mean you're out of this world right now
something is running swimming around in your head right now
and you're one piece from your head to your toes right now like
a great relaxation in a wave starting from your neck and sweep-

ing down and back again I know how it is fellow only I'm sorry you can't have it longer you know Friday late afternoons? ah there you go the final jump rock a bye baby rock a bye baby upsy daisy can't stop a flood now can you I mean the Johnstown flood too once it starts okay fellow now I can go upstairs I mean I'm not needed here anymore you can do it yourself now leaning against a stone wall now you don't even need that now only please don't ruin my best dress you hear me? ah you dog you're peetering out now finished eh? and I touch your hair like a dope don't I? it means I love you doesn't it? you bastard you just try calling me up after this I'll show you what I think of you just try it and you will of course where can you come so easily? oh you poor slob rest now get off me embarrassed a bit like wondering how you ever got there I'm poison right now ain't I? I'm just a hunk of meat now to you you wonder why you can't go for this lovely thing sitting next to you like you know you will be wanting to do by tomorrow at the latest you want me to leave now you want to run away so you can get away from here and I draw the wrap my aunt's around me now you know why? because my dress is ruined that's why can I take it to the cleaner's this way? I can't because it would be embarrassing this way it's not a stain in a place where a lady might get a stain say once a month it's in the front in a most unusual place for it to be that means I'll have to wash it out myself when nobody knows what I am doing as though I went into the bathroom to rinse out a pair of stockings for tomorrow somebody comes in my mother what you doing to your dress? what do I say then? you dog you miserable male it's a joke though really a joke because wouldn't it be funny if when I washed you out of the dress and took it to the cleaners and it came back fresh from the cleaners I put it on Friday and wore it to school Friday and the girls would think I was going somewhere Friday night with not enough time to go home to dress after school and I sang the song all day long fresh from the cleaners fresh from the cleaners and late in the afternoon I went to his office in my best dress singing it would be symbolism sort of wouldn't it?

A nice little kid was lying in the hospital, on a bed that had a another bed planted on the mattress. The kid had a curvature of the spine and the second bed was only a frame that curved up in the center like the shape of a mountain that a kid draws in school. And the kid laid on the mountain with a noose around his head that was attached to pulleys dragging two pails of buckshot, and there were pulleys attached to both his feet counterbalancing the buckshot hanging from his head with the two buckets at his feet. The idea was to increase the buckshot in each of the four buckets each morning until the maximum pull could be achieved without tearing the kid apart. Today the quota was another five pounds in each bucket, making a sum total of forty pounds pulling each way. All the kid could see was the ceiling and the top of his chest. It got so the kid began to complain, he couldn't stand it anymore. He couldn't sleep either. You just can't close your eyes and drop off into the land of nod with forty pounds pulling one way and forty pounds the other way. He grew sores on his back and along his chin where the noose nestled. They brought him gum, to chew for something to do. No go. You open your mouth to chew and forty pounds says no. He tired himself out on a stick of Wrigley's. They brought him an all-day-sucker and he nearly choked to death. He couldn't sleep. He'd live a million years during the night, praying for morning when the ceiling . . .

I'll tell you, a Bronxite was seized after a sales talk to the Mayor of North Pelham in fact. Now what's the angle here? What goes

on in a Bronxite's mind that urges him to travel by bus out to
North Pelham and talk to the mayor of North Pelham? He must
have accomplished a lot of thought the night before. What a line
of attack he must have formulated! A mayor! This is no ordinary
salesman. This is class with a shot of initiative plus. Even so, his
heart must have been going on high test gasoline from the very
moment the idea hit him that the Mayor of North Pelham was the
guy he should give a sales talk to. I can assure you that he didn't
enjoy the bus ride out to North Pelham, he didn't have the time
nor the inclination to contrast the quiet splendors of North
Pelham with the familiar scenes of his native Bronx. Did he want
to turn around and go home every once in awhile? Did his careful plans backfire at him square in the face about a million times
before he came into the presence of the Mayor of North Pelham?
Ten to one they did. And did he bear up splendidly before the
hulk of a Mayor of North Pelham? Did he act like Grover
Whalen would have acted if he were behind these plans that the
Bronxite had laid out so carefully the night before in the security
of his own rather stuffy bedroom and before the mirror on the
bureau as he stood adjusting his summer tie with his plans going
bang bang all the way through him so that he couldn't eat his
breakfast of rye bread and melting butter and coffee cooked in a
small pot?

I tell you, there is nothing worse than failure, and if they
seized this Bronxite after the Mayor of North Pelham sat and listened to him talk for a half hour wearing a mask that didn't say
yes or no behind a good cigar looking just like a Mayor should
look, didn't this Bronxite experience failure, failure first degree?
Say what you want, say this Bronxite was a crook, didn't he try?
Didn't he work on his own? Didn't he exert himself? My God,
didn't he put his life and soul into his work? And if you don't like
the smell of his plans maybe you can suggest a better way to
make a few dollars. Boy, if you figure out the total amount of

energy this Bronxite used up in this whole affair you would have
enough power to tear down the Bronx and create a housing project that would put your eye out! Well, too bad, I say, but at least
this Bronxite who gave the Mayor of North Pelham a sales talk
can rest in neutral now, for awhile anyway, because when the
Grand Jury gets finished with him he's going to sleep peacefully
in the Bronx County Jail, a WPA project with sanitary cells. But
he will never forget his failure, and I say again, there is nothing
worse than failure. It eats into you and makes you feel like all
hell. It gets you very close to yourself but there isn't any fun in
knowing yourself, not by a long shot. I mean, say there is a girl
who was working hard all day in the summer over a machine
where she has to keep on feeding strips of cloth into a line from
which it comes out in neat diabolical designs, and she comes
home say about six o'clock with her head in a merry-go-round
and her clothes sticking to her like a three cent stamp on a love
letter to a girl outside the state, and say she lives with her family
on the fifth floor of a Bronx apartment house, four rooms forty-
three dollars a month, beds in four rooms, and she gets undressed
to be cooler and rest her head, and she draws her slip over her
head and it is wet through and through the straps too and that's
peculiar because she was wearing panties and a slight brassiere so
the slip did not really touch most of her body all day but it is wet
nevertheless, and she lays it on the sill of the open window to dry
because it is the only slip she has and she is really too tired to
wash it out and anyway it is so sticky out it might not be dry for
tomorrow morning if she washed it anyway, and suddenly like all
unexpected things happen a wind comes along, if there is the
least breeze we get it, and carries the slip off the sill and it floats
down five stories this way and that way you don't know what it
is. Now if this girl comes to the window on the fifth floor and
watches her slip drift down into the street that is failure too and
nothing is worse. This is an awful kind of failure, worse worse

than the failure of the Bronxite who gave a sales talk to the
Mayor of North Pelham because at least they caught him and he
can rest now for awhile, but her kind of failure keeps on because
five flights the street get dressed again five flights my head hot it
is the gutter only slip dirt in the street neighbors kids laughing, It
goes on and on, only a punch drunk God could think of it all.

He said, You know what? He says to her, I love you. And she was
soooo pretty. Like a doll, with long thin legs and big feet, her toes
many inches from her ankle bone. It was so beautiful, Everything
was lovely. Like something out of a 35 cent movie. You didn't
need technicolor. In black and white it was packed full of glamour—in a quiet way. Can you get what we mean? Love, in a clean
high-living way. He says to her, you are very beautiful. She wasn't
really, if you are viewing all this from some impartial survey outlook. This isn't Madeleine Carroll. This isn't beauty out of a cat-
alogue. This is the honest truth. This is girls in panties that get
dirty, feet that smell and sweat. Boy, this is love. This is a polished
orchestra over the radio made up of middle aged baldies blowing
away like mad in wet shirt sleeves in the studio. These are legs
that look good, very good, in three thread stockings when the
legs are shaved and the razor leaves a few cuts around the knees
and the blood blackens and hardens as it clots. Her hair, it smells
best when it needs a washing. Then it's got a heavy smell, sweet
and thick. You make perfume out of garbage don't you? He says
to her, I just want to hold you close, near me, just a little while,
not squeeze you, just hold you closely, neatly, like a soft pillow.
That's what he says to her, and she doesn't say anything, only
comes in closer, her eyes down like a bad little girl and her hands
feeling for him, and there you are. One of them goes and dies and
it's the end of everything for the other one. Until somebody
comes along and fills The Great Void. But don't be disillusioned.

You'll get used to it. Go sink yourself in a chartered story in *The Saturday Evening Post*. Go light a cigarette; go inhale and lose yourself for twenty minutes. Only don't get mixed up in those page editorials near the front. Better scan the advertisements at five thousand dollars a page. They make you believe you really got a stake in capitalism. Maybe you have at a-not-so-certain 35 dollars a week. Only don't be cynical. Be earnest, with a wide-eyed interest in something. Like you want to learn everything about something. Like knowledge is supreme and you want a piece of it. Have faith. It covers a lot of territory. You can explain a lot of things by faith. Boy, it covers a whale of territory. You can add two and two and make four any day of the week, but with faith you can make it five and everybody will applaud, You say two and two make four and everybody is suspicious. You say two and two make five and add that you got the total by faith and everybody says you are a nice boy. And they feel nice too. It's like being very respectable. You can rape a lot of women, or even seduce them in a mean way, but if you do it respectably its oky-doky all around. Say a young guy is a stooge without looking like one and say he goes to the University of California for four years, see, and he has an awful urging sex urge all the time, and he has ambitions, not so much money but fame and position, and he thinks heavy things all the time, like about what is time and what is truth and why is nature natural and all that, and it gets him into strange company and he gets very superior in a very obnoxious way and he is very scheming and he almost knocks himself out with plans for this and that and suddenly he gets very bohemian and he finally gets his degree, and say that's in 1923 and he ain't a worker and he hasn't enough of what it takes to become a lawyer or certainly a doctor and very definitely an engineer. He almost becomes a high school teacher in Romance languages but the glamour of life is too much for him to accept that kind of security, so it's 1923 and he gets his family to send him

off to Paris. To study more. And he stays there seven years. Seven
years and he is studying philosophy all that time. Really studying. If you call philosophy studying. He gets a dose of it sooner
or later, but it dries up. He is becoming a man and he loves it. He
loves himself too, I mean. The Sorbonne for seven years and the
University of Paris. Say it in French and its very cosmopolitan.
What he's after is not to have to sit on his fat ass with a hungry
look on his face. Hungry not for food and a pretty clean bed, but
hungry like a hunger for women sleeping with seven a week can't
kill. You know what it is living mean like in Paris as a student
and an American not yet thirty with an allowance? That's what
it is. It takes you seven years to cop the Ph.D. that way. You write
your thesis on Durkheim. It never fails. You grow a mustache,
but a real fancy one with hair and all. Listen, you know what it
means when the girls around the place get to know you by sight
and love to snicker about you behind your back? It's time to go
home then, and that's a ceremony. The members of the Academy
of Paris say goodbye to you and urge you to carry on the work
in the United States. Carry the message of Bergson and Levy-
Bruhl to America. Let us know how the lecturing situation is in
the states. They write letters for you and you land in New York,
lunch with the chairman of the philosophy Department of some
university at the McAlpin and take a year's contract as tutor at
the University of Rochester. Deposit three copies of your thesis
with the New York Public Library and copyright two more
copies. You're established. A philosopher and who knows what
else. But don't get stuck in Rochester. It's too small and too far
away from Columbia University and University Place in the
Village. The Village ain't what it used to be but its intellectual.
Everything is The Mind down there. And the women are aggres-
sive down there. Mention Schopenhauer down there and you got
a harem following you all around, day and night. Talk about
Paris and you don't have to carry money on you any longer.

You're established. So come to New York, by hook or crook. Take an instructorship at City College. The pay is good, considering, the reputation is not so bad, be able to bait the students on Marxism, laugh them off with cosmopolitan references and the administration will appreciate you. You'll be an assistant professor in almost no time. Discover Roger Peet's and buy all your clothes there, a suit every three months. All kinds of tweeds. Start with a brown and end up with a mustard yellow, but choose them heavy and tweedy, like a bushel of Brillo. Be an innovator, smoke your pipe in class, wave your hand to the 14 students sitting around you to light up too if they want to. Make an issue of it with the custodian on the floor. Be petty and make an issue of it if he says it's against the rules. Tell him about study in Paris, in the Sorbonne, where teaching and studying is so intense and wonderful that you can eat your dinner in the lecture room or bring in the girl you picked up outside. Talk expansively and smooth your mustache down all the while. Don't teach a damn thing. Just talk, about anything. Mostly yourself. Read to the class the articles you write and explain why even *The New Republic* doesn't take them. Explain that it's the lack of a philosophic attitude in America that's keeping you in the dark. Tell them what they're missing. But philosophic attitude or no, you're not getting any place this way, Better branch out. It's 1937 so you can make something for yourself out of Marxism these days. Get invited to explain why Marxism is off the beam, why Marx was wrong. Tell it all philosophically. Use Hegel and diagrams and deep thoughts and logic. Make it high class. That's the stuff that may get into the papers. Pester the editors for a chance to do some reviews. But I'll tell you, even this isn't the stuff. You want to become a full professor someday and just sit pretty? Hah, you want fame and position and women running after you just to stroke your walrus mustache! Something to fill out your pants. You know what you ought to do? You ought to specialize in something. Metaphysics? No, you got to be a poet these days and anyway, it takes too long and the company isn't fast enough. Logic? Well, frankly, that's too difficult, and anyway they got the field pretty well gobbled up. You know what? How about The Philosophy of Law? There's a subject. Easy. All talk.

———————————

Do you ever get awfully sentimental and soft all over and feel very confident in the security of your total comprehension that you are wonderful and very handsome or beautiful and so lovable and yearning for real love thinking that you can love very competently with such a feeling and tremendous passion that you and the one you love will both be so very satisfied and truly happy, like after a long cool shower and crisp cool white sheets in a night studded with strange white flashes they call stars? Love, brothers and sisters, it's truly wonderful.

I was listening in on the radio where a tricky little showgirl seems to have made good because they asked her what the glamour stars in Hollywood were wearing and she seemed to know and it fitted in just right because it seems that the glamour stars in Hollywood all wear fur coats created and sold by the man who sponsored the program I was listening in on and then they asked this successful showgirl about herself and she wears the same coats it seems, she said their style and quality couldn't be surpassed anywhere and then they asked her about herself and her career and she read a statement telling when she was born and all the highlights in her climb to fame in the entertainment field and it seemed so easy the way important people in the amusement world happened to see her at the right times and push her up and up all the way. It seemed so easy how it happened to her that I could only figure that either she was some little genius that even an impresario couldn't help noticing or else that she was lucky enough to sleep with every important guy in the entertainment business night after night or early morning after early morning, where we going now? to my apartment oh are we? yes any objection? no, through pursed lips, I mean, it's a matter of personal pride this going to bed with every Tom, Dick and Harry. It's your sense of values that counts and you can walk in and rob the First National Bank without batting an eyelash if you do it pursuant to a fine personal sense of values. I mean, just don't be pushed around, and if you feel you're spreading your legs apart and it has nothing to do even in the slightest degree with the idea of rape it's all right and more power to you. But just as soon as you get to feeling that you're losing something that is all yours and nobody else's, that's the time you're no earthly good, and it's time to turn over a new leaf after taking stock of yourself. Figure this way: if you can truthfully tell yourself I can look the best people in society square in the eye and honestly feel superior then there is nothing I have done and will continue to do that is wrong or for which I am sorry. If you can say all that without effort or strain of rationalization I say let me step up and shake your hand, the hand of a proud person full of pride and self respect. So when I listened to this ambitious showgirl on the radio I realized how foolish it would be for me to ask her whether she was a technical virgin and how much more significant it would be to ask her whether she was happy about the whole thing.

I do not deny that love will come to our showgirl. I only suggest that there are so many angles in her life and her career that love when it comes to our showgirl will have to come into the picture in the guise of just another angle and that it will have to fit in with due consideration for the other angles among which it takes its place. Like they asked her on the radio, we hear rumors from Hollywood that you have been seen around in the company of, and they named a guy in pictures, have you any romantic plans? And she laughed with a naturalness that gave it away that she was used to the microphone, no I cannot confess to any def-

inite plans for matrimony, as though she were contemplating
signing a contract for a new little intimate revue for the winter
season. And then the announcer laughed too and said what about
seeing her in the company of some guy around Broadway, and
she laughed into the microphone again and said yes he is my constant escort in New York since I returned from Hollywood last
month, but it is nothing serious. And the announcer said fine
then there is still some chance for me isn't there? And the showgirl said certainly there is some chance for you. And there you
are, and who can tell but there may be some chance for the
announcer if he shows up at the right moment, unless there is a
bigger fish in the pond at the time he shows up. I mean, after all
he's got a voice that's a pleasure to listen to especially within the
intimacy of a taxi riding through Central Park and his physical
build goes with it unless all this fanfare about calories and
physique is all wrong and after all business is business and it has
its place and time and you need a little recreation too once in
awhile. All right, call that whatever you will, the newspapers
could call it love even though you and I know it's just a matter of
relaxation, a curiosity to compare techniques, maybe she's interested in the polite eager way the announcer looks at her dancing
breasts when she finds it too hot in New York to wear a
brassiere, or the way he is proud to be seen with her on
Broadway walking into Lindy's for a sandwich, maybe she wants
to hold his handsome head on her lap and do a Helen Hayes for
a change, maybe he has only a little room in a cheap hotel while
he's waiting for a call from the National Broadcasting Company
to cover the 1940 Republican Convention with H. V. Kaltenborn
and she wants to remember again how a cheap hotel room can
feel so that she can walk out of it afterwards twisting away from
the chair and the bed and the bureau mirror, running her fingers
over them with her hand in his knowing that she wasn't in this
room just passing through but that she slept here on this lumpy

bed and loved and fixed her hair in this mirror and lifted her skirt over this blatant toilet and swished out of the elevator through the worn-out modernism of this little lobby passed the desk in clinging black acetate so that the clerk behind the desk who had one wife in Flatbush and another wife and little son in Hackensack, New Jersey, felt a sudden hungry emptiness grow through his lower extremities with such a fierceness that the day-old desire to visit which one of his wives vanished with a sense of futility but returned in a hot flood of passion behind his desk after the showgirl walked out of the hotel and he leaned on his elbows over his desk sucking the top of his pen daydreaming away on what he could do with the one in Hackensack, New Jersey, but couldn't do yet with the one in Flatbush.

If you think a strong man has to be a superman to be a strong man, you are wrong about it because I tell you a guy on the street who you'd say was just a little shrimp may be the light-weight champion of the world recognized in New York State and all the other states too. You may think he couldn't even defend himself on a dark night and you'd say any truck driver could take him over in one wallop. I tell you fighting is an art, just like a good doctor in the operating room, and massive shoulders and big arms like girders and bulging muscles and bull necks and iron-set jaws and barrel chests aren't the half of it, though they count. A big bruiser will wallow like a beaten kid before the dancing science of a pretty good boxer. If you could see what I mean you would say it was unfair putting a tough guy against any four round prelim boy. If the tough guy could only get a punch in okay, it would be a fight, but the trouble is he can't get a slug in to save his life, and the little boxer could jump around him jabbing away with a straight left that seems to come out of nowhere and it's not a fight or even a massacre, it's just a sly deliberate cutting up process and all your sympathies are for the guy who weighs sixty pounds more than the victor. It's like a greasy Chinaman using Fu Manchu on a splendid American from Princeton. For a real fight you want two tough guys against each other none of them who know the difference between a jab and a hook, all they know is charge in and see how many punches you can get across before the other guy finishes you and look out he don't smash his heel down on your foot or get a kick in between your legs. That's why a truck driver who goes to see the fights some Wednesday night sits there with a sneer all over his face hollering they're a bunch of bums up at the two machines tabbing away at each other under the lights in high laced leather shoes with heavy white stockings rolled over the tops. If he could get hold of one of the fighters, just hold him around the neck with one hand, he could knock the living hell out of him with his other hand.

It's funny though. I mean, you ask any girl who is picking a ride into New York from say Norwalk, Conn., you ask her who she'd rather ride with, a private car, say even with a radio and a heater, or a truck. She'll say a truck any day. That is, unless she is not so much interested in getting to New York as she is in playing the road for a little business besides. She says a truck driver is a man you can trust. Sitting high in his cab in a leather coat with a sweater underneath and a pair of real shoes against the floorboards, he's a woman's idea of a time in bed, No tricks, no line, no grabbing at your leg once he shifts into third and hits the gas pedal. No crap. A girl knows where she is and who she's dealing with. And if he's open for a date it's a date and no lead on where he can drive off the road a way and muscle in on you to let off a sudden but solid hardon, under the idea I got a date with you next week you ought to be satisfied to be nice to me now a little, and it comes next week and you wait outside where he's supposed to meet you and of course he never shows up like you expected he wouldn't all the time. First place you don't drive a

truck off the main highway, it looks too suspicious, and a truck
driver knows how to take his time anyway, he's not a kid and he's
got self-control. And anyway, he's not out on a pleasure trip, he's
got a schedule to keep and a record to keep perfect if he wants to
hold on to his job until his stomach doubles up on him behind
the wheel in another couple of years or so, and he's bonded for
all the stuff he's carrying in the back locked up there, and he's got
to keep his eyes on the road ahead of him and watch out some
Jewboy in a new Buick with whitewalled tires don't get adventurous and hit fifty and try to cut him off and get his new fender
clipped off for his trouble and then get to hollering blue murder
and taking down his number and promising to sue the company,
you're insured aren't you, and getting him his walking papers
because the ICC and the insurance companies and the company
ain't going to have a collector of judgments driving their trucks
and once they put you out nobody is going to let you drive their
trucks for them, not by a long shot.

A great plane came out of the air without a sound with the
leisurely glide of a clean ivory monster. What a ship! Let them
show you pictures of the history of man's conquest of the air,
from Kitty Hawk to Floyd Bennett Field. From ungainly wire-
bound crates to this chromium fuselage. If they go any further it
wouldn't be fair. This is class and we want to stay here. Or have
you got something even better on your mind? Come on, you
blueprint boys, what's next? But try something that will give us
back our heroes. Something that will remind us of Frederic
March in the uniform of the Royal Air Corps with a yellow scarf
around his neck. I mean, give us back the open cockpits and guy
wires. Let William Faulkner design the planes for Pan American
Airlines. And those fancy offices on Forty-Second Street with the
aging Dartmouth boys behind the low mahogany counters selling

tickets for the Newark-to-San Francisco runs, with a berth! Isn't there any romance left in this world? Do we have to wish for a crash in the Rockies to restore our faith in life the adventurous? Sure, I know, the adventure of construction, the hours of construction, the details of assembly, the uncertainty of weather reports, the years of post graduate work in navigation, the brutality of physical standards, the horror of test flights, the old mechanics of finance, the intrigue of inter-airway lines, the threat of government ownership. But give me the thrill and dignity of Clark Gable carrying the mail over the Appalachians one stormy night with ice gathering along the tips of the wings and the tanks draining almost empty and the altitude needle reading 8,000 then 7,000 and so on down and Witchita pleading "Come in, 347, Come in 347. Are you there, 347? Do you hear me 347? This is Witchita calling you, 347."

I mean after all we got a right to our piece of bread, haven't we? At least if we can't live like men at least we should be allowed to strum a guitar with Nero while Rome burns. I mean, there is a lot of nonsense in such a classical statement, such as, "I will rescue your honor from yourself." But it's nonsense only because the setting is certainly not appropriate for this declaration. My opinion is that this statement must ride and ride supreme, no detours, no nothing. Give us back our aviators, not bespectacled mustached technicians staring avidly at two hundred dials and gadgets driving airliners through megaphones. Our sky birds did well enough with goggles, they didn't need silver framed lenses and wives and five year old kids and two family houses in Bayonne, New Jersey. Give us strong, hard men with lean sky-stricken faces with an eye out and a black patch and a stiff left leg and a suspended Department of Commerce license. It will be time when we all drive around in flivver planes to kick these social dregs out. I mean when we all stop suffering then it will be time to get rid of the sufferers who make it heroic to suffer and thus make our suffering heroic for us. I mean let's not put the cart before the horse.

She had a cute little mouth, like a doll's, with a soft dark mustache hanging over it. Like a mane. It was disconcerting until you got used to it, and even then it was a hell of an idea whoever was responsible for it. Like the white snow, smelting into slush and garbage. You'd think somebody would look into it and do something about it, like fixing the leak in the roof. The best you could hope for was a scissors first and then a little razor in a fit of desperation and hope one night when the hairs were stronger and longer and frightening. Go patch the roof with newspaper. Better in theory to leave it drip all winter, but can you convince the tenants of that? Who ever heard of suing the landlord or the engineers or the Building Department or tearing the dump down altogether? So go make a crazyquilt on the roof and talk about the lousy housing they got in Russia, a father does in a kid of his so the family got enough room to lay down and get a little sleep once every sixth day, Its going to be a long winter, and the English are going to fight to the last Frenchman.

Glen Miller is good. He is standard stuff and he plays his band at the Glen Island Casino during the summer on the Long Island Sound where at night the young couples in white jackets and evening ginghams on sleek full hips drive off the Post Road past the golf course and cross the clean two-lane roadway over the bridge, underneath which the more than white cruisers with lots of brass and mahogany swing at anchor, and drive crunching over the bluestone right up to the door of the Glen Island Casino and the doorman in hat and in white opens the door and they park the car and you eat overlooking the Sound where it is cool and salty and clean like so many showers and girl's perfume and

powder and Glen Miller plays swing but not too rough but
enough to call it swing and all the young people think it is swing
and at least danceable the girls say because they are little ladies
going to marry pretty well so they don't have to cut up and lose
themselves in hot music kicking their feet and lovely legs out like
other girls who would wander into the Village that type of girl
and be tough about it and be good radicals, but all the time Glen
Miller plays melody that goes with the Long Island Sound lapping gently against the beach and the night just like in the movies
and he plays songs of young love and how two young people can
get married just on love without money and the song says we
haven't got a pot to cook in even and one fellow who goes to City
College and saves his NYA money until he has enough to take the
girl to a swell place where he don't like what they must think of
the car he is driving up to the Glen Island Casino doors where the
music of Glen Miller can be heard muffled like through the dark
doors into the red leathered room before the dining room
because it is a 1932 Plymouth sedan and looks it and is a family
car no matter how you figure it so that he can't act as though he
is just a substantial college fellow with his girl and a car he
picked up to knock around with during the summer, it has to be
a Cadillac touring or a Buick roadster or a convertible for that,
but the girl is not thinking so much about the car because even
though it will dirty her just-cleaned linen dress because the thick
seats are dusty you need a car to get to the Glen Island Casino
and this is the first time she is at the Glen Island Casino and isn't
it nice here and ten to one she can't tell one car from another the
only thing she knows about cars is that some are new and black
and others are old like this one and rich people have bigger cars
and she gets out of the car feeling excited and not knowing what
to say right now because she wants to act natural like always
with him like when they go to the movies and afterwards they
have coffee and pie in the cafeteria before he takes her home,

while the boy figures if he has to tip them for parking the car because other cars drive right into the parking space without stopping to let one of the attendants do it and maybe it shows I am better adjusted than they are, I know the right thing to do and they will respect me for demanding and getting the right things even with an old car, this is the car of a friend of mine he rooms with me at Columbia, I come from Alabama studying up north, I didn't come up with a car this year, okay fella, have a cigarette, with a subtle trace of southerner in my voice as though I don't know it's there, though I shouldn't be lighting a cigarette going into the Glen Island Casino, I should be grinding one out under my sole as I take her arm almost not holding it near the elbow going into the Glen Island Casino for dinner and some dancing to Glen Miller we haven't got a pot to cook in, I bet they really meant down on Broadway and 47th Street where they wrote the lyrics we haven't got a pot to piss in and another guy down there at the piano said or a window to throw it out of.

You know what's worth while? When you get through, if you ever do, reading through the Monthly Report of the National City Bank on events here and abroad and its effect on general business conditions, then you're pretty well satisfied with every-thing, everything looks fine and neat and everything is in its proper place by golly and suddenly that watery-eyed little guy shuffles along in pants that drag and tear around the heels and he mushes through Harlem trying to sell a couple of shopping bags to busy housewives and if he has an extra nickel in his pocket or he's feeling full of enterprise he takes the subway up into the Bronx where business should be brisker and trading is done in volume. The only trouble is the stores and the super-markets pass out shopping bags with their own personal compliments with every sale. It's enough to make the little guy with the dumb stare suggest a sort of gentleman's agreement with the stores, namely, you sell the eatables and I'll service the accounts. Come, buy my deep, durable shopping bags, three cents each. I got ten on me. The bustling community buys them all, my whole stock and I take in thirty cents which represents enough to keep me going for a whole week. I live cheaply, my family shifts for itself. I drop in only for a few hours every so often. My daughter is a career woman. She has a secluded corner on 114th Street all for herself. You see, she offers all kinds of extra services to her growing clientele. She frenches with a finesse seldom achieved in the relatively short space of thirteen months of experience. It's because she is diligent and eager to learn. She has beautiful breasts, only her legs are very thin and she's got nothing around her hips, the bones stick out like she was sick. I know, I make free passes sometimes.

So you come on and buy my assortment of shopping bags, three cents a bag. Here feel the quality. You can put in milk, nice bottles of milk, and eggs and butter and meats and vegetables, everything you got money to buy to eat. Me, I shuffle along, it's good for my health, it keeps me in the open, fresh air fiend, that's me. I go home every night and read the Monthly Report of the National City Bank on events here and abroad and its effect on general business conditions.

See? He's a scholar, if not a gentleman. But you want to meet a scholar and a gentleman? Or let's put it this way for variety: A scholar and a gentlewoman. By that is meant a woman who pays her just debts, to the penny. There is Annie, or Anne, or Ann, if you're still reading the Monthly Report of the, well you know what. Ann looks for work everyday, that is everyday except those days she just can't get out of bed. Annie picks up the day old papers and checks off the likeable household positions open. The next day she looks the employers up. The *Times* has the best jobs but she doesn't look them up usually. They don't like her looks and she's afraid of most of them. They make her stutter. She does

that when she's excited. She coughs then too. And begins to
sweat even in the winter. They have such nice houses. *The
Journal-American* is better. The ladies don't expect so much.
Most of them work and only want a girl to watch the kid during
the day. It's nice if you can get a job where you can sleep in, in a
steam-heated house where it's warm and you get as much to eat
as the kid and during the day you are the boss and can open the
ice box whenever you're hungry again. Annie doesn't buy papers.
They cost too much. If you save up you can buy another astrology magazine. Annie is a student of astrology. Astrology is wonderful. It's got all the answers, on everything. It explains things.
Annie lives on 11th Street. That's not so good because most of
the ads you have to answer are uptown and if it's the Bronx that
means carfare. Annie can walk as far as say 40th Street. It takes
her about a half day except if she can get a lift on the way. First
Avenue is best for that. They're not particular who they pick up
there. Just as long as you got a skirt on. If you get picked up say
by a salesman or an insurance man, they got time on their hands,
you can maybe get them to wait outside while you go up to see
the lady and then get them to drive you downtown again. It's nice
then to sit near the door and make believe it's your car and you're
taking a ride say with your husband. Except that you're hungry
and would stop to have lunch somewhere. Because for supper
last night you had a small can of cod fish, some tea and a banana.
You wish you had a new dress and a pair of stockings. You wish
you had something to eat. It all depends on his face and under
what constellation he is born whether he will buy you some eats.
If you studied astrology deep enough you could tell right off. The
other way is to make him buy you some eats. If he is hot in his
pants it is easy if you say you're hungry. Even so you got to watch
out you don't cough. That spoils it except if it's winter and even
then. Some men like slim girls. That's when they have fat wives.
Ones who eat a lot. All kinds of sandwiches and cakes and

chocolate bars. They get fat. Men like thin girls for a change, for variety. So if he buys you a hamburger and coffee and even soup, and even if he sits outside while you eat or goes in with you and watches every mouthful you take, it's no more than right that you should be nice to him afterwards. Only not too nice, some guys will want to do anything in a car in broad daylight. If he says where can we ride, you say down there pointing to below 14th Street way over on the east side where it's like Brooklyn, full of empty streets with big factories with machines making noise inside everybody at work and only trucks passing every once in awhile and the drivers don't make much out of what you're doing parked at the curb of the street. They take it for granted, the ones in the big trucks do. The ones in the little trucks are snot noses into everybody's business. So it's no more than right that you should be nice to a guy if he treats you right and buys you lunch and drives you where you have to go. But, see, if it's a kind of guy you could go for, say like one who would work out under the right constellation and all, then don't give in too much because if you do it's all over quick and he wants to go away and you feel like hell because with him you want to lay against his shoulder like they do in the movies and just lay there against him looking out of the window peaceful like, not saying a word, gee, like you was married to him say, and you both had something to eat together and you were going for a ride and was parking for awhile. So don't let him touch your breasts even though they are small he wants to and you shouldn't let him because that starts it and it's over quick then. Just keep his hands away from your breasts, from inside your dress all the time. Even though it doesn't work out that way ever because he can't help it and if you keep him off too long he finally jumps on you sooner or later and he hurts you pressing against you talking all kinds of crazy things and not saying anything at all and he pulls you to pieces rough like and you can't stop him no matter how you push and all and in a way you don't want to except that it's nicer to just lay against him quietly only he don't like that, and then it's all over quick like and he becomes heavier and heavier and quieter and then he pulls away like it wasn't even him at all all this time and then you know it's time to get out. And that's why it's always best to pick a spot where you don't have to walk too far back from.

You can bet your sweet dick that what you don't really know about cafe society and the Social Register and Debrett's Peerage and *Town & Country* ain't worth even musing about. What I mean is that if you want to eat you have to work. And don't think for one minute that your upper classes don't slave away. Just like you slobs. They don't go around slashing their wrists and jumping out of windows just for a thrill. I guess you think it's a cinch selling bonds these days. Or trying to sing a few songs before a critical mob in the supper clubs without much of a voice let alone a shape to carry them on and put them over. And troubles! Listen, say you're a pair of parents with a teethy son in Princeton, one daughter married to a cheap polo player who rates only one goal and blames it on his horses, and another daughter who you give the whole works, French convent, tap dancing lessons by good old Bill Robinson, one thread stockings and so on and you figure nothing else but an eligible Rockefeller boy, and bang she runs out one night and hitches up with a band leader or a garage mechanic. Trouble, eh? A little fool you raised, but what you going to do about it? If they got married at two in the morning up in Yonkers they're probably kicking up the sheets in some hotel up in Dryden, New York by this time in the morning, or maybe it's no novelty for them by this time, how do you know where she was every night since the *Normandie* docked eight months ago, or the mornings and afternoons too for that matter, you know band leaders and salesmen their time is their own. You'd be heartbroken, wouldn't you, I mean because you had such high hopes for the heiress. Especially since maybe she couldn't be an heiress for much longer the way things were going if some of those high hopes didn't come true pretty quick. So what you got now? A bandleader. He can bring his whole band up to the house and play for you. Yeah, but then you'd have to feed them. All right, say you figure maybe he will give her a divorce once he finds there isn't any money and she can start all over again. All right, maybe he doesn't, maybe he's looking for a vocalist anyway, one who wouldn't cut the orchestra to bits with her share of the dough. Well, there you are, and divorces aren't easy in New York. Gosh, do you know what it costs just to get the lowdown on his background. Boy, you could buy back a seat on the Exchange for half that price. Trouble, eh? You go and raise a daughter with beautiful high shoulders and you teach her how to smell sweetly and wear her hair combed down long and her breasts are nice and small, and bang, she goes to the masses. It makes you want to cry, I know. It makes you cynical, like thinking back on that swell $175,000 duplex apartment in the River House you were going to take when Marguerite married, well, sure go ahead and take the place, decorations and all, enough room for about ten apartments, but take it anyway so that bandleader can keep his instruments there, he can fill the place up with his traps and bass viols and maybe he's got harps and organs and super-pianos in his band, he can keep them all there. Your heart is bleeding a rich red, I know. Let's put oil on the fire, says the Prom Committee at Princeton and hires this bandleader to furnish the music for the Junior Dance and who comes trotting out that night but Marguerite to do the vocals. That's going to be a nice surprise for your ambitious little son, isn't it? Send him a pick ax to dig a small but deep hole in the middle of the waxed dance floor to crawl into. I mean, it all piles up with all kinds of subtle ramifications.

All right, you can't stand it, neither can I. The whole thing is really a matter of remaining solvent. Say you got a yacht, it looks real pretty swinging against the anchor off the 79th Street basin in the majestic Hudson River. And say you get word from the elegant New York Yacht Club to get ready for the annual August cruise. Who is going to pay for getting the tub into condition? All right, you can say you're going to rough it in slacks for a day and meantime polish up the mahogany and chromium gadgets, just in fun you know. All right, but can you polish up a thousand gallons of gasoline and a crew of eighteen? What with unions and all you just can't stand on the drive and hail two dozen sailors and offer them a splendid trip up the New England coast and back just for stoking the boilers and standing watch and all, And uniforms. How will it look with your boat passing in review off Glen Cove and the Commodore stands on the deck of his flagship and looks through his spy-glass and turns to remark to his staff that your boat seems to be full of uncouth sailors in dirty pants? You might just as well holler, hard to starboard Mister Klein, we're heading home! A jolly tar you make!

The overhead is terrific. Say you got a Long Island estate, say you call it Nenemoosha and a sick uncle with nothing to do went and planted the whole thing with flower beds and right now the whole estate is blooming and it smells like a cemetery on a nice Sunday in summer. All right, it's a beautiful estate but there's no room to turn around with the flowers and ferns and hot houses and all. You got acres of land but you can't even take a morning constitutional without tripping over irrigation pipes and earth-eaten gardeners. And there's taxes and interest payments on the place, let alone the water bill, so you decide you'll show some of that initiative that your grandfathers showed when they built the Union Pacific some years ago, you'll send out announcements offering beautiful flowers for sale to your neighbors. You think you can get away with it, you think you can clean up the joint a

bit and take in a few needed dollars? Don't be a fool, friend, it's a
miracle that they let you grow flowers on the place, let alone sell
them. The florists all over the state fall on your neck like you were
poison ivy. If you cut the price they holler, if you raise the price
they holler. It's quite plain that they don't want your two cents in
the industry. As though you were some kind of a dirty foreigner
or something. Sure, what does J. P. Morgan care about such
things? When he doesn't feel good about the way things are going
he says pack up we're leaving for a spell of grouse shooting in my
castle on the Scottish moors. See, he's got an escape mechanism
with a full line of standard equipment. But even J. P. can't really
break away from it all. You think it's a cinch preparing those
statements for the reporters on the course of the depression or the
possibility of a European war by the end of summer? Boy, the
sweat that goes into one of those statements! They tell stories
direct from the closest circles around J. P. how before the boat
docks in New York old J. P. sits up for nights at a stretch musing
on the affairs of the world and dictating about a million words a
night on the subject to a staff of seasick secretaries dropping over
their pads with fatigue and a squadron of little midgets creating a
turmoil fighting with each other for a chance to climb up there on
J. P.'s knees and play with that anchor chain around J. P.'s belly.
And how these Harvard English majors sweat over those treatises
boiling them down to fifty word précis for the morning press
releases. It's a tough job all the way around because you can't
open those innocent-looking dispatch bags which come by sea-
plane every hour and tell what the syndicate's chief lieutenant told
Herr Thyssen and how Herr Thyssen nodded his wise old head in
total agreement and kept saying yah, yah all the time. There's
statements and there are statements and you must know when
and how to use them in the interests of the really fundamental
principles of civilized living. What do you want, another Russia?
One isn't enough in Europe? Sure it's difficult putting up with a

Hitler and all, but you got to be intelligent and foresighted enough to appreciate when a compromise situation is necessary and opportune and being such intelligent and farsighted persons we save the essential glories of Western civilization for the present and what's more for our posterity too. So don't think it's all tea and grouse at Gannochy Lodge out in Edzell, Scotland. The planes come zooming in out of the skies, the telephones keep ringing all day and night, the low grey cars keep whizzing through the gates all week, the carrier pigeons swish through the fog every fifteen minutes, the wireless buzzes without a let-up, I'm telling you the caretaker can't sleep nights just thinking up schemes by which he can eradicate grouse from the face of Scotland. The dope. He thinks it's grouse that they come to shoot at Gannochy Lodge.

What is important about all this is how much failure must you chalk up before you get a situation where even Christian Science must admit failure? I mean, it seems to me that failure is failure if it's a million dollars or a penny in the weighing machine and out comes your fortune whose beneficent predictions you just know can never really happen for you. And if a blond feather-and-bubble dancer who was once one of Sally Rand's principal competitors waits until her twenty-eighth birthday to jump out of the seventh floor window of a well-known mid-town hotel, calling "I'm sick and tired of it all" to John the Roach sitting on her bed with his shoes off, "So long. Goodbye," and lands on 44th Street in her nude body at three o'clock in the morning just missing the cab drivers bunched around the cigar store and dies two hours later in Bellevue Hospital after a priest gave her the last rites of the church as she lay covered by a sheet on the sidewalk, he was in such a hurry, something happens like death and it's relayed automatically to the Vatican where the Pope sends out automatic bulls to every priest and they leave anything they're doing at that moment and race each other to the scene of the happening and he who gets there first can give the last rites and only he . . . well, if she finally jumps, can you honestly say that her failure was such as to justify leaping out like that without even a nightie on? I mean can you give me item for item the reasons why she could have jumped and another could not because the other didn't have enough reasons? It is my sincere and deliberate conviction that you could not, because in your heart and soul you know as well as I do that Thais, that's her professional name, and what Thais went through was and is no different from anybody or anything else. If she was born on Melrose Avenue and never went home after she discovered Manhattan, if she had a girl friend called Babe whose real name was Gladys, if she once danced in the Paradise Restaurant and knocked 'em cold and laughed and laughed and laughed, if her nose was really a bit too puggy and her lips too cupidy but boy did she know her stuff, and if she did live intermittently with John the Roach since he was released from Sing Sing in 1933 and never took no lip from his wife and family up in the Bronx and there was an unpaid bill of $46.90 laying on the telephone table in the well-known-hotel, and Thais the specialty dancer had spent all afternoon and early evening looking for a job until she met Babe and John the Roach in Greenwich Village and got to drinking and got all slopped up and got to thigh holding and breast pinching and Mr. John the Roach brought Thais to her hotel and came up and all and when he was coming out of the bathroom she was standing naked on the windowsill and very gloomy—now if all this is thus and so, do you mean to tell me she's somebody from Mars here on an investigation? You mean you never saw her or anybody like her, or that your sister is different, or you are too for that matter?

————————————————

I was asleep and dreaming and this time it was the World's Fair with lots of sun and bluestone under the feet and the King of Italy was visiting with Grover Whalen smiling in a cutaway with that solid belly held firmly in place like something from an *Esquire* advertisement up in front of the book. The little king had on a hat too tall and too large for him and his hook-nose twitched above his bristling mustache. He couldn't say a word of English and a flock of smartly uniformed Fascists tripped around him, bending from the hips and from the necks to the little king telling him all about it and Grover Whalen was smiling away to beat the band. Everybody was very courteous to the little king, especially the big Fascists, but they weren't going to stand for anything from the little king. One thing out of the way from him and bang they were going to give it to him and give it to him good too, with those little daggers hanging from their belts. No kidding. And I looked down and the little king was seeing the Fair in run down shoes. He was walking around in shoes with high wooden heels to make the little king look taller than he really was, but the heels were run down in the back like they were filed down with a plane. The little wop needed a pair of shoes, and the ones he had on were run down at the heels and they were getting more and more dustier as everybody was taking the little king around the Fair.

The first time you will do it with anything and after that you will do it with almost anything. It isn't the first time only that you think about it a long time because you think of it just as much after that too. You think you are all finished when it's over and you can't imagine how you could ever do it again or want to do it again. But in a little while it grows back on you, like you need a haircut; you can even space it like periodic lunar appearances or I haven't been to the movies for a week now. You're like a different person then. You can't imagine how you could ever feel all through with it. You can do it with anything all over again. You could kick yourself for not taking her address so you could find her again now, and you feel lost.

———————————

He is a wonderful fellow, I am really crazy about him. If my daughter should marry a man like him I would feel very proud. He is a mathematics teacher and an accountant and he is studying law from the big shots out in Washington. Always studying, day and night. He loves books. And he likes recreation too. He likes girls. But he loves to study, always with a book, day and night. Hot it was hot like you can't sit down it's so wet and hot the moon shines full like it was the sun at night and the clouds from daytime stay around the moon so it looks like Joan Crawford in the South Seas at night when they want to show the inevitable is happening with the man and the woman while the moon lays on the dark blue waters off the sand shore all the time it is happening just like the end of Fitzpatrick's Let Us Turn To The Magic Isle Of Manhewati Under The Southern Cross and so we say farewell to Manhewati land of the setting sun and all the time it is happening in the Joan Crawford picture except that was before the Hays office took things serious because not being serious enough makes America's children have bad thoughts and want to imitate the movie stars and the streets get full of walking women and the state penitentiaries fill up with movie fans it ruins the country the influence that was a few years ago with *Scarface* before the *G Men* but nevertheless it is so hot everybody stinks and lipstick on the mouth is greasy and sticky and the elevated is louder than it ever was ice cream from the Bungalow Man yeah maybe some ice water Florrie go upstairs and take ice cubes from the frigidaire in the pitcher bring down with glasses a little water please Florrie go I do enough for you the radio blares from the window on the ground floor through the darkness into the street

lit up by the arrogant street light showing the air like a London
fog with flying things running around like crazy the radio from
fashionable Peacock Court high atop Knob Hill in San Francisco
with wee Bonnie Baker singing in a high voice way down in her
sweet lovely throat holding her mouth wide open laughing like a
baby with Orrin Tucker's orchestra they got a nerve playing the
radio so late and so loud it's so late some people have no consideration for other people say please stop that radio please you got
some nerve it knocks in my head honest to God, bridge chairs
have a hollow sound scraped against the sidewalk like you were
pushing them around the block seven times, remember the time I
think it was two summers yet no last summer no it was two summers when my Harry when I sent my Harry to camp for the summer when the Greenfield boys they were men already it was so
hot they slept on the roof they had beds on the roof mattresses
fixed up on the roof don't you think there was the girl from the
apartment next to mine they moved already it was such a scan-
dal that was the tenant before you moved here she was sleeping
on the roof too listen she was a real one everybody knew it was
an old story Lillian what was her last name I forget already it was
so long ago after that they moved I think to Brooklyn the father
opened a grocery store in Brooklyn to go on the roof like that no
shame no nothing it was all over the neighborhood the
Greenfield boys they talked why shouldn't they they lost something by it? both of them for them it was a wonderful time they
had a picnic you could blame them? I say it's always the girl's
fault every time it's how you hold yourself that's how you are and
that's how people look on you too ah hot hot beds and sheets the
fire escape god help you if it's Saturday and you got a date thank
god for a date but it has to be so hot you wait all week for a
chance to go out and you have to go to the movies where it's 70
degrees says so on the canvas awning painted sky blue and painted snow around the edges like fun it is and if it really is you'll get

pneumonia coming out from inside where so many people in sleeveless dresses bare up to the arm pits and in polo shirts in mesh weave showing hairs curling on narrow chests like under the arms taking up all the seats and making them sticky and the leather damp even when it's so hot they want to hold hands and some kiss look up by the balcony the light from the projection room dances this way and that and the smoke from cigarettes in the balcony only there you can smoke rises in clouds lit up by the light but never gets on the screen like you think it should since it is in the path of the light showing Paul Muni acting with his face this is high class art like George Arliss you go miles to see such acting down on Second Avenue especially in the Café Loyale they knew him when and it's for this it is a pleasure to be a Jew he talks like a radio announcer and they listen to what he has to say like he was the president of the United States, but gee I want to see something where Loretta Young is in a bathing suit showing her beautiful breasts like they made her wear something you can't see on the screen which lifts them up higher put her in the cold water cool and drink from frosted glasses on a rock in the middle of the bay and flash those teeth at Joel McCrea in bathing trunks and David Niven liking her too something to make me think it is cool somewhere where a person can look down and then lift his head back without leaving his neck full of sweat sweat is wet and greasy like chicken soup so that means people make soup like a chicken does so that makes sense I guess you're happy so I am too and come out at eleven-thirty and millions of people standing in line to get in too for the midnight show mammoth cooling system in operation be cool and comfortable it's healthful, you don't need bingo to pull 'em in these days, kids crawling home from the pool hot all over again but it was nice in the water you could stay there all your life for fifteen dollars you get rid of them for the summer a couple of sandwiches a peach ten cents maybe for an ice cream a bathing suit from Hearn's a towel and there you are you got to buy slacks a whole outfit they make it in cotton in different colors and you come home in it beautiful bodies baked a chocolate brown in a few days smelling salty and fresh and cool to touch beautiful kids in tawny hair two molds of fat a hank of leg and a stretch of limb a neat ankle and a broad instep in sandals everything juggling as they trudge up the street lugging the satchel home and I hate it I wish I didn't have to go home to the hot kitchen and the dark stuffy bedroom with a million things in it I wish I was on an estate with a lot of grounds and nobody nobody at all near me for miles around and I lay down on the cool sand and went to sleep with ice cream sodas all around me and never never any more neon lights in my eyes you don't know how much you can suffer a fish is so happy in the water all the time not like in the basin in the fish market where they haven't got enough room to even swim around in the dirty water when the fish man reaches in for one and hits it over the head and it jumps out of his hairy hand and flaps around on the sawdust on the floor and the women scream and the colored man who works there wouldn't pick up the fish because he is afraid of it when it is alive and the fish man in his white apron swears and reaches to pick it up and by this time the fish is bulging its little eyes and pleading for death puffing away for air and sawdust all over its body and he hits it again and it is dead but nobody wants to buy the fish now and the fishman swears again and he has to put it away for different customers who wouldn't know what happened maybe you want a drink? a drink of pepsi cola? two pepsi colas, please with straws, straws yet they want for a nickel a bottle I got twenty boxes in the back yet it should be so hot all year I should worry let them drink up pepsi cola till it busts in their stomachs and they get gas fourteen hours a day I stand on my feet wiping off the counter and paying off notes every month for a hole in the wall seven thousand dollars mortgage three thousand paid in in cash like blood money with

eight hundred dollars paid off so far let them drink pepsi cola
with straws too already so drink and be choked with the coca-
cola man Mr. fancy you think he is the president of the company
talking to me nice now because I buy pepsi cola instead of his not
like he was snotty independent when I had my store on Third
Avenue and there was no pepsi cola yet making signs in the sky
with airplanes and I needed his coca-cola and with their credit
rules like they thought I was a banker I need them now like a hole
in my head I should be a dope and not keep pepsi-cola with bigger bottles and everybody wants pepsi-cola they buy a bottle for
the whole family now it lays them in mind to drink soda so coca-
cola yeah I should worry about tests he shows me which is better soda it's my business which is better a doctor I should be, a
pack of cigarettes? what kind Mr.? a fancy sport he smokes with
taxes up to seventeen cents I should maybe tell this one not to
smoke it's too much money better go buy a candy store with
notes for the next ten years to pay off with your seventeen cents,
taxes taxes taxes for breathing they should tax yet it's not on real
estate they don't tax on rich people they don't tax but on cigarettes they tax so I should pay the rent and the electric and the
counterboy and the notes ah the notes I should stop paying the
notes one week and they take out the fountain they should take
the fountain and the stools and the straws with them to hell and
break a foot too sixteen hours a day and night vacations I get I
don't pay the notes I get vacations plenty it runs down my back
and in my shoes the sweat and vacations I get only school teachers get vacations with trips to Europe and San Francisco and the
mountains they got vacations with two jobs and maids and wives
working in teaching too and my Libby graduated from college a
year already teacher for a year and no job, your change Mr. from
the cigarettes, with the taxes so the teachers can go on vacations
to the mountains go smoke yourself to death go break your neck
fancy ha more fancies with a car with the top down maybe teach-

ers where is your vacation? sit down by the tables sure why not
I should run around the fountain to bring you ice cream why not
I got two feet you should care for my feet I got tables with notes
so you sit down by them for me to wait on you you can't stand
by the fountain like the people I must run around like a chicken
with the head off, sweet-smelling girls with nice faces cool arms
fellows in crew haircuts and gabardine suits the coats on, real
gentlemen rich fathers taller than everybody else standing for
their pepsi-colas you see I'm busy now making for the notes to
pay on Tuesday if I live so long so you must sit on chairs I run to
you a customer is a customer maybe you take more than pepsi-
colas? say coca-colas and I break a glass on your heads ah a fine
boy he is sensible he says he will help me he will wait on his
friends he says I shouldn't bother he will order for them by the
fountain a nice boy a pleasure to his papa I should have a son-in-
law like him for my Libby lime rickeys sure young man lime rickeys fancy drinks for you with your friends the best I can make for
you stop everybody I make lime rickeys for this gentleman fancy
drinks it takes half the day to make but better than pepsi-colas
with coca-colas good like a plain glass of cold water I make them
fancy and you watch my hand shake with lemons with limes the
sweat pours out from me like rain better you should go on the
Concourse the Grand Concourse for such drinks everybody
drinks pepsi-cola and three cent cherry sodas he wants lime rick-
ey for his friends ah it's a life for slaves better he watches me and
he feels to laugh how I make lime rickeys I know from lime rickeys a cutter by trade now with a candy store with notes to pay on
Tuesday so laugh Mr. fancy you be a lawyer and the judge will
watch you lose for the clients a thousand dollars you see how it
feels too so here already here is lime rickeys so go take to your
friends he thanks me I see in his face he knows I am not a maker
from lime rickeys and he thanks me I stand here it drops from my
nose the sweat and he carries lime rickeys to his friends by the

tables like I should be doing for them for the customers I feel like to cry and take my hat and walk out from here goodbye good luck burn to the floor he comes back to me he pays me in a coat yet such a hot night in a coat yet I feel like to say Mr. gentleman you keep the money you did more than me I want nothing from you only peace and quiet you got no service and I should know I should have a big place with air condition and eight soda jerkers in white hats and Gentile faces with smiles all the time and I should come in like the boss every five minutes and look over the cash registers with a cigar in my mouth no cigar a fancy place I smoke no cigar I just walk around with my mouth shut and my eyes open I should have they sit and laugh and talk from nothing on their minds it's hot but they don't know from hotness girls like pictures they are like my Libby should be with them laughing instead with her communisms and her friends they going to change the world better they should change for themselves better they should want lime rickeys they should get it on the Grand Concourse in fancy ice cream parlors with gentlemen with good jobs you think it's hot.

You should have been with us off City Island fishing all day was it hot in a row boat the big Jew's place two dollars for the day the lousy kike sixty cents for bait he thinks he owns this country where did he get the bait anyway from my country from my country he says from his country shit how long was he here came over in steerage we'll show them some day they're not so wise we'll show them yet crabbing we were crabbing caught nineteen crabs sixty cents for a crab net he wanted the Jew we bought one on Third Avenue for forty five cents the louse he wanted us to throw the crabs back they were mostly female he tells us big yellow pouches under them soft and full of eggs, like a round spotted sun, you can pull 'em off don't cook 'em that way pull it off it runs out

then you cook them don't kill them cook 'em all in a big pot till
they die like chicken they taste like chicken certain parts I told the
Jew I was going to haul off and let him have it the mockey, square
heads and lantern jaws long bull bodies and short legs and mop
of hair inch off forehead curly black and parted on one side in
shirt sleeves rolled up on tattooed arms in work pants stinking
from here to high heaven, Scotch-Irish pug-ugly toughs, in the
quiet of their small bedrooms and in the Dutchman's bar and grill
on the corner settle the Jewish question there with a couple of
beers and a Camel or two, and that's why Smith didn't get in god-
damn 'em, we took some stuff with us in the boat it was hot a bottle left in a brown bag and two inches of a pint in Harry's back
pocket what you stopping for Harry? stop too long on this street
the Jews will try to charge you for it, let 'em try let 'em try anything the cocksuckers, sh, sh, Harry, looking around half ashamed
half belligerently sure he's drunk you want to make something of
it, sh hell I'll say what I want this is a free country because we
made it that way and I'll say any god-damned thing I want to if I
want a drink, Christ the bottle slipped you broke the bottle Harry
you dropped it hell let it lay it's all gone now let it lay let the Jews
pick it up, let it lay George until they go away the drunken bums
even if it's on my gasoline station right where the cars drive in for
gas and oil and washes and broken rear ends let it lay until they
go away no use starting trouble with those micks, sure said
George black as night rigged up in his gas attendant's uniform the
best pair of pants he had in a long time with his union button
pinned to his shirt he has to wear it even if he doesn't get union
wages, George you have to take two dollars a day and say twenty-five seventy-five a week because that's all I can pay you now
take it or leave it the union knows too but all they want is their
two dollars dues a month and I will pay that for you, sure said
George I'll pick it up just as soon as they go away because they
will take it out on a black man just as well, iy iy a country a world

it comes to they actually put the Jews and Niggers together why?
give one reason why, Come on Harry we cross the street here let's
have a drink on the other side it's darker, tax-payers closed and
dark at night on Sunday so hot the window panes are warm
against the hand leaving fingerprints an amateur detective could
spot in the entrance to a store places where in the movies the killer
hides after the shooting so dark it is crouched low with his gun
still smoking in his hand a bullet lodged in his left shoulder it's
good it's not my right hand, daddy and Harry in the darkness of
the entrance little Jimmy his yellow hair falling flat over his forehead from the back of his head in rompers with the buttons
yanked out around his middle stinking of baby sweat and dirt
watching this hide and go seek hiding and fumbling there in the
dark over a bottle of bitter stuff it's funny they want to give you
some and you're supposed to say no it's bitter it's like bad medicine, by God I'll make a man of him yet not a mother's boy he'll
be a man, it smells so bitter in your ears and makes daddy sick all
the time like now like he was sleepy and so rough crazy it make
me fraid when he is like that hurts me too when he puts his hands
on me wet like in the water in the boat all day rowing I helped
them row way out I ate a hard boiled egg with bread on the water
all day in the boat the crabs scare me I wouldn't touch them they
got like scissors in their hands with little eyes in front they are so
bad to look at and they run around in the boat till you pick them
up and put them in the bag in the water it's so big in the water all
around if you lean over not too far because you will fall in the
water and drown you can touch the water by the boat like it's
dirty water not like you drink daddy is sick tonight why do they
play like that in the dark place in the store they can't open the bottle like baby daddy is sick people look in the dark place I hold my
hands out so they can't come in I be like a gate they can't go past
me into the dark place and see go away go away I am a gate and
you can't go in in the window is shirts and ties it is dark not like

in the daytime I wish I was home now because I am fraid because
daddy is sick from the bad medicine in the bottle, all right they
wouldn't come back no more the bums so go pick up the glass
they broke in the gutter, sure boss I'll go pick it up just as soon as
I finish reading this page on ignition just as soon as I have to stand
up if a customer drives in for gas, what you think I should let the
broken bottle lay there in the gutter so a customer can run over it
with his tires and make blame on me I have so many customers I
can tell him to go to hell and buy new tires? go pick up now
before flats we make one after the other, okay boss I go now to
pick up the broken bottle just as I was getting that part about the
coil box hookup, because boss I am ambitious to get somewhere
and when I finish that book on automobiles I'm going to get me
a little shop uptown on 140th Street and set me up with tools and
I'm going to be the damnest automobile mechanic in Harlem I'll
make cars hum and sing all day and night and I'll get me a Lincoln
12 and I'll have every little chick in Harlem on my tail day and
night and I'll drive in here to get some gas once in awhile when
I'm up here in this part of town I'll take that looker who comes
around to get the bus to take her to New Rochelle twice a week
after sporting around twice a week here in town I'll take her back
to New Rochelle in my Lincoln 12 and I wouldn't come back the
same night not me boss, the gasoline station resting back in the
heat the arc lights making a hazy daylight in the night 8 gallons
big one dollar smaller 23 still smaller and very small plus tax
there's more to a station than you think because if four pumps
stand there with whitewashed bottoms it means four large steel
tanks underneath the ground like underground bomb shelters
filled with churning colored gasoline three grades of the same
brand the crap the regular and the high test high test for high com-
pression cars late models for faster pick-up ignites faster but in
2000 miles it makes carbon around the pistons and even the best
cars start to knock knock knock.

For how many days and nights he sat looking through the
screened window staring at the same two trees in the back yard
watching each day and each night pass by him as if it meant nothing to waste the time just staring out of the window you would
think there would be an end to days and nights. It was a distort-
ed view all the time you could never really see right because everything was cut up into the millions of little square blocks made by
the screen. You thought you could see a thing as it really was if
you juggled your head quickly with your eyes focused on the thing
so that you could finally get every piece of the thing you were
looking at if you twisted enough but that only jazzed up the
strands of screen so that you saw really nothing just like a person
without his glasses he knows what is before him but he can't make
out the exact details. You wanted to see the girl across the way,
how she got undressed at night instead of just knowing that she
was getting undressed the two joined windows of her little room
closed white with the window shades only the space near the bottom open or a short breeze pushing the blinds into the room for a
brief moment catch what you can. Why does she come home so
late at night to go to bed, does she work during the day and must
she get up early tomorrow morning and if she does she must be
pretty swell to be able to do it all like a girl on her own you can
do a lot of things it seems impossible to do when you are with a
family when you are on your own. Oh lady I don't like the way
you dress, now it isn't that you don't have enough money to dress
right I know you haven't but you'd be surprised at what you can
get at Klein's or Orbach's or Hearns for a little nothing, if you
have the right taste lady. You sweat and strain its worse than a
turkish bath but you can get what fits you right and fine if you
take your time and use good taste lady you really need a fashion
consultant they have them in all the better shops try Best's of

course Bergdorf-Goodman Lord and Taylor Arnold Constable
McCreery's if you aim above your faith let Dobbs fit you out in a
sport ensemble in a breton with a tiny gay feather in the band in
a real cashmere sweater in a good skirt with a pleat in the back in
a jacket to match the skirt full and so well made in a chain of simple little white pearl beads around your neck in two-thread stockings in splendid sport shoes lift your eyes high and superciliously
dilate your nostrils and tighten your mouth and stink lady stink
from here to high heaven of the most delicate lavender sin of my
life purchased by the ounce lady you are a knockout all dressed
up thus and when you come into a room and later make to slip
off your jacket and draw one sleeve off with your hand behind
your back your underslung breasts will jut forward beneath your
cashmere sweater it will gladden the heart of many a man and boy
and you will recline on the couch on one elbow your cashmere
sleeves pulled up over your arms in Vassar technique and you will
float on air with a cigarette in your neatly painted mouth still tight
you will put the fear of defeat in the heart of any man, so don't sit
now in your room under the glare of the 100 watt bulb doing
your nails on the bed for now is the time for every girl such as you
to stand up on the balls of her feet and throw out that awful
wardrobe throw it down the sink flush the toilet get rid of it what
you can't get at Dobbs you can pick up in Klein's and cheaper too
why pay more the exact duplicates don't be foolish the budget
McCreery's stood a loss this year so what you have to worry
about others stop dealing in economics go buy where they know
you but buy with class and discretion buy with such an eye you
can go to lunch in Nassau Bermuda and Maury Paul will think he
is slipping because he just can't place you and the Livingston boy
will say who is that charming creature Brenda? what I don't like
is your makeshift dressing making this and that piece of clothing
serve six purposes throw those gamps out down the pipe a gamp
is for peasants in Europe the ones we sent condensed milk to back

in the twenties with the Red Cross and it mixed us up because it was rich to have condensed milk in coffee it made it like sweet cream in the swell restaurants a good cup of coffee tonight ha Jake? condensed milk from the can on the table with a ragged hole in the top the stuff dripping over and sticking the can it's all right to be so clean taking showers every night but it don't make a debutante out of you if you can't cover that McClelland Barclay body with snappy stuff shave under your arms today and tomorrow it doesn't mean a thing if you can't walk down the street like a visitor from Miami coming to see her poor relatives.

When mamas go away downtown to the place where they make it so no more babies will come only us we go at night while it is still sunny out to the delicatessen on the corner where we have supper. I bet you think you can't get supper in a delicatessen store, only hot dogs with mustard and sauerkraut and hot pastrami sandwiches and beer and cole slaw and potato salad. Well in this delicatessen store there is a sign says seven course dinner fifty cents and they give it to you inside by the waiter who has a bald head but with a few hairs which he parts on the side and brushes across his dome it looks like strings across the top of a bouncing ball. He wears overall pants with a bottle opener in his change pocket and a bill book in his back pocket with the wet napkin he uses to wipe off the tables. You can get a real meal there just like in the restaurant. Papa orders for you chopped liver and it comes looking greyish not brown and with yellow fat on top and it has lots of strings through it like veins and things. You can even have tomato juice the waiter pours it into your glass from a milk bottle. Then you get soup, vegetable soup or chicken soup with noodles which is yellowy with clouds floating on top like white muck and it tastes sour when chicken soup should taste rich and sweetly salty. Then you can have one kind of meat in a big plate divided into three parts with sides for each part to keep that part's food from lapping over into another part. The meat is in one part and in the other the waiter puts potato salad only he puts potato salad in both the other two parts there is so much potato salad. If you take beer you can't get tea and cake after your meat. It says on the menu Apple Pie but the waiter knows what you're going to ask him for because he says no before you can say anything, no apple pie it's too hot to make apple pie it melts before you finish cooking it. Is that really so, though? Pound cake they got though and cookies. And if you didn't have beer with your meat you can have hot tea in a glass with lemon. It's really like in a restaurant, though. You got a waiter and you can learn to holler waiter with your finger up in the air. With paper napkins in the tin box at the end of your table and mustard and ketchup. You can't even get butter here because it says kosher on the window with neon red signs. And the bread and the cookies on separate plates not all together on one plate or just on the table. The cookies are two and they are round with sugar stuck to the tops of them. It's really like a restaurant with so many people coming in and out all the time you are chewing down the supper with steady chews hunched over the damp table from so much wipings which even then don't wipe off all the strings of sauerkraut and cole slaw, with such a hard job chewing away staring into space it's a wonder the fork finds its way into your mouth. Indeed, so many people come in, here's a little family, father Moe, mother Rose and Baby Snooks, ha ha, we call her Baby Snooks she's so cute, the things she says, we don't know where she picks it up. Baby Snooks, nee Beverley, is four years old with a mop of hair page boy, gonna be a glamour girl y'know, in a week-old play suit worn steady a week now so small you don't really have to wash it out after all, though the part around the seat really stinks, to put it frankly. Then there's father Moe, a little gent dressed for the summer in sanforized slacks you put them on when you come home from work, dollar thirty-nine but the thing doesn't really fit around the seat, or is it that Moe hasn't really much of a seat? Nice colors, though. Matches that polo shirt you got on, Moe. You look like an Arabian tent during carnival time in Mestupolia. It's all right, Moe, if you really havn't got much of a chest look at the hair you sprout on it. Come on, Moe, open the collar and let that mat get the air. That's right, Moe, there's a pocket over your breast in that reckless polo shirt of yours, put your cigarettes and matches in it. It all adds to your stature. Then there is mother Rose in a lovely little summer outfit, two for three twenty-five, wasn't it, Rosie? It's a bargain, you should have bought a few more. Nice and cool, it pays to dress well. Nice shoes too. Cut-out toes, isn't it? Cooler. It's a bother cleaning white shoes, though, isn't it? I mean, they get dirty so fast. No stockings? That's a good idea, but is it against your religion to shave your legs? Yes, the hair does grow back so fast and bristles too. Well, whatlitbe, Moe? Three hot dogs and two beers? five ten fifteen and twenty that makes thirty-five cents, please pay when you are served. Okay, Moe, carry the dinner to your table, careful with the beers, better make another trip for the beer. Now eat, pack it in. Beverley, eat nice, remember you're out now this isn't home. Eat your hot dog and we'll go home you'll get your milk. On these hot days a child shouldn't eat much, as little as possible. Gee, I remember the old folks they used to pack it into me all year around. Yeah, that's right, Rosie, and look at you now. I think you're perfectly right bringing up Baby Snooks on psychology. But Rosie, be sure of the brand of psychology you're using. There's so many kinds out these days. Ah, there, look out, Moe, you're getting that mustache full of mustard. You must wear a mustache, Moe? Else you couldn't succeed in the business world? No don't worry, that's not Baby Snooks choking on her hot dog, that joyous lump of fat sticking out of her hot little neck is just the beginning of an incipient goiter, folks. Try iodine, yes, iodine poison, two drops in a glass of water every day, or move out to the Great Lakes region with her. Take a drink of water anyway,

Beverley, helps digest your supper. Ha, Ha, look at father Moe
sauerkraut is all in one bunch on his hot dog and he can't get it into
his mouth and it looks like it is part of his mustache! Maybe you
ought to get two more hot dogs, you both look hungry. Come on,
be a sport. Hot or no hot, you still got to eat, you know. What a
business they do here, and it's all year around too yet. Look there's
old man Klein shuffling in on his cane also in a polo shirt colored
fancily and checkered summer pants, ach 'scooler in such pants,
no, no white it gets dirty too quick, like this it's got boxes on it the
dirt don't show and who wears white pants anyway, bunch conser-
vatives, a little color some design makes something to look on. Old
man Klein lives with his son and daughter-in-law and the children.
They are always out, God knows only where. It comes that a poor
man without teeth has to look for his own eating and he has to pay
yet twenty dollars a month yet to her and she has to tell him if he
don't like it he can move out she's too young yet to lay down her
life to a house her children are grown up and she wants a little fun
out of life yet before she dies. So I'll also have a frankfurter and a
glass beer, please. Okay, Klein, open up that little black pocketbook and count out fifteen cents for this feast. Ach that's how the
money goes, twenty dollars I pay her for the room and for eating
and I must come here to eat my supper. It's home a whole can sar-
dines in the icebox but who can open cans like that? So enjoy here.
He who wishes me bad should enjoy like I am enjoying eating with
such teeth it goes down in whole pieces. I know what I'm eating? It
gets caught in the bridge and I can't get it out. I pay for frankfurters
and it gets caught in the teeth. A black year on the dentist with his
teeth with the whole thing! So take out the teeth already to pull out
the frankfurter. First the top, push and pull, ah here it comes with
saliva all over the fancy polo shirt wipe off with the back of the old
hand, now pick out the frankfurter stuck in the cracks, lick the
meat out with the lips and the tongue, polish with a paper napkin
make shiny like new the big buck teeth, now the lower set pull and

push here it comes, what a mouth full, clean it out, get the five cents worth of dog roll it over those butchered gums get it down into that twisted belly, now get dressed up again put your mouth in shape for your public appearances, now what? you're gonna cough? okay get a paper napkin, now ready? well cough cough up, and spit out into the paper napkin, more? well take another paper napkin, it's free, now spit, only pop, listen, leave the frankfurter be, don't cough it up, let it be swimming around in the beer down in that pot of yours, you hear? How you feel, pop, Hungry? Bloated? Wanna hot dog? Wanna beer? No? well whynchyou go home now and sit on the bench awhile then go to sleep, maybe a few cigarettes Luckies held lovingly in your left hand between the thumb and the first finger pamp up. So go already, Klein, you made a dirtiness on the table, you used up paper napkins with spitting, so go home already. Ah look, here is a young couple, out for the evening. You can tell right off she is a nice girl with a big mouth once she gets over the introductions. He doesn't know what he's in for, he figures he's got himself a girl friend with dignity and class and good background, he doesn't knows she's mnya mnya, so sweet. A figure you have to sew it up to call it human. Soft, you know, and slushy with suprising big hips and heavy legs, very neat though and so good, really a wonderful girl, better grab her quick there's not many around like her, ask her mother, ask her while you're at it. She winces you mention listening to the radio, so much of that swing music on the air, you know, she winces cutely above it all, that's for children, give her Beethoven she went to the Lewisohn Stadium concerts one Saturday night a young man took her. Isn't Shirley Temple adorable? Why don't Janet Gaynor play in the movies anymore? This is really very good, I haven't eaten frankfurters like this over a year now, she smiles with that six inch spread of lip across her puss. He's an accountant, not a CPA mind you, but an accountant and a good one, was always good at figures, in an eighteen dollar two year old suit good material look how nicely it has worn, kinda short around your bottom, kid numbers, though. He likes the idea of her breasts under that cover-all dress. Sometimes they're there, sometimes they're not. But there or not, buddie, you got one big job ahead of you trying to find out. I mean. You don't know who you're dealing with. Goodness looks up from her table, takes in everybody in front of her, sweetly. There's a guy at the little bar grabbing a beer. She looks once and away, musn't look at people, especially men they are such bums. This guy at the little wet bar is tough, bones and red blood and eighteen dollars a week loading and unloading delivery trucks around the city; pants and a shirt, a shirt once very colorful kinda blue with pin stripes of green, faded now in so many washings and sweat, unbuttoned all the way down hairless torso, the sleeves rolled up not two inches at a time but actually rolled up making it a helluva job unrolling them in the laundry. He takes a swig and laughs at something, but laughs all over the place out loud like a crazy kick, In the back the owner tells the customers, when he starts to laugh he doesn't stop, he laughs at nothing, a beer and he laughs all day. Let him laugh the customers tell him. Me, I should stop him from laughing? the owner shrugs, making mustard packages twenty a minute, it's fascinating to watch him at work.

November 20, 1942

Dear Mr. Levin:

Mr. Fadiman has suggested to us, on the strength of your writing in New Directions, that you might find The New Yorker a congenial place to publish short fiction. Although The New Yorker is technically a humorous magazine, our stories are very often serious, not to say grim. We hope very much that you let us see something.

Sincerely yours,
William Maxwell

May 25, 1943

Dear Alvin Levin,

I have read with great pleasure your long piece in the last NEW DIRECTIONS. I am editing for a publisher here an anthology of MODERN AMERICAN SHORT STORIES, and it seems to me that, if you write short pieces that can technically be called stories, there is no doubt you should be in it. Would you care to send me several stories from which to choose? Your best, please, since this is not a causal collection, but a definitive anthology. Of course, I can't say I will put you in until I've seen the stuff, but it seems probable that I will like it sufficiently, if there is any of the requisite sort—of course, I don't mean necessarily a more commercial short-story, but I also don't mean a piece of purely abstract writing. This is a short <u>story</u> collection, not a collection of prose pieces: on the other hand it's meant to be good as opposed to commercial. Do you get it?

Yours sincerely,
Nicholas Moore.

P.S. Payment about 8 guineas per story.

Unpublished Sketches

8 Yrs. Old / Laments Begin Young

You're not any good. You're not any good. Only Ruth is good. You had a blue coat, so has she. You bought the coats together. Same coat. "Ruth what a beautiful coat." Yours looks different. Your coats not good. Your coats not good because its your coat. You're the same age. "Ruth how big you are. But you my little dear are younger, surely, but Ruth how lovely you look." You are small, you know, they tell you puny. Doesn't your mother give you enough to eat? (hah hah) "Ruth do sing for us, such a beautiful talented child." You can't sing. You pray to be sick or to have cramps. But then you couldn't stay in the bathroom long. They'd come in for you soon and they'd ask questions and then they'd be too nice. They were always too nice to you, and they would make you cry, and you were all swollen and red and you had to go in with the rest of the company and you couldn't find a place for yourself.

"No you don't know how to Charleston, Ruth you try it." You tried to be like her. You couldn't, "poor child." You couldn't wear silk stockings. You didn't get invited to parties. And you were secretly glad. (You didn't need them.) They didn't invite you because you weren't nice. You didn't sing or dance or recite. Shame on you. Shame on you. Shame, shame, shame. You sucked your fingers and you liked to drink milk. But children weren't supposed to. Ruth doesn't have to. She can have half coffee. "My what a good child you are. Drink your milk and everything. Funny you look the way you do, but then again you only nibble at the rest of the food. Ruth eats more'n anyone else at the table.

It's a pleasure to watch the child." "After dinner you'll recite for us won't you dear?" You shook and prayed, don't ask me to recite. You knew they would. Just to show you up. Her father looked at her and then at you and you felt yourself getting all red and wanted to shout stop it, stop it, I know I'm not good like she is good. And again you would pray—you begged the evening to soon be over so then you could get into your bed and cry and hate and wish to die.

Sargeant Mike

When it came her turn for saddling Nelly arched her head and neighed through distended nostrils as she pawed the floor and danced around impatient to get started off. They buckled her belly and dressed her head in the regalia that set her off distinctly as one of the 9th. She was the queen of every horse on the street, and it was too bad she didn't have much competition during the day.

Fully dressed she kicked around uneasily in the yardway. Then Sargeant Mike appeared at the stable door and she neighed a morning salute, sending forth two snorts of hoary flame as her master strode into the yard to rub Nelly's misty nose.

His face smooth from an early half hour shave and ruddy from the early morning wintry blasts, Sargeant Mike stood six one and a half in his booted feet, like Nelly, every inch of him part and parcel of the heroic 9th. With a quick studied leap Michael was in the cold saddle, arranging his big coat and gathering Nelly's reins. With the rest of the 9th they both trotted into Tenth Avenue, and stood prancing, twenty across and three deep in front of Captain Hendricks for morning dismissal. Then, finally, at the wave of the captain's hand, they were off, Nelly and Mike, eastward crosstown for patrol along the Canal Street sector.

They were both a sight to behold on this bleak and friendless morn. The sargeant, his big coat buttoned back across his mighty legs, holding Nelly with a steady grip between his sturdy knees as she danced crosstown, lightly and with becoming grace, breaking ever so often into a neat little sidestep trot until the sargeant took a steadier hand, juggling two orders of hot coffee inside the burly walls of his, her master's fat stomach.

Like a benevolent despot riding among his people Sargeant Mike surveyed the scene with deep concern written all over his honest face. The people were coming into lower New York to go to work this crisp winter morning. Of all those who came to just work many stayed to look for work. And others just wandered around, walking along, stopping at the corners for the lights, and then walking on again, moving to stop the gnawing companionship of despair, turning a corner, looking through the windows. The Sargeant knew his charges well; he could spot a "drifter," as he called them, a block away, something in the timing of their walk.

The gloom settled early, as though it had never lifted since the break of day, and the horseman felt the ominous threat of stark tragedy as he rode through the deep canyons of the city. All around him his futile subjects scurried through heavy plate glass doors, from the entrances of subway dungeons, into the storied dungeons in the sky, to sit chained behind finger marked desks and stand locked to huge machines of Devil design, leaving their protector, our horseman, alone guarding their mercantile frontier. The Sargeant thrilled in his saddle. He felt the dramatic content of the situation.

With stern understanding plastered all over his young Lochinvar face, he rode into the east where his people needed him most. This was the way of life, Mike, and its only a man with understanding, with charity of soul, that can figure it all out. Life is just like Ivanhoe, no one can say different. Its all a dramatic novel, a tale of heroes and villains, with brave daring things always to be done. Mike drifted into the days of yore.

The lone horseman counted off the rivers he had to cross: Tenth through to Eighth was a desert plain, bleak and desolate, the waste land of abandoned locomotives, stables turned into auto repair hope, small cafeterias under the shadow of the snaky ridge called West Side Highway; Eighth, Seventh, Broadway, Sixth, Fifth, Fourth, all huge tributaries flowing South from their source at the foot of the Bronx Hills up north. And Sargeant Mike rode them heroically, pausing at their banks only for the lights to change green, to charge majestically across between motored fleets drawn up facing his sides, on either side, in practiced attention. Nelly acted with decorum, pausing only at her masters touch, her rump high in the air at all times.

Mike, with imperious dignity, could check the scene. He could bend over to give an erring driver hell, could urge a hot chestnut vendor on his way, could unobtrusively eye the girls emerging from the underground tunnels and hurrying up the streets in tip toe haste, soft milk fed blobs of flesh moving gently under drawn coats to the rhythm of moving legs. Mike searched high and low for his Lady Isabel, dearly loved by all who knew her and long lost since she was stolen from her father's castle high in the stony heights of the Palisades on the night of her betrothal to our hero.

Janet Moris

Up in the central part of the Bay State of Massachusetts the wooded ground-frosted campus of the century-old women's college became a storm center as a determined group of alumnae brought indignant demands for the resignation of the college trustees who had last week appointed Dr Hamilton Frey as the college's first male president. Bristling women wrote to each other on expensive pale blue initialed stationery. flooding the whole eastern seaboard post offices and urging concerted action in the interests of the school.

Overnight a "committee of one hundred" took distinguished shape and within a fortnight sixteen sectional meetings were planned in the homes of the butler-equipped alumnae members in the central eastern states of the Union.

Meanwhile Dr Frey visited the peaceful campus of his future academic post. He was overwhelmed by the seductive swishings of so many tweedy skirts against so many tall, thin, and healthy legs. The new president made several tours of the college. "So many mouths to feed, so many holes to fill," he calculated and he was pleasantly shocked at his own spontaneity. The president was a former professor of English, of an old New England family, married late in his career to a rich women who had earned her B.A. at this same college. Needless to say, Mrs. Frey sided with the board of trustees.

In Washburn Hall, at the north end of the campus quad, things were quiet enough for all the revolution that was taking place in the college's history. A tin white moon made clear shadows across the walks and against the ancient dorms. A crystal clear night begging for the snow.

Inside, Miss Janet Moris, up from New York and finishing her third year on a personality scholarship, sat before a bridge table trying to finish a two-composition-page letter to her dearest friend in the city.

The things a girl could tell her friend, the things a girl could tell her mother, the things a girl could tell the whole world—but cannot. A girl can't even tell herself the things that would explain the whole wretched mean. The best you can do is try to bear it through. Janet felt lousy. She felt the salmon on the slightly wilted lettuce of supper. She was still really hungry, but the thought of food nauseated her right now. She lay her head on her hand, staring at the wall.

It would be so nice if some tall, big fellow would call for her right now. He could be riding up for some reason and think of her. He would ring the bell now and she would hear it here upstairs, and downstairs one of the girls would open the door and be surprised it was a man and she would quietly admire the way he looked and talked and then he would say he was calling on Miss Janet Moris and the girls would tell everybody it was for Janet and Janet would wait until they called her and she would fix up and put on her coat and she would run downstairs into the sitting room and he would stand up and they would both smile to each other and then Janet would introduce him to the girls and then they would go outside together while everybody watched them go and their car would make a swift, purring noise as it crunched over the pebbled road going off the campus. And she would be so nice and they could have a lot of fun together. He would have a lean, hard face.

There was nothing to be happy about and you had to be happy all the time. Janet returned to her letter . . .

"The final bit of news is Winter Dance which comes this weekend. I have finally decided to go. Until today I've been scanning high and low for a ride to NEW York for this weekend— not that there would be anything doing at home, but I thought it would be nice and wouldn't have to sit around and feel so bad watching all the college, practically, having a swell time with their male visitors. However, I couldn't find a ride and I haven't the money to go by train—so I shall stay here, pay fifty cents, and go to the dance stag and probably not have a good time. Did I say probably? Honestly, I don't know why I'm going either.

So you see, dear, even tho I've filled up two and a half pages already, there is nothing much of interest that happens, except little things. On the whole, I've been feeling pretty low—I could do with a man very well! But—the days go by pretty quickly, so that life's not *too* unbearable. And pretty soon we go home for

Spring vacation which lasts until April 8th. So—life goes on—

Much love

Janet."

Janet sighed. She folded the sheets into the envelope. The envelope bore her name and the house and college seals, all in imposing dignified taste. "Gee, why can't things be as nice as they look, like this envelope. Damn it, things were supposed to be so swell up here." She licked the flap, her mouth growing dry and sticky.

She went to the closet. Her roommate's coat hung next to hers. It was a lovely lapin fur. Janet's carefully selected swagger coat, from Klein's, looked meager against it. "The hell with her and her coat. I hate lousy lapin anyway," she said aloud, cute like. What have I got against her anyway, she's got her own troubles too. She slipped into her own coat, flung up the broad collar with a reckless scowl on her face and strode out of the room, putting out the light and slamming the door behind her. "I don't care, I'm better than anybody around here," she told the hallway.

She felt sore enough to feel better now. The chill night air hit her in the face. She had to button her coat around her neck, letting it bellow open around her body and swing behind her. It was colder that way but that's the way she felt. Janet wanted to be cold and angry. If a fellow could see her now, she thought, he'd fall right in love with her. She strode along the walk, wishing she had taken a cigarette with her, she felt in her pockets for the pack.

The ground was bare and hard. Most of the girls were inside the vined buildings. From the long bay windows of the main library there blazed the yellow glare of so many domed lamps. "I wish, I wish—oh I don't know what to wish."

Janet turned toward the library, and inside she sent the letter down the mail chute, Then she walked upstairs to find someone in the reading room to talk to.

At 8:30 the Middletown mail truck rode onto the dark campus and Postman George McGrady was at the wheel, looking the place over once again. He intended for as long as he and his wife could remember to send his daughter to the college just as soon as she graduated from Middletown high school in June. Just as part of his salary was deducted to make up his pension fund, so had he and his wife taken part of his quarterly for Winifred's tuition at the college. It lay there in the Farmer's Bank now, snug and quite enough for her four years with enough for her extras that she would need to stand up with the girls whom you could see on Saturdays in Middletown spending the afternoon.

The postman descended into the basement of the library and emptied the mail box into his bag, and he suddenly grinned to himself as he straightened up. He shook his head in wonder; he never saw it to fail. Every time he got to the college on his route he had to take a leak and there wasn't a men's room in the place. It was the funniest thing.

He climbed the flight of stairs into the lobby. He looked the place over for the 311th time in the last fifteen months. Like a blind man figuring out his surroundings for further reference he leaned against a tall pillar near the entrance with his bag between his legs, deciding with satisfaction on the places that would become part of Winifred's life next winter. From under his peaked, grey hat he smiled to the girls as they passed him, to and from the lonely campus, with their notebooks under their arms, fatherly like and with understanding. Then he hitched his pants of grey denim, lifted his sack, strode out into the night, and drove his high green Ford truck back into the city.

Janet's letter was carried from the Ford into a large, bare room and under the glare of huge yellow lights it was stamped and dropped into the New York box. Men in shirt sleeves and sweaters, with holsters around their waists, worked in the big room. Then the permanents, with loaded revolvers hanging from their belts, dumped the New York mail into the rear of several Fords which started off in a burst of spitting motors to catch the New York Express.

Number 872 thundered its way southward at 12:03, picking up the mail along the route without making a single stop. Middletown was too small to earn a stop on the express. A cold north wind blew the engine smoke into bits as soon as it left the engine stack. In south Connecticut the yellow beam of 872's headlight penetrated the bleak darkness as the line swerved a bend, lighting up the rows of steel tracks ahead, sending fire-fly sparks off the rails spreading south into the sultry beat of the Florida shore, and suddenly picked up the signals of the onrushing Boston Special, pushing its way northward and carrying a soft-scented letter destined to disturb the equanimity of the college board of trustees. As the engines roared past each other the engineers leaned on the sills of their cabooses and waved stiff greetings; the lights of the cars rushed by, yellow behind drawn curtains.

More than six hours before, in New York, William who was Miss Althea Rowland's house man had borne that letter from the high Chippendale desk in the study on East 54th Street to the post box on Park Avenue. He had hurried out of the house and returned immediately after trying the flap again to make sure the letter was securely inside. The lady was having dinner tonight; William had only time to throw a jacket over his serving clothes and leave the snug warmth of the house when Miss Rowland said he wanted to catch the earliest mail out of New York, he made haste in returning to the house.

She was in the library now, with her guests waiting for William and the cocktails. Known as Ally to the class of 1900, she sat before Dr and Mrs Goslin, and her two nephews and their wives, repeating to them the contents of her letter which informed the trustees she was changing her will because of her objection to abandoning a tradition which never saw a man as president of her alma mater.

Law School

If I see a hen that is evidence that there is an egg, but only because I take judicial notice of the facts of life.

Oh well, sic transit.

A blond man on 59th street hearing a crash rushes up to feel the damage . . .

A girl, pretty as a picture, crossing Times Square unmindful of the traffic is almost hit and smiles at the driver suddenly almost on top of her.

Honey boy, she calls him.

Kids pulling away on purloined cigarettes, their privates straight and hard in the wild reckless abandon of the night.

The lecturer with his wife running after him keeping him sober. She looks drunker than he does. That's because she keeps him in clean starched shirts twice a day. Been doing it for years. He knows biology.

Helena wants to read a good book on sex. Isn't it a bit too late now?

I warn you, if we waste more than three hours I'm going to get mad.

Lowder, lowder. What you yelling for, he isn't saying anything. I want to make sure of that. I got a bar exam coming on.

Ads for bad breath. Kissing, loving. Anyday, now, they'll be showing the real thing.

Home alone until 1. Parents away. Then down to the Astor Bar, of all places.

Winter: frost on the moon.

I copied my style of hairdress from the Dionne Quintuplets.

He's a male who made domnei his career. He used to sit on the Vassar team.

It was inside dope, gathered from 5 continents, the 7 seas and the secret archives of the Vatican.

My God, I've discovered a new school of philosophy.

Wanna eat something good? How's about some Fetsil, some medwurst, and bonor arter lingon, svensk og norske? Or do you want just a glass of cold water?

You're a Communist, aren't you? I mean, you lean that way, don't you?

I must refer back to Shakespeare again.

Girl married over week-end. Sits in lunchroom feeding another girl, practicing tending infants.

Policemen, like two nuns walking, always driving together.

What's 8 times 5? Can I say 5 times 8?

In the next war I want to be a carrier pigeon.

He's an anemic Casanova.

What's so wonderful about getting married? She's been sleeping with him for months.

The girl was wearing a pill box hat held to the top of her head, on an angle, by a wide band around under her face. All she needed was a muzzle and a leash. She had the face for it too.

Ayude a las madres y niños chicos. Boycoteando la Americana Japonese.

Ayude a pueblo China boycoteando a su enemigo el Japón. No ayude a la matanza de niños inocentes. No compra nada Esta Tienda vende solamente mercancía hecha en USA. Ni Japoneses, Alemania, Italiana.

One night the window dresser on Fifth Avenue went crazy. He was roaring drunk.

Shalamith, a girl's name.

Armonk, a town.

The city of Shanghai is so high in terrible ruins, full of stones and rocks. And all the death is women and children. You call this a war?

Look, he reneged on me!
Jumping jive, all take five!
She lost herself in statistics again.

Do you write moving stories about life? That's all I write, see. And I got so much of it out in the market lanes that the only way I can keep track of whether or not I have "arrived" is to read rather studiously the daily papers, particularly the book review sections. Publishers show a startling disinclination to communicate with me concerning the literary merits of my moving stories about life. I do not know what they do with "the self addressed and stamped envelope" I enclose with every manuscript. Only quite recently was awakened one morning by the postman who left me four splendidly decorated and exquisitely apportioned little magazines. The point is my name was printed on the cover of each of the little magazines. The point I wish to make is that this was the first news I had received in four long months concerning a very moving story about life that I had written one winter night and had thereafter sent on its glorious way through the U.S. Postal Service.

What I want to know is, if a woman is bow-legged, is she that way all the way up?

I am a little tot
I have a little pot
In it I do a whole lot
So what
Call me a pisher.

She went to the toilet like a boy. She was sluggish all the time. It got so I couldn't look at her.

Patient dies and the doctor continues the operation for another 20 minutes.

There's a house in the Village. Part of the entertainment is living demonstrations on how to kiss the right and wrong way, how to lay a girl the right way. And a man is as good as his gonads.

Wait till the Jews hear that the Catskills are dissected plateau on a pene plane.

If a kid drinks up the water in the fish bowl he's suffering from a disorder of the pituitary gland (excessive thirst) and not from some high class neurosis.

Menstruation is the monthly discharge of an ovum, and if no impregnation the ovum disintegrates and bleeding results.

Growth ceases as soon as sex develops.

Disorder in male is impotence; in female it is sterility.

Underactivity of gonads is acromegalia (big muscles).

Pituitary glands are the size of 2 aspirin tablets.

Merchant counting money in bank, a Holbein character.

The soldiers are guarding the line with fixed bayonets.

This is a city of dead fish and worn out frying pans.

She was a clean rich girl with an exciting body. Grade A stuff, in glasses.

I'll boycott that picture. It was the lousiest picture I ever saw.

De Rashun poiges. De are o disgraceful ting. Ven wil de trut come out from Rasha.

It takes a long tall brown-skinned gal
To make a preacher lay his bible down
For 20 years I thought to sin was like to me
But I'm going to get mine till I die.

Like Mr. Edward G. Robinson with a cigar in his mouth and a gun in his hands, both smoking.

Before you know it a whole lifetime has gone by and how can you retain even a part of what you have done? Why don't you write a diary?

How does he look taking off his shoes?

Not them, they divide at the belly.

If the truth was written about him on his tombstone, it wouldn't be an epitaph it would be a police record.

A hard patrician nose, a hawk, you mean.

A nurse's uniform is crisp and sibilant like oyster shells.

Money has but one language.

Kapulyah Graf Putansky. Minsk-gabernia.

The summer sun is a big round splitting orange.

The announcer was a castrated eunuch urging me to buy soap.

New cars in the show room neatly arranged on bubbly tires staring though the plate glass window with round glassy eyes.

The Bowery bum has a tremendous liquid capacity. He fell with the greatest of ease.

Blond haired fellows from Groton and St. Mark's.

Dogs in Central Park in coats and hats shoes raincoats over-shoes fur coats and pipes.

She was destined to blush unseen.

There's a lonely dignity about an old car, a jalopy, a load. A small red tail light against the tall back rear of this archaic heap, against the dark night of the street, chugging away, puffing up the street, the pistons going as best they can, the oil squirting through where it doesn't belong, upholstery fading pitifully against the respectable background it once was. Eating gas and shooting oil, rolling along in a cloud of smoke, four wheels on their last legs.

White limbs and red lips, a chorus.

Pickup threatens to call a cop. Starts to holler for help. Guy starts to plead with her as though she were a cop handing out a ticket for passing a red light.

Ah, the happy Spring and the somber Fall.

Who am I? 1% solid, 99% fluid. On a hot day I could disappear in a vapor.

He felt for her breast. She said, its all right, its still there. She looked bad. My mother-in-law looked better three days after she died.

He had an ekymosis on his left eye. They swatted him good.

Horsey faces, beautiful breasts, fine long full legs and jazzy clothes.

Danny came up the street and I said to Danny, I say, Danny what's the matter with you Danny, you're all doubled up, you been eating green apples, Danny?

Listen, Miss Louder than I.

It was a 4-H Club project.

I was walking around in the 7th A.D., taking in the sights.

He was one of the Yankee-Doodle Uptown Boys.

What? Snot, ten cents a whole lot. Sore? Put Vaseline on it. You're mad? Stick mad. I haven't any gum. I'll buy you some. Go to hell. Go double and save me the trouble. You're another, and my ass is your brother.

Yeah, she's supposed to be married to him.

Love and money are the biggest assets to a bar's business.

It was a thick soft snow.

There was bitterness and impotent fury whirling inside him.

The cigarette ashes crumbled soft and flaky on his vest.

It was stealthy furtive music.

Soap was liquefying in the dish.

"Slaves we were unto Pharaoh in the land of Egypt, and the Eternal, our God, brought us forth from thence, with a mighty hand and outstretched arm." (4 questions)

Herschel, you come here! Herschel, you come right here, Herschel! Pointing to the first base to his side. Come, Herschel, so I can get off from here. Look hit it like this Herschel, he shows him how to hit, smacking his hand against his ear and twisting his mouth viciously. Like this, Herschel, Just like this you hit it.

The cat sneaked by with eyes a blazing yellow.

I was exhibited naked to eternity.

Rich girls attending Traphagen School, mostly for their own designs.

He looks like something a lobster would see in his ono-matopoetic vision of disappointed specs all about him.

I'm no dope, I don't fool with the government.

He was wiring poetry with footnotes.

Daylight saving time means more time, another hour, to worry.

I found time for *Anthony Adverse* and *The Citadel*. Now I got to find time for *Gone with the Wind*.

Veries does a rumba sitting down.

I don't think I would ever marry a man who snores.

Sure, that's why I look so terrible today. I was away over the week-end and he snored every night.

Ninety year old woman on subway, on way to visit her brother who fell and broke his hip. I really shouldn't be out because I have to have me left breast cut off. Do you think it will show?

This is New York, and you got to keep talking. (Negro on Sugar Hill)

Look, it don't even hurt, she exclaimed, slapping her head with the ruler in desperation.

How you doing? Swell, its only September and already I've made the *Times* 100 Neediest Cases.

A carpenter with a neatly wrapped saw under his arm, wait-ing for the trolley, fingering a nickel in his palm.

Old Negro selling a victrola on his porch.

Tall rangy girls with slim broad shoulders, with red hair and grey eyes and they look better without stockings, really. On the other hand there is the girl who is the very embodiment of the Siren Call, voluptuous and heavy-burdened with sex appeal.

They got a kid, he goes around after a party drinking up the left overs in the glasses.

She was a graduate of Women's Medical College of Pa.

The moths, three of them, made a tapping noise as they dash around and around from corner to corner under the electric light.

He makes 20 dollars a week and spends 23 in the French Casino.

Nicodemus

What is love, mused Nicodemus, the riding kid, as he cruised cross-town by the way of 167th Street, bearing east. This question needs clarification, and quickly too, for the masses are doomed to eternal bestial exchange of spermatozoa and nothing more unless the words of truth are brought to them. For, he considered, the age-old definitions are mere empty pretenses, meaningless, useless, futile. We sing their phrases blindly, without understanding, without attempting to understand—and better so perhaps, for to understand or to try to understand the intricate maze of nonsense is to sink deeper into the sloth of nothingness.

I must clear my mind of what is known to all and build within it the structure of what I know, he figured as he brought the car to a stop to wait the event of the green light on Broadway, at the metropolis of the Heights, gateway to the Jersey lands where politics and public service streams glossily out of the MOTOR VEHICLE BUREAU'S office in Trenton, sturdy foundation for the Empire side of the George Washington Bridge, land of bus terminals, noted for its bakeries, basking in the reflected glories of nice residential apartment sections, Pinehurst Avenue is its capital, densely populated with tenants who can pay their rent, more or less.

Let me not be humorous about this question, he asked himself as he started off with the light, waiting first for the path to clear in front of him of crossing people, let me come to valid conclusions without the aid of quips. Is love a thing, something you can touch, feel, see, buy or sell? No jokes, now, he warned himself. The truth, clean and fresh. No, it is not such a thing. Not a bundle of joy that grows happily out of the love of the fellow for the girl and the love of the girl for the fellow, like an altar standing to the side with strings of toughest golden sinew flowing in straight clean strands to the shoulders of the fellow and to the shoulders of the girl.

All around me girls are pulling up their skirts with willing hands, and fellows find sudden difficulty with buttons of their pants. This would be love and the strings of the altar grow taut and vibrate in the sun of early day. But it hardly seems so simple, so true. The strings of the altar are a tarnished gold; in spots along their shining surfaces a clashing hue of bleached color shows itself, gaudy and really hostile for all its shoddy imitations of the purer strand. Pessary and contraceptive rule the day and to recline upon the couch of intimacy is a bit to defy the order of the day in seeming ridicule of the pleasures of erotic play.

Nicodemus hit the Washington Heights Bridge now, built so high above the Harlem River that ships of any size, cared they to see the Harlem River, could pass with ease, their highest smokestack still seventy-five feet below the level of the bridge, built like a gallant roadway, broad and smooth with sculptured rails, with no obvious supports, no headpieces, no sides, just a straight pavement of several hundred feet across, connecting West Bronx with North Manhattan.

In the fast pace of the car, driving along the whitewash line stretched down the center of the bridge, Niccy mused the inconsistency of girls, their desire to flaunt the existence of the guides to life when they were in truth its leading exponents. Each penis, circumcised or not, points in one leading direction, spermatozoa accumulate and fill the vessel walls, but this has not the slightest connection with the dream of love. So rare the girl who realizes this, so rare the fellow who appreciates this. What function urges this mad decision to spread the legs yet caution guards against the full expression of the charging flow? What angry, righteous glare defies the shock of convention with the lying tales of wild delights? That logic, be it Marx or Lawrence, can reconcile the child-learned rules with their useless violation? Who foots the bill when the last great vestige of a woman's pride lays beaten and low, stung through by the act of revolt that waged stridently and blindly against the stubborn wall of stupid stability, the stability that the woman would be last to challenge or destroy because within its marshes she ever seeks the path of happiness?

And man, the bestial fellow, whose mind is supposed to rest belligerently somewhere below his belly button. How frantically he turns to sleep or writhes in remorse after that mind has functioned! With what dialectics he can staunchly prop up his argument, however, once the mind begins to contemplate further expression on the morrow! Poor beggarly fool, messiah of the new world when his mind is at work, like a pop gun ready to squirt when he sees the white of her eyes. But particular too, choosy about the place to land, obsessed with a fixation that this one place be the only one when really any would do.

Is this love, Nicodemus asked the cop on the Bronx side of the bridge, standing deep in conversation with a woman lost up here in the curving avenues of West Bronx. Is this the sauce for poems, epics, silver anniversaries? Indeed it is not. This is mere rationalization, as a political of the leftist school would say to refute his opponent's curious mixture of the general with the par-

ticular through a roundabout system based on common sense
and kitchen logic.

Nicodemus was at work on a crystal clear idea, one of
momentous social significance, worthy of great chapters in the
Book of God, worthy of long columns in the *Encyclopedia of the
Social Sciences*; an idea piercing and glowing for all its truth,
born amid the curious convulsions of Niccy's brain as he sat on
his rump squarely behind the wheel and guided his four-wheeled
vehicle down First Avenue, south past 54th Street. An idea dangerous and destined for the junk heap for all its truth because it
had its conception in the very heart of a world that sees in truth
only the efforts of advertising agencies to make lies presentable
and reasonable, and more important, livable.

But Nicodemus seeks no affirmation, no praise, no seat of
honor; the windshield is his audience, and he speaks clearly at it,
through it. The idea: that men are not men, that they manifest
motion not for their own life but solely for the life of one great
other; that hopes and plans to give some meaning to life are nonsense since there is no life for them to interpret for themselves,
only the life of one great other whose sight they know not, whose
method they cannot perceive. That we are but the enlargement of
our own blood system, each man a corpuscle, red or white or
black or yellow, in the super blood stream of one great other.
That we flow in ordered channels, through arteries or veins, carrying out a purpose, but one not our own, a purpose in the one
great other. That our futile meanderings are just so much waste
if we attempt to conceive of our own motion as the end in itself.
That such wishful thinking is a mite more sillier than the notion
that our own red and white corpuscles lead lives of personal purpose. That such is the course of life and who knows but that even
the one great other is some corpuscle for an even greater other,
until the whole of everything, not only worlds, planets, univers-
es, but the fullest appreciation of the word *everything* is all tied

up in this business of doing corpuscle duty all the way up and down the line. A line like the curve in calculus, one ever approaching the vertical base line but never reaching it, the line headed for infinity, on a clear track with plenty of fuel and under automatic control. Only the dopes can't get it through their skulls that the line never touches the base, though of course on the blackboard it looks very certain that if you draw the line out far enough the two chalk lines have to meet. And the dopes do make them meet somewhere up near the top of the blackboard, and that's why they flunk Math 2.

In this business of corpuscles there are no independent meanings, no ivory towers with good or bad addresses, because it makes no difference what the address is, the result is the same; you're all little corpuscles and it makes no difference where you live just as long as you keep on pumping that diaphragm up and down for your allotted number of years for the one great other. Let the actuaries of the Metropolitan Life Insurance Company work out the number of years you got to pump away, their figures will be no surprise to the one great other because that bird knew all along and for all he cares the insurance companies all operating under the State Insurance Law can fold up or call in their mortgages or take over the government, it means nothing to him just as long as his little corpuscles live out their time for him, in misery, in pain, in happiness, in comfort, just as long as they live out their span.

And that's the way it is. After all, the Mayo Clinic can tell us all about the personal life of each corpuscle in our blood, but does that make us go around worrying whether number 56809832, living up in the left shoulder is happy, whether his environment isn't all it could be, whether or not he suffers from sickening frustration, whether he is jealous of number 46678944 living down there near the navel? It does not, Of course there are the routine explanations, that the energetic corpuscle will work out his own salvation, that 56809832 gets around to the navel and even better parts in so many seconds, but who is interested, after all? Nobody but the individual corpuscle, and his interest is useless, it gets him nowhere; he can cry or laugh, it matters not just as long as he lives out his allotted span. But does he realize all this? He does not. So what have you?

Nicodemus, the riding kid, figured all this through between 54th Street and 14th Street, a long ride, really an adventure any time between eight in the morning and eight in the evening, what with First Avenue divided in half, one part going up and the other part going down and only a whitewash line separating up from down, and let a cop catch you as much as touch the line with your tire wheel and its a ticket for you, pull over to the curb, lets have your license, buddy; ten dollars first offence, pay the cashier, you don't have to see the judge if you plead guilty and take your medicine like a man, standing on line in the county court house, clerk's cage to the left, send your wife down to pay it for you, the city doesn't care, it only wants your admission fee, no you don't buy seats for the movies here, wise guy, don't you see we have no marquee here?

And each part has three lanes, one at the curb for the parked cars, fix a tire, how much to straighten this fender, some Sunday driver ran into me yesterday, stop for a pack of Camels at the candy store, the boss's car, a new Buick, Western Union boy's Ford; then the lane for the trucks, watch them big babies, those drivers think nothing of cutting into the outside lane if they can get the chance and a foot of extra space to lumber through, with a mirror sticking far out of the cabin into the street and a couple of flash signals on the rear of the truck, those drivers sitting hidden high up over the motor play the two ton for everything she's got, nothing wasted, not an inch, and tough, get behind one of them in a private car and you're lost for sure because the outside lane is fast, see, private cars racing downtown, doctors to

Bellevue, money men to Wall Street, lawyers too, security men, chauffeur driven too, and as tough as the truckmen, and they wouldn't give you the time of the day, the aristocrats of the road, nothing less than a two year old model; its loads, three, four, five, six, seven, eight years old, that skirt the lanes, trying to get ahead, make up time, time is money, a few dollars anyway, no insurance on these junks, its enough you have to buy gas and pay storage, sweat behind the dirty wheel and swing over behind a truck as that line moves and yours stands befouled a moment, now you're stuck on that lane and try to get back to the private car lane, just try it, can you move over in two feet with the cars riding to the side of you bunched together? the drivers with murderous glares at you, a foreigner, an interloper, trying to muscle back, next time stay in your own line, you four eyed bitch! And for what is all this? So you could make a delivery of that rotten mattress on the back seat and get back to the shop as quick as possible. But for what, you dope, for what? Don't you know you're only a little corpuscle and it doesn't matter? Nicodemus told himself severely.

For what, and for when? I tell you it's a joke. But who laughs? Nobody. I tell you, Mr. Max Eastman, this is for your book, that monument on Laughter. I bet it's too subtle even for you, though. Even for that walleye psychologist who figured all this laughter business out scientifically before you sat down to give us your slant on the business.

Twenty-Third Street now; take it to the right, across town, see the pretty sights, and think carefully: this used to be the northern boundary of Little Old New York. Ask Edith Wharton, she knows. Remember the old trolley line? the archaic street line, flanked by wide sidewalks and brown stone houses, the gas lights flickering, the swishing skirts? Remember? Well, look at it now, sweetheart.

Pussy's Car

Lets see what's going on around here. Its the middle of the night and the kid sits up in his crib and starts hollering, Boppa, Boppa, I wanna go pishin! He's trained like a little dog and he don't do it in the bed anymore, even at three o'clock in the morning. Its the same time of night, or morning too when the fellow is taking a girl home, its Saturday night see, and a girl is awfully nice at that time, tired out and natural like she really is with her face soft and a little greasy by this time and smelling like she really smells to herself, you know how nice a girl can be when she's tired and still on her feet but longing to be in bed on her side with the covers over her shoulders. Tremulously girlish, something to associate with oddly exciting things like clean sunshine and fresh water gushing and bubbling in mountain streams; things you never see but know and feel about. And look, he goes to school yet and she doesn't really remember the name of his school, its a name with a St. Not St. John's, but something like that, and he wears a draped suit which is full all around and nice and tight around his behind and that makes him look full and healthy and substantial and his pants are cut short so that you can see his socks a bit and he kisses the girl goodnight and her mouth smells of chewing gum and thats sweet and human and his mouth is dry and tastes of stale tobacco and if they kiss hard parting the lips and touching tongues, they both taste the cavernous depths of the throat and the sensation is swift and kind of sour and full of sulphur and its all very familiar and they know each other very well and they stop and she says something casual like look, there's Pussy's car and Pussy is in it, Pussy is the lady who lives across the street and she runs around even though she's over forty and she gets her car and a lot of other things with her Pussy, that's what her husband says when he gets mad at her and says things he doesn't want to say. Then there is the guy who reads all the papers every night. He stays up all night reading the news and comments on affairs. He sits with a long scissors at his elbow, cutting out the really important facts. He smokes many cigarettes, the kind you get with coupons stuck on the back and save for cash or premiums, and he collects items that deny certain allegations, like the one where somebody very important denies the allegation that he once told President Roosevelt to mind his own business, or the one where a very clean and handsome square faced scion denied the allegation that his family ever sold more Chase Bank stock than it had. Now on Park Avenue below the 90's the street lamps along the gracious boulevard rise in a long slow straight wave up and down, north and south, and people with money in their pockets and cold fine faces breathing out good liquor walk east and west in top hats and good shoes and Worth gowns and pointed breasts giving out in long drawn out words. And in a drug store a fellow closes himself up in the telephone booth and fishes a nickel out of his pocket and slips it into the slot and dials a number slowly from the back of a card written in red pencil and waits until he says I want to speak to Ethel and she says what the hell do you want at this hour of the night and he says what you doing and she says I'm in bed and he says can I come up and she says if you got the price and he says I want to talk to you and she says you can go to hell but she doesn't hang up so he says I'm coming up right now and she says and I'll yell to them downstairs to kick you into the street if you do. And up in the Club one flight over the street Little Augie wanted to go bowling and Nick says you go take a hosing for yourself, he wasn't so drunk on the gin as the rest of them were, so he decided for them they should go to the cat house and they did but they were so drunk they didn't feel anything and the girls got scared about a raid and finally got them out of the apartment and they stumbled down the stairs, only Jose wanted to go down on the elevator for his money and they said it wasn't working so late and Jose said anyway and they

left him and he walked into the open elevator door and fell down
three flights and they started looking for him and he was hollering hey fellows, hey you guys! and the police fished him out and
he had a broken arm and a broken collar bone and in the ambulance Jose kept saying Jesus Christ, Jesus Christ. And all the time
Paul Whiteman may be the King of Jazz but Benny Goodman
may be the King of Swing which isn't saying much for jazz, at
least Horace Heidt seems to be hep to something called Sweet
Swing and Sammy Kaye is very enthusiastic and a little too
much? And in south Harlem where it meets Central Park and
thereabouts a tall thin negro waited for a brown skin girl in black
bottom stockings to come home along this time and as she
stepped out of the taxi and started across the street to her bed
and sleep he followed her into the hall and grabbed what she
made that night from inside her dress and ran like mad and she
didn't dare open her mouth except struggle futilely because she
couldn't come too near the cops for anything. And everybody
wants to knock off a piece of romance and Broadway is not the
place where a million lights flicker and a million hearts beat
quicker because in a little cafe with a hundred notes on it still to
be paid off and regularly too in a booth near the back a guy
bought the woman a roast beef sandwich and a beer and felt for
her breast and she looked at him and said to him its all right, its
still there and later that night she said seriously thinking it over
why don't you buy a balloon instead of all this and stay home
with yourself and play. And off 42nd Street earlier this guy in the
soiled Admiral's uniform was telling everybody about the girls
inside, introducing lovely Marcia Trent, one-hundred-and-twen-
ty-pounds-of-glowing-feminine pulchritude, in swinging swaying
static tempo. And in the lobby of the Hotel Taft a thirty-two-
year-old woman with a good figure was watching the entrance
and thinking that many girls can get undressed, in fact most girls
do but few of them know how.

December 4, 1944

Dear Laughlin,

*Came Thanksgiving I said let's write to Laughlin and
see what's what with good writing for a change. I
think I was happier a few years ago when it was all
LITERATURE and not just writing, writing, writing.
Today I'm in writing, but deep, and its like the grocery
business. Not like the old days. Today its distribution,
binding, printing, picas and "available labor supply". . . .*

Alvin Levin

The Old Man Is Recouperating from a Hell of a Long Illness
(1943)

She closed her eyes softly, tilted her head back and started clucking her full red tongue through pursed lips to the tempo of the muffled slide trombone, beating out tense rhythms, with her finger pointed to the ceiling, gliding in front of every piece of furniture, scarcely moving her body, only her tall, hard legs swishing pajama pants under her flowing Chinese dressing gown. "Duke Ellington is my husband," she confided slowly to Herman, pausing for a moment in front of his chair. "My friend Marcella is Cab Calloway's wife," she said leaving him in a whirling dip that sent her shampooed braids flying like whips around her neck, as the cats finished the jam in a riot of noise.

"Good number, that," she estimated as she flopped into a chair, her legs stretched out in front of her.

Herman didn't know what to say. She scared him silly. He figured all he needed to do was get up and sit next to her on the chair. She sure was hot stuff, one of the real ones; the only thing they're good for is a bed. He sat still, a silly grin on his face, thinking up something to say to her.

"You're a good dancer," he said finally, taking this as an opportunity to examine her legs thoroughly under their silk pajama pants.

"Oh, I'm pretty good," she admitted. Then she went into a long account about a fellow she met on the boat on her vacation trip to Bermuda, he was the swellest dancer she ever danced with, like oil. It was a long story; she told it with her arms clasped over her breasts. "Ferguson had million dollar legs," she concluded.

Herman nodded understandingly. The announcer introduced another number. "There's something to really dance to," she cried jumping up to show him. She took a few steps.

"It's really a lindy number. I don't like to lindy, you have to shake your shoulders and that spoils the dance." She showed him. Herman couldn't stand it much longer.

She tch, tch, tched, through a partly closed mouth. "Look, watch me mix truckin' with the Peabody." She went through a series of leaping contortions that had Herman ready to jump from his chair. "You know, I don't like that dance either." She stood still, dancing on the balls of her feet, "it's like a Polish wedding dance with everybody running around like drunken hyenas."

"What do you like the best?" Herman wanted to know.

Freda pursed her lips and thought, still swaying to the music, "Oh, I don't know, the Susie Q is all right, I guess I like to truck, though."

"Come here, I'll dance the next one with you," he said, suddenly standing up.

"O.K. big boy, come on." She laughed to him.

"Let's wait for the next number to start," he said for no good reason at all. She stood waiting. "I don't dance as good as you." he warned her foolishly.

"What? with all your experience? And all your bragging! I don't believe you, mister," she mocked him as he stood there a picture of excited misery. "Anyway, I know your type."

"What do you mean?"

"I know, Herman. You don't think I'm that dumb, do you?"

"I don't know what you're talking about," he said, and he really didn't.

"Come on," she said taking his hand. He grabbed her and they were off. He danced a little too studied, trying his best to fall into her swing. She finally took the lead, glancing at him with a laugh every once in a while. Nobody spoke; he could only feel her body next to his, frankly socking against him. He began to breathe heavily, he couldn't stop it or slow down.

"You dance like a Westchester smoothie," she said.

"What's that, good or bad?" he wanted to know, displaying his ignorance.

"Oh," she shrugged, "it depends on your taste."

"Oh."

He studied the situation carefully, he started to twice and stopped, then he hugged her tight and kissed her roughly, somewhere near her mouth. Still pressing her to him, he sought her mouth, fiercely, kissing her all the way from her cheek to the corner of her lips. She wiggled out of his grip and pushed him away. "You got a nerve. What's the matter with you, anyway? Don't you ever do that again." She wiped her face with the back of her coat sleeve. "Gee, what nerve!"

She looked at him standing in the center of the room, with the same silly grin on his face. "Go on, sit down, you big baby," she told him. She sat down on the other side of the room.

Freda looked around with weary resignation: "Well, that's that, I suppose."

The radio still played and she listened, beating out the time. "Listen, don't carry on so," Herman said from the other side of the room, "this isn't the first time you were kissed, and you know it." He was still hot and awfully frustrated.

"Of course I've been kissed before, and I'm not ashamed of it, but there's a difference in being kissed and being mauled around. Anyway, how do you know I want to be kissed by you?"

The old man called from his room. Freda rose to leave. "Excuse me." she said politely.

Herman watched her go. God, what a girl! He'd give anything to lay her, anything. It wasn't so bad kissing her like that. He got a feel too in the bargain and she wasn't so fast in pulling away either. She had a fellow living with her now, what did she see in him? He must give her plenty of it too; she could certainly take it, matadme. Maybe when she came back . . . but it was late already, what a dope he was to stay at the club all evening when she was here alone with the old man. If he'd only known they were all going to the movies.

Over the old man's bed pan, Freda figured it out, that she'd better send him home right away. Let him stay around and he'd start things that would land her in trouble. Anyway she was tired, the old man was a nuisance, all day long. I'll call Murray up in the morning, maybe, he'll meet me in the apartment in the afternoon for a little while.

She put the old gent to sleep, giving him a rub down and two pills; his temperature was up two tenths again. Some fun, big boy, take as long as you want to die. She came back to Herman, her hair combed out over her shoulders, ready for bed.

"You'll have to go now, it's late," she told him. He was sitting where she left him, a sheepish look on his face. But she made out everything was forgotten. "Thanks for keeping me company," she told him. He got up and took his hat. He didn't know whether to grab at her or not. "Would you like to have me take you out on your night off?" he asked.

"With you? I'll have to think it over before I decide."

"We'll go dancing."

"Would I be safe with you?"

"What do you think?" he parried.

"I'll see, Herman," she said seriously, walking towards the door. It was dark on the landing. She reached over and kissed him on the cheek.

"Is that all I get?" Herman was delighted.

"Yep, isn't that enough?" she pushed him to the steps. "Good-night, and don't think of me too much."

"Lemmee kiss you good-night too." Herman wanted to play.

"No, get going," she said. She had him down three steps by now and he had to keep on going. "O.K. Good-night Freda," he laughed over his shoulder, "I'll drop in tomorrow night."

Freda went back into the bathroom and put her hair into braids again. She crept into bed hoping the old man wouldn't wake up until six at least. She read until they came back from the movies. Honey could melt in her mouth.

Freda came back late. She rushed into the house, a bundle of carefree wickedness. Sarah, at the sink, was sore, quietly boiling. Freda saw it but she didn't give a damn; let them holler their heads off, if they didn't like it they knew what they could do.

"Was Mr. Schwartz all right this afternoon?" she asked as she shrugged her shoulders out of her coat.

"He was all right until a while ago. He's used to his rub down at four o'clock you know, and I had to give him some tea just now," Sarah said righteously.

"Oh. it's too near his supper for tea," the nurse said, unbuttoning the side of her dress as she stood in the kitchen door. She looked around. "Is anybody here?"

"No, it's all right, you can get undressed here," she replied from the sink. Like hell you can you good-for-nothing! Say where do you think you are anyway; pretty soon you'll be running my house for me, if you're not running it already. Telling me it's too close to his supper! I'm glad you know what time it is at least!

Miss Radally trotted into the bedroom, in her slip, trailing her clothes over her shoulder.

"Hello, pop," she called as she passed the old man's room, "I'm back. Did you miss me, pop?"

"Oi, Oi, Oi," sighed pop slowly from the depths of his bed.

Sarah boiled in wrath. "Do you want to feed him now, Miss Radally?" she called icily.

"I'll sponge Mr. Schwartz off first," nursie calculated as she struggled into her uniform. That old witch, I'd like to smack her right in the teeth!

"Well, the food is on the stove," Mrs. Schwartz said. "I'm going out for a minute. I haven't had a breath of air all day."

So what do you want me to do about it, lady? "O.K.," said Freda lightly, bouncing into the kitchen, "I'll attend to it." She moved over to the stove, patting down her uniform as she walked. "Everything ready?" she asked politely.

"Ready? Of course it's ready. Do you think I've been playing all day?" What kind of talk is that, you good-for-nothing. I can't stand it any longer. I'll go off my mind. It's too much for me!

Freda smiled, friendly like. She put her hands on Sarah's shoulders and danced her around. "I like you," she told the woman. "I've met a lot of people and I know a nice one when I see one. You ought to take a rest."

You and your ways to get around people. Take your hands off me, you whore! "Did you have a nice time this afternoon?" she asked, acting friendly like, too.

"Oh, swell. I met a lot of people I wanted to see. I was a little late, wasn't I? There were so many things I had to do," she explained.

"Well, I'll be back in a little while," said Sarah. "I want to get a bit of air after being in here all day."

You mean you got to go over to your sister's and talk about me a little more, you sneaking bitch! "Papa, I'll be right back in a minute," his daughter-in-law called into his room.

"It's all right. It's all right, you can go, Sarahlle. It's all right by me. Go and have a very good time," pop advised his bed.

"I'll be right back, papa. I'm only going to the corner." She didn't want him to get the wrong impression. "I feel dopy, I need a little air."

"Go and have a very good time," he told her again.

Yeah, go and break your neck, nursie suggested as she prepared a basin of lukewarm water over the sink.

"Well, I'll be right back," she said to Freda as she passed to the stairs.

Freda took the bowl into the old man's room. "Well, tell me, did you miss me much this afternoon?" she asked him brightly.

"Ai, Miss Nurse, I don't know from missing anymore. I am a sick man. It's through already the missing," he told her as he prepared for his bath. "So give me a wash off, and that's all already."

"Oh, so you're tired of me already," she said, piqued like.

"Ai, shiksele, when I got my health I ain't so tired of you, when I was healthy I went in the winter to Florida and in the summer to Saratoga Springs with hotels all the time and I wasn't tired of girls like you. So wash up and make an end already." Pop and Freda understood each other perfectly.

The nurse did a thorough and efficient job. Pop lay back on his puffed-up pillow, a clean little Santa Claus, smelling from rubbing alcohol and baby talcum.

"Well, how do you feel now, pop?" asked Freda with satisfaction, rubbing her hands in alcohol.

"Fine, fine," muttered the old man, smoothing the cover under his arms, "like the Pope I feel, and he should feel like me tomorrow, that's all I ask."

"Ah, go on, you know I make you feel good. I bet you're the only one here who appreciates me." Freda entered the temperature on the report card. "They love me here, they do."

"So they love you. What can I do about it, Miss Nurse? I pay her ten dollars every day and she worries that they love her."

"O.K. Mr. Rockefeller," she laughed, "stay here and I'll get you your supper." She danced out of the room. Temperature up four tenths again; some guy!

"Say, can I put the radio on for awhile? I want to hear the WHN Request Program."

Pop mumbled something, so Freda went into the living room and turned on the radio. A full hour of requested recordings with incidental commercials between numbers. Swing, baby, swing. I gotta be a rug-cutter! Freda was hitting it up all by her lonesome in the living room, until she remembered grandpa's supper. She made the radio louder and ran into the kitchen.

"Wet your lips, pop, here I come with the best little supper you ever ate!" she called in to him.

With the rest of the family the supper went off fairly well considering that Mrs. Schwartz complained on seven occasions how tired she was after working all afternoon. She really felt better since she let off steam in her sister-in-law's house awhile ago. But there was still enough steam left for anyone who came her way to listen, and her husband and daughter were in for it, sure enough. Freda ate with a good appetite, the life of the table; she went off swell with Morris who enjoyed her. Libby tended to side with her mother. Dessert was finally dished out.

Libby was on the telephone in pop's room, laughing away for the past half hour with somebody on the other end. The old man lay Oing away under her occasional uncertain stare of misgivings. Freda helped in the kitchen with the dishes, Sarah washing with a polite silence that was supposed to be deadly in effect.

Freda had to laugh to herself. It didn't look at all like anybody was going out of the house tonight, and when she thought of Herman coming over and trying to get her alone she had to laugh. The poor slob! His mother would be over too, she'd come with him.

"Who was it?" asked Sarah when Libby came out of the bedroom.

"It was Esther. She met a fellow Saturday and he keeps calling her up," Libby told them, taking a chair in the kitchen and starting to fix her nails.

"A nice fellow?" mother wanted to know.

"How do I know, I didn't see him," Libby said over her nails.

"Well, what does Esther say, does she say she likes him?"

"Sure she likes him, I guess; she's going out with him."

"Who Esther could go out with!" remarked mother from the sink.

"What do you mean? What's the matter with Esther?" Esther was her friend, her best friend this month.

"Who is Esther? Did I meet her?" asked Freda.

Listen to her; everything she has to butt in. I tell you our lives ain't our own anymore, mused Sarah.

"Sure, she was here last week. You remember, the girl with the blonde hair, the tall girl, you liked her dress."

"Oh, I remember, yes, she's a nice girl."

The bell rang. Herman, I bet, figured Freda. Sure enough, Hermie and his little mother. They came into the kitchen with their coats on.

"Hello girls," greeted Herman cheerily, chummy like.

"Hello Herman," smiled Freda waving a dish towel at him.

Libby raised her eyes for a hello. Herman's mother started in.

"Well, how is papa feeling tonight'? Is he asleep?"—anxious like.

"No, Mr. Schwartz is still up," said nursie professionally. "You can go in to see him." She put the towel down and made off for the old man's room.

"Take your coats off," said Sarah, making a face at Miss Radally behind her beautiful back, for all to see.

Hermie laughed discreetly; he knew that nurse!

"You can come in now," called Freda from pop's room. "Visitors, pop. Your daughter and her—her handsome son."

"Who needs them, Miss Nurse? Who needs them, I ask you," he turned crankily in his bed. "All right, so send them in already."

"Hello, papa, how do you feel? Better?"

"Yeah, better I feel. I should feel like this tomorrow and I'm dead already," he groaned.

"Ah, you'll be all right, grandpa," cheered Hermie, standing as near to nursie as he dared.

Stinker, you! Give back the nine hundred dollars and the fifty dollars for the license and keep your compliments, grandpa glared.

"Yeah, better I'll be," he said mournfully.

"How's his temperature?" Hermie asked the nurse, confidential like, just like the doctor.

Listen to him! Big stuff, all right. "It's about the same," Freda answered confidentially. Herman nodded his head, professionally.

Pop's daughter sat near the bed. "Look how hot he looks," she told nursie. "Maybe he needs something now?"

Mind your business, you old hen. Nursie went to the bed, she moved the covers a little. "No, you're comfortable now, aren't you, Mr. Schwartz?" she asked him for the visitors' benefit.

"Sure, sure, why shouldn't I be comfortable?" he piped.

His daughter wasn't so sure, she didn't like the way the nurse was handling him, too free like. "Papa, would you like me to make you some chicken with soup for tomorrow?" She turned to Miss Radally.

"It will give him strength," she told her.

"Well, a little broth is good for him, but he had some chicken soup yesterday, didn't you, Mr. Schwartz? You don't have to bother, though, because Mrs. Sehwartz cooks all his meals," nursie told her. Say, what do you want to do, raise the roof off this place competing with your sister-in-law.

"Never mind. Say grandpa, I'll bet you'd go for a nice plate of mama's chicken soup right now, wouldn't you?" said Hermie grinning knowingly at the old man.

Mr. Schwartz gazed back at him with disgust written all over his wizened old face.

"Go ahead, ma, buy some chicken and make some soup," said Hermie, liberal about such little things. He was all enthused about the idea. Act right in with the family, like one big happy bunch, show Freda you're all right.

Mr. Schwartz suddenly hollered for the bed pan, so they all had to get out. Hermie winked to Freda as he passed her.

"Aren't you going to the club tonight?" she asked him.

"No, I don't think I'll go. Say, you don't think I go there every night, do you?" Herman didn't want her to think that's the only place he had to go at night.

"Huh? Oh no, I just thought you were going tonight. I saw you were all dressed up." Didn't I *know* you weren't going tonight!

"Dressed up? oh this." Hermie waved his hand down his pressed suit, negligently.

"What you and me doing tonight?" he asked her, kidding.

"Oh, anything you say baby," she whispered wickedly.

"So where is the bed pan already?" Mr. Schwartz queried.

"Coming, coming, papa," sang out Freda as she raced to the bathroom and came back with the white seat, passing it right under Hermie's nose as she passed him into the bedroom and closed the door behind her.

Herman went into the living room; everybody was sitting there. Gee, if he could only get her alone. But Uncle Morris was set by his radio and the "girls" were talking about playing a game of casino. Libby was in her room, doing her homework. Herman was growing frantic. He had to get Freda by himself for a little while.

He stood there in the center of the room, feeling them out. "Do you have to go shopping, ma? You said something before about getting a chicken."

"No, I wouldn't get a chicken for tomorrow." She didn't want her sister-in-law to know about her usurpations in pop's room a while ago. That's all she needed! Her Herman didn't know. "I'll get what I need for tomorrow on our way home."

"Sit down awhile, Herman. Are you going to the club?"

"No, I'm not going to the club," he answered angrily.

"Well take your hat off in the house," said Sarah. Herman had his hat on, on the back of his head.

"All right, all right, don't get excited, I'll take my hat off," he answered her, taking his hat and flinging it on the piano.

"Listen here, Herman, don't get so fresh. You know I don't owe you anything," Sarah told him, growing excited.

"Herman, take the hat away from the piano and hang it up," his mother soothed.

"Jesus Christ," the fellow cried, "this is some house!"

"Listen here, you don't have to come here! Nobody sent for you," Sarah cried standing up. "Did you ever hear such nerve? Who the hell do you think you are anyway? Big shot all of a sudden!" She turned to her husband. "You sit there and listen to all this and you don't say a word. Did you hear him? You'd think we owed him something!" She was blazing now. "It's not enough what I have to put up with all day. This thing has to come in and finish my day for me."

"Take it easy there, Herman, take it easy, where do you think you are anyway?" said Morris, performing a special favor for his wife.

"All right, all right, what are you all flaring up for all of a sudden? What did I say anyway? My mother too!" Herman explained.

Freda danced in then, a picture of grace and beauty. All eyes turned to her. "Mr. Schwartz is feeling better now," she told them with wide-eyed innocence. "You can all go in now."

Sarah and her sister-in-law went in, Sarah giving Herman a

nasty look as she passed him. "We'll go home pretty soon, Herman," his mother told him as she passed.

"O.K., O.K. Take your time, I'm in no hurry," he told her.

That left Freda with Herman and Morris. That uncle of his wasn't going to budge. "Anything special you want on the radio?" asked Morris, the host, from his chair.

"Oh, anything that's got some rhythm to it," she told him. She leaned over towards him. "Let's see what the program says," she said taking the paper from him. "Is it O.K. if I look at this a minute?"

"Sure, sure," he said giving her the whole paper.

She found the radio section. "Gee, Henry Busse is on at twelve o'clock, and Count Basie at eleven thirty," she remarked reflectively.

"You're used to staying up late, aren't you?" asked Morris, smiling.

"Well not when I have an early shift; that's at seven in the morning," she told them both. "But otherwise I don't get to bed until about two every night. You hear the best dance orchestras at that time. Recordings mostly."

"Some life, eh, Uncle Morris?" Herman asked, grinning for effect.

Morris didn't know what he was talking about but he smiled back. Freda said: "What do you mean, some life?"

"Oh, nothing," said Herman, he didn't know either.

Freda found something she liked. "Try eighty-five," she told Morris at the controls. He did. Some snaky stuff came in, filling up the dimly lit room with loud swing rhythms of the orchestra. Freda jumped up, her breasts shaking visibly under the starched front of her uniform. She tilted her head back, looking the men straight in the eyes as she turned from one to the other, impishly laying her full red tongue on her lower lip as she rocked to the syncopation of her hands before her, beating out a two-beat tempo on an imaginary keyboard on the level with her bosom; she shook her head in short rhythmed jerks. She stopped and laughed to them; they laughed to each other, the men did, marveling at the abandon of this creature.

Herman didn't want to appear on the side of his uncle, against the girl. He wanted to show her that he understood her, felt the way she did. The orchestra was playing a slower number. "That's their theme song," said Freda, sitting down again.

"Now we know that orchestra is going off the air," explained Herman to his uncle. Hermie knew all about bands now, he was well versed in swing, he could tell uncle what it was all about, he and Freda here.

Freda sat still, demure-like in front of the men. She caught Herman watching her. A laugh burst out of her, "What's the matter, Herman," she asked with a grin, taking Mr. Schwartz into her confidence.

Wide-eyed, with a red face and mouth agape, Hermie only said: "Nothing, why?"

Mr. Schwartz turned to Freda. He wanted to know what was the matter, too, what he missed just now. "It's nothing, just a little secret Herman and I have between us," grinned Freda and making Herman wish with all his might that uncle would get out of the room for a minute so he could get a hold of her.

No use. He was wasting his time, and she was having a good time with him. Teasing him, like the little whore that she was. Boy if he could only bring her down to the club with him, would he be the stuff. He could see the fellows watching him with her, trying to get a dance after he introduced her around. She'd knock them dizzy. Boy, when Herman picks them up he picks them right! If he had her for just a little while he'd get tired with her. They're all alike those Polacks, crazy shiksas. You couldn't trust them from here to the corner. But just this once to get his hands on her!

"Look at the baby pout," imitated nursie from her chair.

"Who's pouting?" Hermie wanted to know.

Morris didn't know what it was all about. He wanted to read his paper a little anyway. He left them to their smart repartee, it was just as though he had left the room, but not as far as Hermie was concerned. He couldn't get her out of his system.

His mother came into the room with Sarah. "Do you want to go home, Herman? He's tired," she told them, "he's working hard all day."

Herman looked up at them like a tired business man. "No, it's all right, you can stay here a little while. I'm not tired," he said.

"We'll play some cards then," said his mother. "You want to play a little casino, Sarah?" she asked.

Sarah wanted to, so they went into the kitchen. Hermie was left alone again with Freda and his uncle at the radio, deep in the *Bronx Home News*. For appearance's sake the nurse went in to see how Mr. Schwartz was getting on. On her way back she stopped at the card game. She lit a cigarette from her side pocket and came into the living room.

"Like this was her house," complained Sarah to her sister-in-law.

"Well, Herman," said Freda settling herself next to him on the sofa, "what are you doing this evening?"

"Me? oh, I'm just resting tonight. Here, let me have a cigarette, will you?"

"Sure, here. You don't smoke regularly, do you," she passed him the matches.

"Oh, pretty regularly," he said. "I just forget to buy them, that's why I haven't any now. You don't mind if I take one of yours, do you?"

"No, of course not. I hate anybody who makes a fuss about whose cigarettes they smoke. You can have all I got."

"Is that all I can have of yours?" Hermie wanted to know;

he was playing again, tickled pink that she was sitting next to him. He inhaled deeply for her benefit, hoping he wouldn't choke letting the smoke out, or feel sick. He felt he should have taken one of his cigars with him tonight. He wondered if his uncle over there would see if he took her arm right now.

She bent across him to flick her ashes in the tray at his side. He smelled the heavy scent of her hair as she withdrew. "Freda, can you take a walk with me?" he asked her in a low voice, eagerly.

Freda grew very motherly. After seeing Murray all afternoon she could afford to be, with this guy. "Look, Herman, why don't you find yourself a nice Jewish girl who will be nice to you and who your mother will like? You don't want to go for a walk with me. You shouldn't stay away from your club on account of me. Honest, there are so many nice Jewish girls around who are just for you," she told him.

What the hell! Who did she think she was anyway? Did she think he wanted her for a steady girl friend or anything like that? She sure must think he was a dumb guy if she thought he was falling for her that way. The dirty prostitute! That's what she was, trying to rope a guy in! Just as soon as she saw he was a fellow with a good job she tries to hook him. So that's why she was playing hard to get! O.K., sister, I get you, but you don't get me, see? Boy, I'd like to take your pussy away from you, as if you had one!

"Well, I guess I better be going, it's late and I have a lotta work to do tomorrow," he told her, manly-like as he rose from the sofa. Boy, if my uncle weren't sitting here now I'd sock it right into you so help me!

"Atta boy, Herman, go on home and get your sleep," she told him, laughing as she rose with him.

Herman was sore as hops. He rushed into the kitchen. They were playing cards.

"Well, come on, are you coming?" he demanded, his hat on.

"You said you didn't want to go home yet," his mother complained. "You said that and we started to play, this is the same game."

"All right, all right, you can stay, I'm going home, I'm tired," he started to leave.

"Wait, Herman, wait, I'm coming, wait," his mother dropped her cards. "I thought you wanted to stay awhile. I was sure you said so. So wait, I'm coming with you, Herman." She turned to Sarah, shrugging her shoulders. "So we'll finish another time" she told her. Sarah gathered in the cards.

"Your son is crazy, that's all I can say, he's crazy," she told her sister-in-law. "If he was my son I'd have his head examined."

"Listen, did I say anything to you?" Hermie wanted to know, belligerently.

"Listen here, Herman, you can't talk to me that way, do you hear? I wouldn't stand for it, especially not from you. Big shot all of a sudden. You can get out of this house and you needn't come back until you've learned to talk to me differently," Aunt Sarah cried, dashing the cards over the table and then picking them up again.

"Sh, Herman, sh," his mother pleaded with him.

"Come on, ma, let's get out of this house. They're all crazy here," he took her arm.

"Morris, Morris, do you hear? Come here a minute, Morris! Look how he sits with his ear in the radio and don't hear a thing that's being said in his own house. Morris, come in here a minute and hear what your nephew says about this house! We're all crazy here!"

Freda tried to butt in. "Mrs. Schwartz, please try to control yourself, please. It's not good for you. And Mr. Schwartz is in there sick. Try to take it easy." She tried to get Sarah to sit down.

Morris came in, in his slippered feet. "What's going on in here? what is it?"

"What is it, he asks! Try to listen for a minute to what is going on around you! Listen to your nephew, he says this is a crazy house, everybody is crazy here!" his wife cried out.

"Listen here, young man, you'll have to change your ways when you come here," said Morris turning to Herman who stood in the doorway with his mother, looking sick and foolish, his hat pushed back on the top of his head. "We've got enough going on here without you making any trouble."

Sarah was crying now, holding her head in her hands as she leaned over the table. "And now what's the matter with you?" demanded her husband, pointing the *Bronx Home News* at her.

Freda ran to the sink for a glass of water. "Take it away, take it away!" jerked out Sarah. "Water she brings me. I can't stand it any more. It's too much for me, I can't stand it no more. I'll go crazy. I tell you!" she sobbed.

Libby came in slowly from her room, holding her reading glasses in her hand and sucking at the stems. "What is all the hollering about here? What's the matter?" she asked.

"It's nothing," said Freda. "Your mother is just tired, that's all."

"Well you can all be heard way down the corner," Libby told them.

"All right, come on, ma, let's get going," Hermie told his mother, tugging at her arm.

"Wait Herman, wait a minute," his mother told him. "Sarah, stop already the crying. I'm sorry, Herman is sorry for everything. Stop already, you'll be sick, Sarah," she pleaded with her.

Sarah sobbed on, making only theatrical attempts to halt her tears.

"Listen, Mr. Schwartz hears you," said the nurse, hastening into the old man's room.

"It's time he heard what's going on here. It's time he knows what I have to stand for in the last eight weeks!" Sarah told them.

"Mama, stop it," demanded Libby, "stop it right away, you're acting foolishly and it's not getting you anywhere either." She stamped her little foot and then took her mother's head to her sweet ample bosom. "Mama, please stop this nonsense. Aunt Elsie, take your son and please go home," she told her aunt.

Now it was Aunt Elsie's turn to get sore. "Come, Herman, let's go home," she told her son, hurt-like.

They left. Herman said, "Good-bye everybody," at the stairs. "Yes," said his mother as she went down the stairs before him, "Good-bye." Then she reminded herself, "I forgot to say good-night to grandpa," she said.

"Oh, he wouldn't know the difference," said Herman, "Come on, let's get out of this joint."

"Sarah, say good-night to papa for me, I forgot in all the excitement," she called back up the stairs.

In his room the old man wanted to know what they were hollering about this time. Nurse soothed him back on his pillow and told him it was nothing, his family was only having a little meeting.

"Meetings, meetings, they should hire a hall for such meetings." The old man was half asleep. He was slowly waking up. "With my money they should buy a ship and go fishing with it," he told her peevishly.

Morris came into the room. "How are you, papa? Did they wake you up?"

"Who was waked up? I wasn't even sleeping. I was laying here telling myself stories, what else I got to do?"

"It was that dope Herman. He's a crazy dope, coming here and making trouble. He got Sarah excited, but it's all right now."

"Dope, dope, he ain't such a dope, was he the dope to take from me nine hundred dollars and fifty dollars for the license?

Who was the dope, him or me, you tell me that," he pointed a shaking finger at his son. Freda was bending over him. "You tell me too," he told her.

"Come on now, Schwartzie, don't worry about anybody but yourself," she told him, raising him on his pillow.

"That's right, pa. Just get well and everything will be all right. Don't even think of Herman, he's a dumb kid."

"Nine hundred dollars, and they tell me not to worry yet," marveled the old man.

Freda was convinced that Herman ought to be shown a lesson. The damn fool! What a stinker! And what a ride he gave his mother and the poor slob has to take it from him just because he supports her. Gee, I'd like to run that guy cockeyed for just a week! Hot in the pants he was, like a kid on a spree, and then he doesn't even say good-night! Freda, my girl, you've been stood up, and by that, by that palooka because you tried to steer the stinker straight!

Well, she gave popsie the best little rub down he ever had, she gave him his medicine and took his temperature; still up all right, and let everybody in to say good-night to the old man. He started repeating over and over again, "Good-night, good-night, my children, good-night." She ushered them out quietly. Sarah, still sniffling went to bed; Morris followed her. Freda was still wide awake and wanted to stay up awhile with Libby in the living room and listen to the radio turned down soft, but Libby had a class early in the morning so she said good-night sleepily, her hand over her yawning mouth, and Freda found herself alone in the kitchen with nothing to do.

She started to play solitaire but gave it up pretty quick; how anybody could sit alone and play for no reason was beyond her, they had to be bughouse or it would drive them bughouse. She threw the cards down and thought about Murray for awhile. He was a swell guy, sometimes. O.K. this afternoon. Had to get that dress out of the cleaners tomorrow. She sat drumming her fingers against the table. The only time she could think when she was alone was when she was doing her nails. She finally bent over to take her stockings off to wash. What a beautiful leg you have, she told herself, feeling it along the back and around up her thigh. Scram, she told herself, rising and going to the bathroom.

December 13, 1944

Dear Levin—

*It was good to hear from you again. What are you
writing these days? I really think it is a terrible shame
that you don't write more. You have a wonderful gift—
a sort of special vitality—and if you don't put down all
that Bronx stuff in permanent form the world will
have cause to feel you have not discharged your obliga-
tions to it. Now that's a fact!*

*I don't say this in any personal frame of reference
because I plan in the next few years to do a great deal
less publishing and more of my own writing. But I
have always felt that your gift was a very unusual one
and that you ought to take it more seriously. . . .*

> *Best wishes,*
>
> *Laughlin*

NOTES

LOVE IS LIKE PARK AVENUE: First published as "A section from his projected book" in *Literary America* 4, no. 2 (Winter 1936), pp. 168–174.

MY SON: First published in *The University Review: A Journal of the University of Kansas City* 5, no. 3 (Spring 1939), pp. 172–173.

A COOL DRINK IS REFRESHING: First published in *The Parchment* 10, no. 3 (May, 1939), pp. 14–19.

ONLY DREAMS ARE TRUE: From *New Directions in Prose & Poetry 1939*, edited by James Laughlin IV (Norfolk, CT: New Directions, 1939), pp. 387–390. *Contributor's note:* "Alvin Levin is a young New York lawyer. He is at work on a novel."

AND I TOOK A WIFE: First published in *North Georgia Review* 4, no. 4 (Winter 1939–1940), pp. 25–27.

LITTLE ALVIN'S STORYBOOK: *Little Alvin's Storybook* (Cincinnati: The Little Man Press, 1940) was published as part of the second issue of *The Little Man* chapbook series. *Contributor's note*: "THIS MAN ALVIN LEVIN just got out of college and lives in the Bronx, NYC. He spends part of his time being an attorney-at-law, the rest writing a swing review for a hepcat magazine, reviewing book for magazines like the Nation, and running around New York taking people's pictures with his little camera. This is the first time his stories have been published in a magazine, but more will come soon in THE LITTLE MAN."

MY BABY NEEDED A MOTHER: First published in *3 New Guys*, the second issue of *The Little Man* (Cincinnati: The Little Man Press, 1940), pp. 1–9.

I BET YOU THINK LIFE IS A MERRY-GO-ROUND: First published in *The Little Man*, issue 4, *The State of the Nation: 11 Interpretations*, edited by Robert Lowry (Cincinnati: The Little Man Press, 1940), pp. 84–95. *Contributor's note*: "Alvin Levin is a young guy taking the great 1,000-to-one shot, taking it with a sad grin, too, that he can some day call his own a real nice window to throw it out of. So far he has three bachelor's degrees. He also has five suits, an electric razor, a 1936 Ford coupe, black, with a radio."

LOVE IS LIKE PARK AVENUE: FRAGMENTS EXCERPTED FROM A LONGER WORK: First published in *New Directions in Prose & Poetry 1942*, edited by James Laughlin IV (Norfolk, CT: New Directions, 1942), pp. 311–371. Contributor's note: "Alvin Levin has been published before in New Directions and also in other advance guard publications, notably those of The Little Man Press. He lives in New York City and is now in the pamphlet publishing business, having abandoned the law, for which he was trained. The excerpts which we publish here represent about a third of the whole manuscript of *Love Is Like Park Avenue*.

THE OLD MAN IS RECOUPERATING FROM A HELL OF A LONG ILLNESS: First published in *New Voices: Atlantic Anthology*, edited by Nicholas Moore and Douglas Newton (London: The Fortune Press, 1943), pp. 150–163.

p. 2   *Briffault*: Robert Briffault (1876–1948), a French writer, social anthropologist, and surgeon, held controversial views about the decline of the West and against male domination and marriage. His novel *Europa: The Days of Ignorance* was a bestseller in the United States in 1935.

p. 4   *August Heckscher*: Heckscher (1848-1941) was an industrialist, New York real-estate developer, and philanthropist whose Children's Foundation sought to improve the lives of children living in New York's tenements.

p. 7   *Joan Crawford supper club*: The actress famously honeymooned with her second husband Franchot Tone at the Rainbow Room in 1935.

p. 10   *Neo-Kantian*: In Levin's City College milieu, the Neo-Kantian schools influenced serious ethical discourses on everything from socialism to progressive Jewish theology.

p. 16   *coco cola*: A spelled-out colloquial pronunciation of Coca-Cola.

p. 28   *Leonard Q. Ross* is the pseudonym of Leo Calvin Rosten (1908–1997), the humorist who published stories about the night-school "prodigy" Hyman Kaplan in *The New Yorker* during the 1930s. *The Strangest Places* (1939) was a collection of sketches about people and places in New York City.

p. 30   *Hurricanes are no fun*: Refers to the New England Hurricane of 1938, also called the "Long Island Express." The cataclysmic death and property damage that resulted from this storm is referenced, like a flood mark, in the work of other writers, notably Sylvia Plath.

p. 32   *Radio's Happiest Family: The Goldbergs*: A popular family situation comedy.

p. 35   *Muriel/Mabel*: This is the same person in the story. It seems that Levin allowed for this discontinuity since the names of characters, perhaps, were considered as much an authorial intervention as punctuation.

p. 37   *College*: City College was called the "Harvard of the Proletariat" for its many Jewish and other minority students.

p. 40   *the Terrace*: St. Nicholas Terrace, by City College.

p. 42   *1930 Packards*: Levin probably means the Club Sedan, which featured a capacious and enclosed rear seat suitable for trysting.

p. 42   *Character Committee*: To be admitted to the bar in New York, law school graduates had to be approved by this advisory body.

p. 50   *crum*: A spelled-out colloquial pronunciation of the pejorative "crumb."

p. 55   *twenty-ninth floor*: A discontinuity. The story begins with the same apartment "sixteen flights up."

p. 63   *shine in my moiling side*: A "shine" is a shot of hard liquor.

p. 64   *Pessary*: A diaphragm used in combination with spermicide.

p. 68   *Not with a Club . . .*": Canto 1304, by Emily Dickinson.

p. 69   *"I've come a long way . . . "*: "It's No Use Raising a Shout," by W. H. Auden.

p. 78   *the Rothschilds*: George Arliss (1868–1946) played Benjamin Disraeli in Disraeli (1930) and Nathan and Mayer Rothschild in *The House of Rothschild* (1934).

p. 80   *Davega's*: A New York sporting-goods chain.

p. 82   *germs and you could get sick*: An allusion to the common fear of polio.

p. 84   *hoover apron*: A wrap-around house dress distributed by New York City relief agencies during the Depression. Also called a "Hooverall."

p. 95   *peetering*: Also a spelled-out colloquialism. The extra e is a vulgarism to imply urination.

p. 105 *H. V. Kaltenborn*: Hans von Kaltenborn (1878–1965), an American radio commentator for CBS, was known for his polished diction, commentary on world affairs, and his coverage of the Republican and Democratic conventions from the 1930s to 1950s.

p. 109 *crash in the Rockies*: An allusion to the death of actress Carole Lombard (1908–1942) on January 16, 1942.

p. 109 *Witchita*: The misspelling may be mimetic: how the character sees the word with "witch" in it.

p. 109 *flivver*: A nickname for the Ford Model T and for any small, cheaply made vehicle.

p. 110 *Glen Island Casino*: A popular Big Band Era restaurant overlooking Long Island Sound in New Rochelle, New York.

p. 117 *River House*: A New York City Art Deco landmark apartment building at 435 E. 52nd Street.

p. 118 *Nenemoosha*: An honorific for the Indian woman Oweenee in Henry Wadsworth Longfellow's poem "The Song of Hiawatha."

p. 120 *Sally Rand*: Rand (1904–1979), an exotic dancer, invented the bubble and fan dance that was popular in burlesque theaters.

p. 121 *Paradise Restaurant*: One of New York City's venues for such big bands as Glenn Miller's Orchestra and other entertainments (at 1619 Broadway).

p. 123 *Bungalow Man*: In this context, someone from the suburbs. Inexpensive bungalows—Sears sold bungalow kits that shipped by rail—and the suburban lifestyle were promoted by the self-styled "Bungalow Man," Henry Wilson of Seattle.

p. 124 *Knob Hill*: A common misspelling of Nob Hill, a San Francisco neighborhood.

p. 125 *Café Loyale*: Café Royale was a gathering place for actors in the Yiddish Theater at Second Avenue and 12th Street.

p. 135 *Maury Paul*: Paul (1890–1942) was the "Cholly Knickerbocker" of the *New York Journal–America*. The leading New York society reporter and expert on "the 400" wealthiest New York families, he coined the phrase "Café Society."

p. 135 *Livingston boy*: A member of the Livingston family whose estate could be seen from the Hudson River, one of "the 400."

p. 135 *gamps*: In standard dictionaries, gamp means a large, baggy umbrella (after the one carried by Mrs. Sarah Gamp in Dickens' novel *Martin Chuzzlewit*). Levin's use is from an alternate meaning tied to the character's morbid occupation: the disposal of dead people's garments. Hence, *gamps* means old or unstylish clothes.

p. 137 *Baby Snooks*: A mischievous little-girl character played by comedienne Fanny Brice (1891–1951) in the eponymous radio show.

p. 137 *Mestupolia*: Invented toponym of Russian-Jewish origin.

p. 138 *ach 'schooler*: House Yiddish for "ah, it's cooler."

p. 139 pamp up: From the Yiddish word for moist or soggy, thus the wet end of the filterless cigarette is on display.

p. 139 *mnya mnya*: Russian-Yiddish, meaning *nice, cute*.

p. 140 *Lewisohn Stadium*: An amphitheatre and athletic facility on the campus of City College, New York.

p. 144 *the 9th*: The New York Police Department's Ninth Precinct, located at 321 East 5th Street between 1st & 2nd Avenues, patrolled the tough neighborhoods of Lower Manhattan.

p. 150 *Middletown*: A discontinuity. "Janet Moris" begins at an unnamed college, presumably Smith, in Northampton, Massachusetts. Then the story relocates to Middletown, which is in Connecticut and the site of Wesleyan College.

p. 152 "Law School" is based on a disordered and possibly incomplete manuscript. Spaces indicate page breaks and the sequence is volunteered.

p. 153 *domnei*: A derivation of *domna* from the Latin domina (lady, mistress) alludes to *Domnei: A Comedy of Woman-Worship* (1920), by James Branch Cabell.

p. 153 *Fetsil, some medwurst, and bonor arter lingon, svensk og norske*: Swedish and Norwegian delicacies, including lard sausage (fetsil), salami (medwurst), and beans (bönor) and peas (ärter) with lingonberry sauce.

p. 155 *Rashun poiges*: "Russian purges" in a Bronx accent.

p. 156 *Kapulya*: A Jewish town in the Imperial Russian Pale of Settlement and part of the administrative district (*gubernia*) of Minsk. Graf is German for count, a title also used by the Russian nobility.

p. 158 *Veries*: Count de Veries was a radio journalist whose columns advised readers where to tune in to find the best swing stations on the AM band at night.

p. 162 *Encyclopedia of the Social Sciences* is a seminal reference source edited by E. R. A. Seligman (1861–1939) and Alvin Johnson (1874–1971) that comprised fifteen volumes by 1935.

p. 168 *the place where a million lights flicker and a million hearts beat quicker*: The famous lyric from the title song of the film *The Broadway Melody* (1929), the first sound film to win an Oscar for Best Picture.

p. 170 *Recouperating*: This spelling of "recuperating" was left uncorrected by Nicholas Moore in his *New Voices: Atlantic Anthology*. The spelling seems to come from folk wisdom about the necessity of money and health.

p. 171 *truckin' with the Peabody*: A fast-moving one-step dance in which couples raced (i.e., truckin') around such venues as The Savoy Ballroom, Roseland Ballroom, and Club Fordham. The Peabody was considered a dancer's dance.

p. 173 *matadme*: Spanish idiom meaning "kill me, please."

p. 176 *shiksele*: Yiddish for a young pretty gentile girl, less pejorative than *shiksa*.

p. 177 *rug-cutter*: Swing Era slang for a jitterbug dancer.